. . . he arose

on limbs and joints that had suddenly regained something of their youthful suppleness and strength, and stalked toward the door. The girl screamed at his approach, and broke free of her paralysis. She ran into the little kitchen behind her. There was no door leading directly outside from the little kitchen, and she went for the only window.

The man who had once been the Dark King, and now would be again, caught her from behind. Now she slumped in his grip, and seemed to have no voice for screaming left. But a moment later the girl broke free, with a spasmodic effort. Careening against the table in the center of the room, she snatched up a kitchen knife. The Demon blurred into action once more; one of the yeoman's hands, suddenly sharp-taloned at the end of an arm unnaturally elongated, swung past Vilkata's shoulder to strike. . . .

Tor books by Fred Saberhagen

A Century of Progress
Coils (with Roger Zelazny)
Dominion
The Dracula Tape
Earth Descended
The Holmes-Dracula File
The Mask of the Sun
A Matter of Taste
An Old Friend of the Family
Specimens
Thorn
The Veils of Azlaroc
The Water of Thought

THE BERSERKER SERIES

The Berserker Wars
The Berserker Throne
Berserker Base (with Poul Anderson, Ed Bryant,
 Stephen Donaldson, Larry Niven, Connie Willis,
 and Roger Zelazny)
Berserker Blue Death
Berserker's Planet

THE BOOKS OF SWORDS

The First Book of Swords
The Second Book of Swords
The Third Book of Swords

THE BOOKS OF LOST SWORDS

The First Book of Lost Swords: Woundhealer's Story
The Second Book of Lost Swords: Sightblinder's Story
The Third Book of Lost Swords: Stonecutter's Story
The Fourth Book of Lost Swords: Farslayer's Story
The Fifth Book of Lost Swords: Coinspinner's Story
The Sixth Book of Lost Swords: Mindsword's Story

MINDSWORD'S STORY

THE SIXTH BOOK OF LOST SWORDS

FRED SABERHAGEN

TOR
fantasy

A TOM DOHERTY ASSOCIATES BOOK
NEW YORK

THE SIXTH BOOK OF LOST SWORDS

Copyright © 1990 by Fred Saberhagen

A Tor Book
Published by Tom Doherty Associates, Inc.
49 West 24th Street
New York, N.Y. 10010

ISBN: 0-812-51118-2

First edition: December 1990
First mass market printing: June 1991

Printed in the United States of America

0 9 8 7 6 5 4 3 2 1

MINDSWORD'S
STORY

ONE

BETWEEN two lofty jagged mountain spines the rocky land declined in frozen swirls that bottomed in a deep depression, forming at its lowest point a narrow and almost circular hollow shielded from human observation by tall crags on every side. Around noon on a summer day a man alone was climbing toward this hidden place. He had begun climbing far below, and he was headed directly for the unseen hollow with fierce determination, as if he knew that it was there.

The climber was a strong and active man, though without any particular skill or experience in the art of ascending mountains; more than once today he had come near falling to his death when a handhold or foothold betrayed him. Dogged resolution had so far sustained him in his effort, though several times in the past two hours he had come near despairing of his survival.

The one fighting his way upward with such dedication was tall, dark of hair and beard, handsome in his own dark careless way. His age was approaching forty, and at the moment, breathing hard in the thin mountain air, he was keenly aware of every year.

The man's lean body had been worn leaner by much recent travel and other difficulties. He was dressed in the clothes of a soldier or a hunter; his jacket, much faded but still faintly blue and orange, might have been part of a uniform when it was new. He wore a small pack on his back; at the left side of his belt swung an empty sheath of a size to hold a long sword, balanced on the right side by a long practical knife. Despite the difficulties of the ascent, the climber evidently considered none of these items dispensable.

At the altitude where he had begun his long climb, the day was warm and sunny, but up here on the high slopes, somewhere around timberline, the summer afternoon was beginning with a light, cold drizzle, spiced with an occasional stinging pellet of snow or hail. Gusts of wind dragged rolling mists across the mountain's face, more often than not obscuring the climber's view of what lay ahead of him and above. Nevertheless he pressed on.

Already at many points in his ascent the climber had paused to rest. Now he did so once more, clinging in a brief truce to the nearly vertical rock. While catching his breath he examined his surroundings carefully, as if he expected to see something out of the ordinary. Also, he seemed to be listening intently, in hopes of picking up the sound of something more meaningful than wind.

Soon he advanced again, with unflagging determination.

His hopes, whatever their foundation, were soon justified, for presently he was granted evidence that his goal was near. As the climber's line of sight topped the next stony barrier he was able to see, no more than thirty meters above him and ahead, the notched entrance to a circular pit, which he knew must be the bottom of the hidden depression between crests.

At this sight the man paused, nodding to himself. Because of certain clues he had been given before he began to climb, he felt certain of what he was going to discover in that desolate place. And if any confirmation were needed that he was very near his goal, he had it now. Because now he was beginning to hear the voices.

The voices, which sounded more in his mind than in his ears, were strange to him, not just unfamiliar but extremely odd. In truth, as the explorer knew, they were not really vocal sounds. But he could not help hearing them and thinking of them as voices, these songs and cries that were so much more than the noise of the wet wind. There surged around him an utterance as of a multitude at worship, singing a polyphonic paean above the gusts.

The climber moved forward another step, and now a new sign appeared to assure him that he was on the right track, and had not far to go. The rocks ahead of him remained properly dead and motionless whenever he gazed straight at them. But all the landscape near the corners of his vision had now begun to move. The effect was such that the entire mountainside around him appeared to be on the verge of swirling away in an ecstatic dance.

Rendered momentarily dizzy by the illusion of dancing rocks, the seeker paused again, closing his eyes. The mountainside beneath his hands and feet felt stable, and with his intellect he knew it was. He understood perfectly well that the dance and the ecstasy were in his mind; but that rendered them no less rhythmic or ecstatic.

Having moved a little closer to his goal, the climber was able now to hear the magic voices more clearly, though still the words were indistinguishable. Some of the voices sounded human and some did not, but all of them were shrieking together in a great chorus of triumph and rapture.

The one who sought opened his eyes and studied the way ahead.

Although much of the mountainside was obscured by blowing mist, he knew that, physically, the worst of the climb was over. From where he stood, the surface he had still to negotiate angled more and more back toward the horizontal. Within the space of a few breaths the tall dark man, standing erect now and moving up on legs alone, was

almost on the threshold of the notched entrance to the
hollow in the rocks.

As he drew steadily nearer to that point, the fanciful—or
perhaps not so fanciful—idea crossed the climber's mind
that perhaps no other human being had set eyes upon these
cracked and moss-grown stones since the old mountains
had thrust upward from the earth.

Once more he felt himself rendered a touch unsteady by
the superhuman power of magic that loomed ahead. Once
more he paused to close his eyes, trying to regain an inner
balance. Standing there with eyes closed and arms out-
stretched, the man thought that now he could *feel* the
mountain dancing. It was as if the whole earth around him
were acting out the joy of certain victory, of success
extended to eternity . . . though what victory, or what
success was being celebrated, was more than any mere
mortal in his place could tell.

Opening his eyes, the adventurer found himself still
groping like a blind man. Trying to make his mind a blank,
he forced himself to forge on, one shuffling step after
another.

And now at last he had reached the very threshold of the
entrance to the secret place, a point from which he could
see directly into the hollow before him.

Ahead, through swirling mist and wind, he beheld a
broad cup of dark rock, irregular in shape, some forty
meters across here at the sculpted bottom. The whole
bottom of the cup was deeply littered by an age-old detritus
of stones and rough soil eroded from the surrounding cliffs.
Tough grass and other small plants, only enough of them to
emphasize the barrenness, grew very sparsely in that soil.

In almost the precise middle of this desolate hollow,
surmounting a natural cairn of tumbled stones, an upright
Sword was poised.

The cruciform dull black hilt stood uppermost, over a
long blade. The metal of that blade, straight as a ray of sun,

and as naked as the surrounding rock, appeared unnaturally bright in the dull, cloud-filtered daylight. It flashed
intermittently, sending forth momentary gleams as brilliant as the sun that hid itself above the wind-rushed
clouds.

Considering the Sword's position, the discoverer sur-
mised that it must at some time have fallen—or been
cast—from somewhere high on one of the surrounding
cliffs. The weapon had landed point first atop the rockpile,
wedging itself indestructibly in some fine crevice, or perhaps cracking open its own niche with the force of its
falling weight behind that unbreakable point.

But it was very hard to think, or plan. In the visitor's ears
and through his mind, the voices that were not voices
roared and sang unceasingly.

For a moment the tall man tilted back his head, the wind
whipping his dark hair and beard, his eyes squinting up
into the rolling, rushing clouds as if he hoped to be able to
gather from them some sign, some trace, concerning the
one who had discarded or accidentally dropped this god-
forged weapon here.

How long might the Sword of Glory have been here,
waiting to be claimed? The visitor could not be sure, but it
might well have been for years. He could picture how in
winter that bright Blade would stand here meters deep in
drifted snow, and how in spring and summer it must be
washed in floods of snowmelt and of rain. But not the
smallest spot of rust showed on that steel; and the man who
stood before it now would have been willing to wager his
existence that this weapon had not lost the faintest
increment of keenness from either of its long, finely
tapered edges.

Possibly, he thought, the Blade had worn a sheath when
it fell—or was hurled—into its present position. That it
stood entirely naked now was easily explained—over a
period of months or years, any covering of cloth or leather

could have been nibbled away by the sharp teeth of scavengers, small mindless creatures unaffected by the magic they uncovered.

The absence of a covering, however, created certain problems for an approaching human being.

Hesitantly, advancing step by step with many pauses, the climber continued his progress toward the matchless treasure. As much as possible he kept his eyes averted from that gleaming Blade, and he tried without success to close his mind against the glare, the influence, that poured so boundlessly, like some effortless reflection of a melting sun, from the thing atop the mound of rock, the artifact that had been wrought at a god's forge from magic and meteoric metal.

The discoverer knew—but the knowledge was of little help—that the glare afflicting him was not really in his eyes. He reminded himself as he advanced—though the suggestion did him little good—that the roaring voices, those of beings forever balancing upon the brink of some orgasmic triumph, were not really in his ears.

Useless efforts to protect himself, useless. The finder knew an almost overpowering urge to fall on his knees and worship—not the Sword itself, no, but someone, something, he knew not who or what, except that the object must be transcendent, and the Sword called him to it.

By now the man, gasping and trembling more in his excitement than from physical effort, was almost near enough to reach out and touch that dull black hilt. But some basic instinct of survival, justified or not, warned him that he must not do so yet.

When he dared to peer more closely at the hilt, he saw the small white symbol that he had known must be there, the device of a waving banner.

"It *is* the Mindsword, then," the trembling explorer whispered to himself. "It can be nothing else."—As if there could have been any doubt. But the mere sound of his own voice, which he could still manage to hold steady, his own words, which he could still contain within the bounds of rationality, helped him to master his excitement and his nameless fear.

He knew that many people, standing this close to this uncovered Blade, would have turned and fled in helpless terror. Many others would have fallen down in mindless worship of they knew not what. The discoverer, being a proud, able, and determined man, did neither. With tremendous stubbornness he had forced his way here, risking his life, to take possession of this prize. And he was not going to be deprived of it now.

But at the same time he feared that he might be unable to collect his treasure without help.

Yet again the adventurer squeezed shut his eyes, trying to establish some measure of composure. Closed lids shut out the sight of the Sword, but could not banish its majestic, insistent presence. In the depths of his mind and soul he could feel how the universe swirled around him. Half-born emotions only partially his own, fledgling hopes, stillborn ambitions, washed over him in a bewildering torrent. The man's brain echoed with the redoubled roar of a vast multitude of voices, some human and some not. All of them were praying, praising, worshiping—who? Or what?

He thought that it would prove impossible for him, strong man that he was, to remain for an hour within a hundred meters of this naked Blade when he did not control it. He had to possess his prize quickly, before it drove him mad or forced him into flight. And before he could touch it directly he had to cover it with something, muzzle its powers, put a sheath on it somehow.

The difficulty was not entirely unexpected; it was no accident that an empty sheath of the required size hung at the discoverer's belt. But he could not slip a sheath on the weapon in its present position, and he still dared not perform the simple act of reaching out to pluck the Mindsword from the rocks.

Surges of unidentifiable longing swept through the adventurer as he hesitated. He felt stabbed by pangs of deathly devotion to some overwhelmingly great but tantalizingly unspecific cause. Bright barbs that might have been sun-twinkles from the metal came dashing against his sanity like crests of poisoned foam.

Moving a half-step closer, he stretched out a hand toward the naked Sword—and then at the last moment dared not touch it.

Groaning, snatching back his trembling arm, the man fell back a step. And then another step, and yet another.

But this man was not going to give up. There might be another way. With unsteady fingers he began to unfasten the empty sheath from his Swordbelt.

With the detached sheath clutched in his left hand, the man gave a sound like a despairing giggle, and bent to pick up some small rocks. These he tossed, one after another, in the direction of the black hilt, trying to knock it over. At last one of his small missiles struck the Sword, which tilted but did not topple under the impact.

Laughing madly now, the man threw bigger stones, pitching them harder and harder, knowing that no rock he could ever throw, nothing he could ever do, could crack even the thinnest extremity of those sharpened edges.

At last he lobbed a larger stone that hit the Sword directly. The treasure fell, anticlimactically, making a slight noise. Obligingly its blade had now assumed a tilted position on the rockpile, the bright point uppermost, angled some degrees above the horizontal. And now the Sword's capturer could approach, sheath in hand, and—without needing to touch his prize directly—could begin to bind and tame his quarry, to hood it like a falcon with the mundane empty leather.

Slowly and carefully he got the point started into the sheath, then worked the sheath along the blade. In its new position the Mindsword rocked, slowly and precariously, with every indirect pressure from his hand.

The madness in the air, and in the rock, began to weaken.

The man could not have said how long the task occupied him, but eventually it was done. The simple covering was effective. The world was stable again, the many voices muted into—almost—perfect silence.

Now the latest possessor of the Mindsword could freely grasp the hard black pommel, feeling in it no more than the subtle power that any thing of great magic might be expected to possess, the sense of tremendous forces bound and coiled and waiting. Now he could pick up his great prize and buckle it on tightly at his belt. And now the world around him was perfectly worldly once again, consisting of little more than rocks and wind and rain. Somewhere birds were crying in the moving mist. He had not noticed until now that there were birds nesting and flying and hunting amid these lofty rocks.

For a quarter of an hour after the Sword was sheathed the newly armed adventurer sat on a small ledge, resting with his treasure at his side, experiencing a reaction of weakness.

Then he was on his feet again, and briskly on his way. The hardest part of the long descent, down to where he'd left his riding-beast, must be completed before nightfall. Early in the morning he'd ride on, in the direction of Sarykam. He had a great gift now to give. A truly worthy gift, to place in the lovely hands of the Princess Kristin.

TWO

IN a small village at the foot of the Ludus Mountains, not many kilometers from the spot where the adventurer had very recently obtained his Sword, but at a considerably lower altitude, a blind albino man sat huddled in one corner of the small main room of a solidly built though sparsely furnished hut.

Few people could have determined the blind man's age by looking at him, but certainly his youth was decades past. His angular body, now slumped and blanket-covered in a crudely constructed peasant's chair, would still have been very tall but for the fact that he never stood fully erect. Long ringlets of unclean white hair hung past his bony shoulders, entering into confusion with a once-white beard now colorless with old stains of food and drink.

No mask or bandage concealed the empty sockets of his eyes; long-lashed lids sagged over spots of raw softness in a face that was otherwise all harsh masculine planes and angles.

The blind man had lived in this hut, or in another very similar dwelling nearby, for the past fourteen years, rarely stirring out of doors for any purpose. Apart from his blindness he was not physically crippled, though his lack of deliberate movement, together with occasional nervous tremors in his limbs, suggested that he might be lame.

Actually the chief cause of his immobility lay in a disability of his will. For fourteen years he had been obsessed with certain events in the ever-receding past.

This afternoon two visitors were standing in the blind man's hut. Both callers were men, and both wore the humble dress—common furs and homespun cloth—of inhabitants of the nearby village. Half an hour ago the pair of visitors had tapped at the unlocked door of the blind man's house, waited with habitual patience for an answer that never came, and at last had let themselves in, calling loudly to announce their arrival. Since then they had been standing deferentially in front of the albino, waiting for him to show some awareness of their presence.

At last the one who sat huddled in the chair deigned to acknowledge, by a certain stillness of his body, a cessation of the long-continued nervous movements of his hands and feet, that he had perceived his callers' existence.

Seizing the opportunity the moment it arrived, the elder visitor spoke softly.

"Lord Vilkata?"

There was no immediate response, even when the quiet salutation was repeated. For some time the man slumped in the chair pretended not to hear his callers. They did not take offense at such behavior; it was only the Lord Vilkata's way. Since their rescue of the blind man from deep snow at the foot of a nearby cliff some fourteen winters ago, many if not quite all of the villagers had been convinced that he was one of the vanished race of gods, in fact the last survivor of that august company. Therefore, his hosts believed, his presence in their village was certain sooner or later to bring them inestimable benefits. True, their life so far had remained as harsh as ever despite the albino's presence; but at least no disaster beyond the ordinary had befallen, and who knew what might have happened were the Lord not here?

The blind man for his part had accepted deferential

treatment, and the regular satisfaction of his bodily wants, as no more than his due. Beyond that he had made few demands upon his hosts. Some of the demands he did make were quite incomprehensible and never met. Others were quite clear. From the first day the guest had insisted that his rescuers call him by what he said was his proper name. So long as the villagers did that, and fed him as well as they could, and kept him warm, and allowed him from time to time the company in bed of one or two of their more comely daughters—then he would deign to speak to them.

Sometimes he even listened to them as well.

"Grandfather?" This was the younger visitor, trying out a theory of his own, that after all these years the eminent guest might be ready to answer to a simpler title.

The experimenter might have saved his breath. The Lord Vilkata took no notice of him.

The senior of the two visitors said nothing for a while, and remained impassive. He had been perfectly sure that the experiment would fail.

After a while the senior tried again, sticking to his own kind of patient communication. "Lord Vilkata?"

"Yes, what is it?" This time the snappish answer came at once, sooner than the elder had expected. Something out of the ordinary was perturbing the blind god-man today.

The elder visitor asked gently, deferentially, what the honored one's trouble was.

The reply was quick and petulant: "My trouble stems from the Sword, of course. What else?"

They were back to the incomprehensible. The two visitors, standing before the huddled figure in the chair, silently exchanged glances. It was nothing new for dear Grandfather—everyone called him that, outside his hut— to talk about the Sword, though none of his hearers knew what "the Sword" might be.

For some time after his rescue, long years ago, the

honored guest had talked of almost nothing else but this strange Sword of enormous importance, and the elders of the village in those days had expended much effort and time in a useless attempt to discover just what he meant. For hours on end, sometimes seemingly for days, their guest and prisoner and lucky charm had harangued the people who had saved his life in an effort to get them to organize search parties, go out into the mountains, and find this mysterious weapon that so obsessed him.

During the first few years after their guest's arrival the people had listened to these tirades patiently—taking shifts when necessary—and tried to understand. Of course the villagers knew in a general way what swords were like, but really they knew and cared nothing about them beyond that—they had their spears and slings and clubs for hunting, and for those rare other occasions when weapons were essential. They harkened tolerantly to the blind man's urgent mumblings, and sometimes to soothe him they pretended to search, but really they made no effort. Only madmen would waste strength and time combing the mountains for objects that were not needed and perhaps did not exist.

Before he had been three years among them, the villagers reached a consensus that their honored Grandfather was quite mad. They accepted the fact that he was mad, as holy men and old men sometimes were, but his madness did not diminish his holiness or his importance to the village. The value of a resident lord, or god—the distinction was not a profound one for the villagers—really did not depend on anything he said, or anything he did overtly. They soothed their guest and prisoner as best they could, and told him pleasant lies to keep him quiet. Yes, Great Elder, excuse us, Lord Vilkata, soon the weather will improve, and then we will climb back up into the high country and resume the search. Next time we will certainly find your Sword.

Eventually the honored one had seemed to forget about

the mysterious Sword, or at least he spoke of it less and less
frequently. Instead he spent what strength he had in other
lamentations, chiefly for his lost youth and fame and
power.

But today the older of the pair of visiting elders was
growing worried that those early days of fiery obsession
might have come back. Because:

"Someone," Old Grandfather was croaking now, "has
found the Sword, and is carrying it away. Taking it away,
farther and farther, while we sit here and do nothing."

Once more the two men who stood before him exchanged glances. "What Sword would that be, Grandfather?" the younger visitor asked, quite innocently. In the
early years of the god's visit this man had been only a
simple villager and not an elder, too young to pay any
attention to talk about some unessential Sword. So his
question now was no attempt at mockery. But still it was
too much for the albino, who lapsed into incoherent abuse.

Where once high intelligence had ruled, inside the skull
of Vilkata the survivor, now stretched a ravaged mental
wasteland illuminated only intermittently by flashes of his
former intellect. The mind of the quondam Dark King
ached in its concentration on a bitter craving for revenge
upon the world in general. Revenge, for the impertinence
of the world, in having dared to escape his domination! A
sharper and more localized craving for vengeance was
centered upon Prince Mark and Princess Kristin of
Tasavalta—and to a slightly lesser degree upon the
Tasavaltan people—for what Vilkata considered good and
sufficient reason.

Inextricably mixed with these cravings for revenge there
persisted a monumental regret for the Mindsword's loss.
Somehow, on that last day of Vilkata's power, that very
nearly peerless weapon had slipped out of his possession.

On that day, in staggering retreat with a band of fugitive
gods, crossing the mountains at no very great distance

from this hut, Vilkata had been either carrying the Mindsword or wearing it at his belt—he could not now remember which. That black day had seen the Dark King in full flight from his last battlefield, where Soulcutter in the hands of the Silver Queen had finally snuffed out his bid to rule the world. And then within hours he'd somehow lost his own Sword—condemning himself to spend the next fourteen years trying to remember exactly where and how.

He seemed to remember that, at one point during the disastrous retreat, the god Vulcan had been carrying him on his back . . . but that might have been only a dream, or nightmare.

By the time the Dark King had lost his Sword, he'd already been half mad, suffering the psychic pain of terminal defeat, and on top of that, the acid despair engendered by that other Sword, Soulcutter. That output of the Sword of Despair had begun on the battlefield to eat into Vilkata's innermost being.

On that day, on that particular field of combat, the dull dead force of Soulcutter had proven even stronger than the Mindsword's blazing, dazzling call to glory. Vilkata's host, thousands of warriors fanatically loyal to him and ferociously triumphant, had in a frighteningly short span of time degenerated into something less than a mob. His large and powerful army had become little more than an assembly of lethargic bodies. The warriors were slumping to the ground, all their blood still in their veins and their bones unbroken, but their strength melting in a lunatic inertia. The great mass of helpless men had been slain or taken captive before they could recover. Only those few who remained physically close to Vilkata, deep inside the zone of the Mindsword's power, had been able to survive. And even those survivors were badly shaken.

But since he'd fled the battlefield he'd seldom thought about the battle. Ever since that day, most of the Dark

King's conscious thought had been expended in a fruitless effort to recall just how and where and when during the terrible retreat he'd lost his Sword. He'd been separated from it somewhere in these very mountains, of that much he was certain. The region was thinly populated, and wherever he'd dropped the treasure, it might still be there.

Alas, these local people, his faithful rescuers, had proven useless in this urgent quest. Vilkata was beginning to wonder, though, if they might not know more than they pretended. It was quite possible, he had recently begun to realize, that they wanted his great Sword for themselves. Might they have already found it, and lied to him of continued failure?

No. In his clearer hours he knew that his mind had tended to wander since his loss, but rationality still prevailed. He'd have known, he'd have felt the change, if anyone had picked the Mindsword up. And, as the remnants of his once-mighty magic had continued to assure him, no one had done so.

Not until today.

Today someone else *had* seized his treasure. The full horror of the fact was slowly being borne in upon the man who had been the Dark King. He could even, behind his sightless eyesockets, conjure up and nurse a fragmentary vision of the one who held it now. . . .

Suddenly screaming renewed abuse, he drove the pair of village elders from him. If they could not comprehend his problem, at least they must be made to leave him alone so he could think. When the two men were gone, some of the women who usually tended to him still remained in the hut—he could hear them moving about in the next room—but they would know better than to bother him.

Vilkata lapsed back into his dark solitary thoughts. The nervous, unconscious movements of his hands and feet soon resumed.

By sunset, the women had also departed, save for one girl, the youngest of several who currently took turns sleeping in an outer room against the possibility that their guest-god should awaken and require something during the night. When the older women looked in on him before leaving, the blind man had let them know in a few savage words that tonight, as on most nights, he preferred to sleep alone.

Though his empty sockets were utterly dead to light, Vilkata was always able to tell when sunset arrived. There were certain changes in the faint sounds of village life that drifted into his small house from time to time, alterations in the sound of birds and insects, and a subtly different feeling in the air.

On this particular evening, the sun was not long gone before another change occurred. This alteration began very subtly, and was almost impossible to define at first. Only one long skilled in magic could have noticed it as soon as the blind man did.

It was also completely unexpected, and it caused him to hold his breath for a full half minute when he first became aware of it.

But there was no mistake. A very different sort of visitor was soon going to arrive.

Vilkata's senses, long trained to the implements and materials of enchantment, had been able to detect the approach of this caller from afar, though he doubted very strongly that anyone else in the village had the least inkling of who—or what—was coming.

Not the least doubt now. There was a subtle smell of sickness in the air, a feeling like an uneasy shifting of the world beneath the blind man's chair, so he could easily have imagined himself perched on the mast of some ship far out of sight of land on the great sea, with storms surrounding him. This evening there was for a little while a more unusual manifestation, a heavy throbbing as of a distant drum. This last Vilkata was able at once to recognize as no mere human sound, and indeed it proceeded from a source that was ordinarily well beyond the reach of human ears.

From the moment when the man who had been the Dark King first detected his approaching visitor, he entertained no doubts about its nature. Most humans would have been terrified, but Vilkata was not altogether dismayed. The time had been when he, by choice, had spent more hours of each day with demons than with human beings.

The knowledge that a demon was swiftly approaching, the first such visitation he had experienced in fourteen years, was not now the total surprise that it would have been a day ago, or on any day when no one had laid hands upon his Sword. Still the event shocked Vilkata into a mental state more closely approaching normality.

The drumming sound soon faded and disappeared, but the other manifestations grew rapidly in strength. This evening the first overt sign of the newcomer's immediate presence was—happy surprise!—a welcome return of vision to the blind man. Not ordinary vision, no, rather a lurid and distorted approximation, more colorful than ordinary human eyesight and keener in some respects. Despite this seeming acuity, Vilkata knew well that the demonic mode of sight was even less trustworthy than that enjoyed by common folk.

"I can see," he suddenly whispered aloud, into what had been the unrelieved darkness of his hut. Now the stark outlines of walls and furniture, the colors drab, were plain in lightless night. His first reaction was that of a man awakening from dull sleep to horror and ugliness. Was *this* the room in which he spent his days, and years? This shabby hovel, cramped and dirty—

Before Vilkata could complete the thought he heard the demon's voice. The syllables sounded in the man's ears as any human might have heard them, light desiccated sounds evoking thoughts of dead leaves swirling among dry bones.

"Receive and enjoy my humble gift of sight, Dark King," the demon said—and its tone was reassuringly deferential, as of old.

Vilkata thought that he recognized—or rather that he ought to recognize—this particular demon. In the old days he had known many of the foul things—many. He ought to remember this one's name. . . .

The man mumbled his response, as if he were speaking to himself, unaccustomed to any real conversation.

"I can see my room now—but not my visitor." Still the thing's name eluded him, still its individual presence hovered tantalizingly on the brink of recognizability.

"I hesitate to show myself," the dry bones scraped.

"I know your nature, visitor. That would indeed be hard to mistake. What can you have to fear from me? Be bold and show yourself, assume whatever form you choose. What is your name?"

Without further hesitation the demon took form in Vilkata's vision, appearing as if from nowhere, adopting a shape utterly incompatible with its voice—or with its real nature. The chosen form was that of a naked woman. Vilkata was not surprised. In all the dealings he'd had with demons in the days of his power, naked humanity was one of the most common illusions they projected.

Distrustfully he stared at this almost-convincing semblance of a female human body, lusty and youthful. The woman-face was blurred in detail, as usual in these visions, but what did that matter? The rest of the body, the sexual regions in particular, was very clear. Long black hair fell around full breasts. The firmly rounded thighs were slightly parted, the painted eyelids half lowered, the red lips

smiling. The nameless female, archetype of a palace cour-
tesan, sprawled wantonly in a crude chair across the room,
her body unadorned save for a long string of pearls.

The Dark King knew well that as a rule these erotic
images lacked substance. He commanded sharply: "Put on
a different shape, I do not care for that one."

"As you wish, Lord Vilkata." The woman's lips moved
to form the dry demon's voice, and even as they moved,
they changed. In a twinkling her shape had become that of
a male human, an anxious-looking, honest, sturdy yeoman
of early middle age, unarmed and clothed for rough
service, standing beside the chair in which the woman had
been sitting. Briefly the yeoman's shoulders sprouted rudi-
mentary wings, which disappeared again the moment
Vilkata frowned at the manifestation.

The eyeless man who was no longer blind prodded, in a
suddenly strong voice: "I asked you your name."

"I am Akbar, Lord Vilkata," said the yeoman in humble
tones, going down on one knee in the center of the shabby,
uncarpeted wooden floor. "Perhaps you remember me."

"Akbar. Yes, of course. I do remember now." The demon
of that name had been one of the most cowardly and
otherwise contemptible of the host who had served the
Dark King—though by no means the least powerful. "You
may rise."

The figure of the yeoman bounced up briskly to his feet,
capable-looking hands clasped before him. "Long have I
sought to find you, Dark King. I am anxious to serve you
again, and I promise to do so as faithfully as before."

Well, Vilkata could believe that kind of promise; because
no demon, least of all the dastardly Akbar, had ever served
anyone with any kind of faith. But all of their race were
very powerful, and if you had the power and skill in magic
to control demons, knew their limitations—and were
willing to accept the risks—they could be very useful.

Suddenly the man in the crude chair frowned. "Why

have you come seeking me now, after all this time? It must have something to do with the Sword."

The yeoman bowed. "My master is as clever as always."

"Ha. Perhaps I am still clever, perhaps not. But there are certain things a man does not forget—what is it, then? What do you want?"

"It is with great humility, Master, that I propose—dare I use the word?—a partnership."

"Say on."

Vilkata listened carefully as the thing went on, always speaking with great deference, to suggest what their relationship should be: from now on it would stay with Vilkata, or at least be in touch with him frequently, and help him. His magically renewed vision would persist indefinitely, even when the demon itself was elsewhere. Akbar could also provide the aging man with new strength and energy, perhaps even some change in appearance, physically renewed youth—and, a matter of even greater importance, it would take him near the Sword he sought to recover.

"Take me near it? Does that mean, in plain language, that you will help me get it back?"

"Of course . . . and there is revenge, Master! I do not forget what is most important. I can help you attain the revenge you seek to have upon your bitterest enemies."

Suddenly Vilkata was aware of a pulse beating in his own head. Blood returning, as it seemed, after years of almost-suspended life. "Yes? And what then?"

"What then, Master? My poor intellect does not permit me to follow—"

"I mean, what do you intend to gain from this partnership of ours?"

The thing's dry, androgynous voice continued to be fawning, soothing, in contrast with the sturdy, honest yeoman's figure: "All I ask in return from you, Great Master, is that you give me certain preferential treatment.

When you have regained the power that once was yours—
and, if and when the Sword of Glory is yours again, that
you should appoint me as your second in command over
whatever forces of human beings and demons you then
command. Your viceroy, over whatever lands you may
then rule."

The albino's voice had become as dry as the demon's
own. "No thoughts of having the top place for yourself, I
suppose?"

"Above yourself? Not I! No, no. Never! Remember,
Great Lord, was I not content to be subordinate in the old
days? When you ruled a kingdom, Master, and that Sword
was yours before?" The yeoman spoke so earnestly; what a
fine, sturdy peasant he seemed! "Was I not content?"

The thing seemed to be asking the question seriously,
really hoping for an answer.

"I suppose you were," Vilkata grudgingly acknowledged.
"That is to say, I don't recall any particular effort at
rebellion." In fact, as this conversation progressed he had
gradually come to remember more and more about Akbar.
Yes, definitely a cowardly sort of demon. Self-effacing,
forever trying to avoid risk and responsibility, always
seeking first of all to evade the pain of magical punishment
and the possibility of destruction. One of the more easily
managed demons, certainly. The very one he might have
chosen to meet, had the choice been his, in his current state
of weakness.

"There you are, my lord. I see that you do remember me.
Why should you not, with my help, be able to regain your
Sword?"

Wind whined, stirring the dry leaves; for a moment the
yeoman's face was blurred into a caricature. "You were a
fine master, a great and intelligent master. I am not clever
enough to be a master over clever men and demons—not
without direction from above—but you assuredly are."

The thing was waiting for an answer.

"Of course I will accept your offer," the Dark King said after a moment. What choice had he, really? It would be pointless, he thought, for him to issue warnings, to say anything of his abiding suspicions. At one time his magic had been quite capable of managing demons, including creatures vastly more formidable, because less cowardly, than this one. His powers might be shaky now—but fortunately there was no need to try to establish magical control over Akbar just yet. The demon was coming to him willingly, and Vilkata saw no reason, given time and a chance to regain his physical and psychic strength, why his powers of control should not eventually be dominant again. Gradually, subtly, he would regain the upper hand. . . .

"Our pact is concluded, then?" the sturdy, hearty yeoman asked him anxiously.

"Our pact is made, and sealed. Where is the Mindsword now?"

"It is not far from here at all, Master. Not very far. Allow me to show you, Master, what I see."

And in a moment, by means of his demonically provided vision, just as on occasion in the old days, Vilkata was once more able to behold a physically distant scene. This picture was of a rider traveling alone, wearing the Mindsword at his side. Magic and symbolism informed the vision, so that the Dark King perceived the weapon of the gods as a pillar of billowing flame, long as a spear.

"Take me to it!"

"I shall, Master, I shall! Never fear. But that Sword, as you know, is very powerful. We must take no chances. We must have a plan."

"You mean the fellow might detect us when we get near him, or even as we approach, and use the Sword on us? Is he a magician, then?"

"*Perhaps* he is not . . . but consider that he has managed to obtain possession of a Sword that other magicians have sought for many years, and failed to find."

"Indeed he has done that . . . and he might well get wind of us, and draw the Sword at an untimely moment—yes, there is that."

Vilkata had no wish to spend the rest of his life in the abject adoration, the selfless service, of any other being.

"There is that, Master, as you say. We would not want him to draw the Sword when we were near. The danger is very real."

Impatiently the Dark King waved a hand before his face, and the wraith of that distant, unknown rider vanished. He, Vilkata, was once more gazing with eyeless and demonic vision at his immediate surroundings, the dark, drab, ugly room of his long exile.

"Of course," he said. "And I—wait." His voice turned sharp, and he directed his vision toward the small room's only door, which now stood closed. "Who's there?"

He knew, even as he spoke, that the person outside must be only the village girl who had stayed for the night, roused to a fatal curiosity by the sound of a strange voice in the Lord Vilkata's room. But it would certainly be best to make sure.

There was a whisper and a blurring in the air. Without visibly occupying the intervening space, the figure of the yeoman, moving with inhuman speed and silence, was already standing at the door, pulling it quickly open.

Just outside, the slight figure of the young girl stood revealed, her face startled, empty hands beginning to rise before her as if in an effort to ward something off.

The yeoman holding the door open bowed lightly toward Vilkata.

"A pleasant morsel, Master," the dry leaves rasped, "for the two of us to share tonight. For each of us to enjoy, in his own way. What remains will be appropriate as a small present for these villagers. A token of your appreciation of their years of hospitality."—

Vilkata began to laugh. His mirth rose louder and harder, as he had not laughed in years. Meanwhile the girl seemed to be petrified.

"Bring her in," the Dark King commanded presently.

But the yeoman only bowed himself aside, out of deference, it seemed. "Nay, you, Master, shall of course be first."

Vilkata looked at his new partner. Then he arose from his crude chair, on limbs and joints that had suddenly regained something of their youthful suppleness and strength, and stalked toward the door.

The girl screamed at his approach, and broke free of her paralysis. She ran into the little kitchen behind her. There was no door leading directly outside from the kitchen, and she went for the only window.

The man who had once been the Dark King, and now would be again, caught her from behind; the back of her simple dress tore in his grip as he pulled her back into the room. Now she slumped in his grip, and seemed to have no voice for screaming left.

But a moment later the girl broke free, with a spasmodic effort. Careening against the table in the center of the room, she snatched up a kitchen knife.

The demon blurred into action once more; one of the yeoman's hands, suddenly sharp-taloned at the end of an arm unnaturally elongated, swung forward past Vilkata's shoulder to strike.

The knife fell from the girl's hand. Her face, suddenly bloody, grew blurred in the Dark King's demonic vision, as she slumped forward into his ready grasp.

THREE

CROWN Prince Murat's destination on his lonely ride was Tasavalta. Slightly more than a year had passed since his first visit to that realm. In the course of that visit he had met Princess Kristin for the first time. Murat had spent only a few days in her presence, and had not laid eyes on her since his hasty departure from her land. But throughout the intervening months the image of her lovely face had never completely left him; the impression of grace and beauty inspired by her chastely clothed body had endured.

Now, on the first day after Murat had found the Sword, Kristin's presence was brighter and clearer than ever in his mind's eye as he rode alone toward her homeland, traversing the desolation of the southern foothills of the Ludus Mountains.

Around midday the Crown Prince was roused from certain improbable daydreams concerning himself and the Princess by the discovery that he was being followed. Glancing back along the way he had come, he caught a glimpse of a single rider on his track, no more than two hundred meters behind him.

Setting all daydreams aside for the moment, Murat began to concentrate intently on matters at hand. Guiding his riding-beast into a maze of tumbled, almost house-sized boulders, he circled back to intercept his own trail, and at a carefully selected point of vantage waited to surprise the man who followed him. Disdaining to draw in his own defense the weapon he was carrying as a gift for the Princess, Murat instead unholstered an ordinary battle-ax from its place beside his saddle. Then he waited, listening to the approaching sound of hooves, ready for whoever might be coming.

Moments later a young man, armed, rode into sight, almost within arm's length. Murat drew back his ax—

"Father! Don't strike!"

The weapon was lowered, as the man who wielded it recoiled. Then the Crown Prince leaned forward in his saddle, staring with the stupidity of total astonishment into the eyes of his only son. Only in the last year or two had the youth grown into his full stature, and for a moment his father had failed to recognize him.

"Carlo!"

"Father!"

The ax was quickly reholstered, by a fumbling hand. After a moment or two of awkwardness—father and son had not seen each other for many months—they dismounted and embraced.

"You are looking well," Murat commented at last, holding his son at arm's length. Carlo, dark and round-faced, well dressed and well armed, was not as tall as his father, but in a year or two he would probably be physically stronger.

"And you," the lad responded, "are looking tired."

In the next moment explanations, and demands for news, poured out on both sides.

Carlo had left Culm only a month ago, and could report on what was happening there. Unfortunately the conditions that had turned his father into a semivoluntary exile still obtained. The aged Queen, Murat's stepmother, still ruled, with her sickly consort at her side. And the royal couple, like many others in the homeland, still blamed Murat for failing to bring home the healing Sword of Love.

Without being asked, Carlo added to his report the information that his own mother and his sister were now living with his mother's relatives. "I told Mother that I meant to find you, Father."

"And had my dear wife any message for me?"

Carlo, suddenly downcast, had to admit that she had not.

Murat, having expected no other answer, shrugged; years ago his wife's feelings and opinions had largely ceased to interest him. Then, seeing his son's sad face, he smiled and tried to cheer him up. "I am glad that you came looking for me."

Carlo brightened at that. He began to explain how, with considerable difficulty, he had managed to track down his father.

Then he asked, in a puzzled voice, and in the manner of one who really wanted to know, what his father was doing.

The older man gazed on his son with quiet satisfaction. "I have been on a quest of my own."

"A successful quest?"

"Indeed! Very successful!" Murat, clutching the black hilt at his side, in his turn explained something—not all—about his search for, and recovery of, the Sword.

"But that's wonderful!" Carlo was suitably impressed. "And where are you going now, Father? Back to Culm?"

"To Tasavalta."

The youth shook his head, uncomprehending. "Tasavalta again! But why?"

"For a very good reason. On my last visit to that land, a year ago, I did someone a great wrong. Now at last I am able to do something to set the matter right."

Carlo was frowning. He didn't understand. "But—the Tasavaltans will want to throw you in prison, won't they? Or worse?"

"Princess Kristin will listen to me. Especially when I present her with this Sword as a gift."

"You intend to give it away? To the Princess in Sarykam?" The young man's perplexity grew worse.

"Yes, that's what I mean to do. Come, if you're ready, let us ride on."

The two remounted. As they rode on, side by side, Murat's son was silent for a time. Then, still looking troubled, he said, "I hear that Prince Mark has a short temper. If they really believe that you have wronged them—" Carlo broke off, looking worried.

"Mark is generally away on some adventure. If he happens to be at home, well, I'm not afraid to face him. Short-tempered or not, he is said to be a fair man, and he will listen to me."

Actually the Crown Prince spoke with somewhat more confidence than he felt. It had already occurred to him that in the unlikely event that Kristin's clod of a husband was on hand when he, Murat, arrived in Sarykam, his welcome could well be unpleasant. But Murat had determined to take the chance.

Carlo, riding beside him, kept turning his head to look at the black hilt. At last the youth asked: "May I hold the Mindsword, Father? In the sheath, I mean. I won't draw it, of course."

His father considered the request seriously, then solemnly shook his head. "I think not. I have pledged not to draw it, nor to give it to anyone except the Princess herself."

"I'm sorry, Father, but I still don't understand why you intend to give it to Princess Kristin and Prince Mark."

An edge crept into Murat's voice. "I thought I had explained. A year ago I stole the Sword Woundhealer from that lady's treasury. In doing so I wronged her greatly, though at the time I had convinced myself that what I was doing was the proper course of action. Now I am determined to make amends."

Carlo was silent. Murat wondered suddenly if he was thinking that his father had wronged others also, in times past, and never made amends in such grand style.

At last the youth spoke again. "Isn't there some other way for you to right the wrong you feel you have committed against Princess Kristin?"

"This is the way I choose," Murat said shortly, and tapped the black hilt with his palm.

Carlo, well acquainted with that tone, did not argue.

Shortly before sunset the two travelers stopped to make camp for the night. The subject of Swords was not discussed again between them before they slept, Murat lying with the sheathed Sword as close to him as a lover's body.

In the morning father and son traveled on companionably toward Tasavalta, speaking of peaceful matters, using the time to renew their acquaintance.

Early on the second day after Carlo had joined Murat, the pair became aware that they were being followed. No such luck as a single stalker this time, but rather a band of eight, who definitely had the look of bandits. When father and son tried to outdistance their pursuers, four more riders appeared ahead, posted in just the right spot for tactical advantage, efficiently cutting off the travelers' escape.

Father and son slowed their hard-breathing mounts to a walk, and presently to a halt. A ravine to their right and a rock wall to their left formed practically impassable barriers. The two found themselves trapped, effectively surrounded by a dozen mounted men who were poorly clothed, heavily armed, and plainly devoid of good intentions.

Murat had not yet voiced to his son his worst fear: that these might not be merely ordinary brigands, but the agents of some great magician or other potentate who had somehow learned that he, Murat, now possessed the

Mindsword, meant to have it from him, and felt confident of being able to achieve that end. The Crown Prince had been aware all along that his finding might well have shaken the threads of several complicated wizard-webs.

"Father?" Carlo awaited orders. The young man was pale, but bearing himself well; he had already drawn his own sword and looked ready to fight to the death if his father should command it.

Murat had as yet unsheathed no weapon. The pledge he had made to himself, in his own mind, never to draw the Sword for his own benefit, was indeed a solemn one. But now circumstances were gravely altered. Now not only was his own life at stake but his son's as well, and not only their lives but possession of the Princess Kristin's treasure.

While Murat hesitated, the band of ruffians were closing in calmly and efficiently to their front and rear, little by little improving their already overwhelming position, edging their riding-beasts momentarily closer and closer still —except for three who remained well out of sword-range, holding bows and arrows ready.

Until now the highwaymen had gone about their business without wasting breath on words. But now at last the bandit leader, one of the four who waited ahead, called out to his victims, demanding that the pair dismount and hand over all their worldly possessions. As he pronounced this ultimatum, the robber's voice and attitude were rather cheery. If, he said, the surrounded pair surrendered their material possessions without fuss, he would graciously allow them to keep their lives.

Murat, his right hand resting lightly on the black hilt, replied in a firm princely voice. "I think that we will hand over nothing."

"Oh, no?" The bandit leader sounded neither angered nor surprised by Murat's defiance, but suddenly tired and rather sad. He was a squat man, with a long graying mustache, who occupied his saddle as if he might have been born there. "Well, then, your fate be on your own heads." But still the brigand delayed, giving his men no command to attack, squinting at Murat now as if trying to settle some new doubt in his own mind. Presently he added: "Your clothing will be worth more to us if we can get it without holes or bloodstains. I grant you one last chance to reconsider."

"Instead," said the Crown Prince, raising his royal voice once more, "I propose a rather different arrangement. If you and your men will let us pass, and go promptly and peacefully on your way, I will refrain from drawing my Sword."

There was no immediate reply from the mustached man. A great many people knew about the gods' Twelve Swords, and quite a few had seen at least one of them at some time. For a moment the bandit leader did not appear to react at all. Then he said in the same tired voice: "Anyone can craft a sword with such a dull black hilt."

Murat did not respond.

With a gesture the weary-looking robber ordered his archers to nock their arrows.

And Murat, feeling a profound reluctance mixed with an unexpected fiery anticipation, drew the Mindsword from its plain sheath.

His own first sensation was one of surprise. The naked Sword now in his grip and control had much less effect on him than it had had when he approached the unclaimed weapon. Now the vast power of the gods' magic went flowing outward, away from the Sword's holder in all directions.

The bandits' riding-beasts, as well as Carlo's, exploded in rearing and plunging excitement. This was caused, Murat supposed, by the sudden turmoil gripping their masters' minds and bodies. One or two men in the enemy ranks were thrown, but no one save Murat, not even the victims themselves, paid much attention to this fact. Each of the men caught in the web of magic had to respond in his own way to the wrenching internal change imposed from without. Some of the bandits cast down their weapons violently, some sheathed them with great care. Several of those who were not thrown dismounted voluntarily, while others went galloping in little circles, shouting incoherently like drunken men or lunatics.

Among the bandits only their leader remained physically almost motionless. He bowed his head for a long moment, and his rough hands gripping the reins went white-knuckled.

His shoulders heaved. Moments later, he raised a tear-stained face to plead with Murat. "Forgive me, lord!" the robber cried in a breaking voice. "I did not know you—I could not see you clearly when we approached, I did not realize—"

"You are forgiven," Murat called back mechanically. His chief emotion was relief that the armed threat had disappeared, that his life and his son's life were safe. And at the same time he knew horror at what he had been forced to do. The Sword in his right hand felt very heavy; on drawing the Blade he had raised it overhead, but now he let his right arm sag down slowly to his side.

Suddenly remembering Carlo, the Crown Prince reined his riding-beast around. His son, sword still drawn in his right hand, was just bringing his own plunging mount under control. And with a pang Murat saw that Carlo, like the bandit leader, was weeping.

The young man stretched out a hand toward him, and choked out words. "Father . . . are you all right?"

"Yes, of course I am. And you?" Hastily Murat sheathed the radiant steel in his right hand.

Carlo sobbed. "If—if any of them had hurt you, I'd—I'd have—I don't know what."

Deeply moved, and vaguely alarmed, Murat rode closer to his son. "Put up your sword, Carlo. It's all right now, they can't hurt either of us."

Meanwhile the bandits, all of them now dismounted and empty-handed, were prostrating themselves among a litter of discarded weapons, groveling before the Crown Prince.

"Lead us, Master!" one of them cried.

"Lead you?" he whispered, startled as if he did not understand at first. Later he was to wonder why he had not understood at once.

Instantly the plea became a chorus. "Lead us!"

"Take us with you, wherever you are going! Don't abandon us here!" shouted another bandit. It was a cry from the very bottom of the heart.

Murat cast one more look around him, while his left hand, trembling, sought out the black hilt once more. The Mindsword's radiant power was sheathed, quenched for the time being, but its presence persisted strongly in the surrounding light and air, as the sun's heat might linger in low country after the sun had set.

Gradually the men who were prostrate on the ground, and Carlo weeping in his saddle, managed to regain full control of themselves.

"Get to your feet," Murat curtly ordered his new devotees, as soon as he judged that they were calm enough to listen to him. Being an object of worship was already making him uncomfortable.

Now instantly obedient, his former enemies got to their feet only to advance on their new lord with empty hands raised in supplication. They clustered timidly yet eagerly around the Crown Prince, daring to clutch gently at his boots and stirrups, relentlessly importuning him to become their leader.

The gray-mustached man who had been their leader before the Sword was drawn now came pushing his way through and ahead of the others, pleading as fervently as any.

"Master, allow me to introduce myself. I am called Gauranga of the Mountains, and I place myself and my poor company of villains entirely at your service. I am their leader, and the only one with any skill at all in magic. We are not much, perhaps, but we are the most accomplished and successful band of brigands for many kilometers around."

Murat could not help feeling a certain sympathy for the poor outcasts, despite their recent murderous intentions. But other concerns still dominated his thoughts.

"Are you sure you're all right, Carlo? The Sword's influence fell upon you also. I didn't want that to happen but as things were I couldn't help it. I'm sorry—"

"I'm fine, Father," the lad interrupted. And really he now looked perfectly well. Then his young face clouded again. "It was only when I thought—when I feared that they might hurt you—"

"Yes. Well, they didn't." The Crown Prince turned his head to speak sharply to one of his new devotees. "Let go of my stirrups, you, and stand back a little—that's better. They didn't hurt either of us."

Murat, inspecting his son, felt reassured. It was unlikely, after all, that Carlo could have taken any real harm. Historically the Sword's effects were very often only temporary; and what was more natural, after all, than that a son should honor and love his father?

The condition of the bandits was another matter. A few minutes ago, they had all been thieves and murderers— and they had hardly changed in that respect, Murat realized. They would grab up their weapons instantly if he were to point out to them someone he wished robbed or murdered; grab up their weapons and fight for him, win, or die in the attempt.

In a few more moments he and Carlo were ready to move on. But a dozen men on foot still surrounded them, begging not to be left behind.

"What do you want of me?" Murat demanded of them irritably. But he realized it was a foolish question even before the words had left his lips.

"Be our leader!" the bandits clamored eagerly, almost in unison.

Now Gauranga, the former leader of the robbers, spoke up again, enthusiastically offering for Murat's consideration a scheme his band had long contemplated. There was a certain walled village that the robbers knew of, a settlement so large and strongly defended that the risks of attacking it had been judged unacceptable. But now, in the service of their glorious new leader, they would gladly stake their lives in such an effort.

"But the lord must not risk his own life!" Another bandit broke in, suddenly aware of the peril implicit in his former leader's proposition. "Our new lord must stay in a place of safety!" Others growled their agreement.

Before Murat could decide how best to placate the gang and get them out of his way, another bandit had the floor and was arguing that the lord would be in no real danger even if he were to join in the attack.

"The Sword he carries will open the eyes of the villagers, even as it did ours." And then, as the elated bandit went on to explain, all the inhabitants' treasure, their food and drink, their gold and their daughters, would become instantly available for plundering. Once the whole village belonged to the lord, he could distribute its wealth among his followers as he chose.

At this prospect a joyful babble arose, only to die out again as soon as Murat broke in firmly. "No! No, I am not going to attack any village, and neither are you. I command you all: from this moment forward, attack no one unless I give you permission."

There was a murmur of surprise at this, though nothing that could have been called an objection. Briefly the Crown Prince regained the quiet, respectful attention of the group.

Then a question burst from one of the worshipers. "What is your name, Lord?"

Another pleaded: "Will you tell us your name?"

Again a general clamor mounted. From the exaggerated tones of pleading and worship in the men's voices, someone just arriving on the scene might have thought that they were mocking the silent man in their midst. But he, who had experience of the Swords, knew better.

It was Carlo, his adoring son, who shouted out his title—Crown Prince of Culm—and then with huge pride claimed the Crown Prince as his father.

A disproportionately loud cheer arose from the small group.

"See?" one of the thieves demanded triumphantly of his fellows. "I knew it all along! Real nobility!"

"The greatest!"

With a quick, reluctant salute Murat acknowledged the newest round of cheers. He felt weary. He needed time to think. "Very well, you may come with me, for the time being."

Renewed cheering answered him. The Crown Prince was thinking that this was certainly the quickest way out of the situation, and such an escort ought at least to discourage other bandits from attacking. The presence of this gang would reduce his chances of having to go through this all over again.

While he thought of it, he sternly ordered his recruits to protect, obey, and honor his son as well.

"He shall be second only to yourself, sir."

"And," Murat reiterated, "there must be no more robbery and murder. Not while you serve me."

Still the men raised no objection, though now several of them looked thoughtful. Murat could imagine their concern: if robbery was now forbidden them, what were they to do from now on, how were they to survive?

One man cried out—it was not an objection but a plea for help—that they faced an immediate food shortage.

Murat and Carlo exchanged looks. Together, their two packs did not contain enough surplus food to provide more than one meal for so many.

"Enough!" Murat shouted into a fresh murmuring, and once more obtained instant silence.

"I have changed my mind," he said. "I order you to go on about your business. Depart from my son and me. Obtain food as best you can, but kill no one for it." It seemed to him a reasonable compromise, under the circumstances.

He ought to have known better, but the reaction caught him completely by surprise. Stricken faces turned toward him. One howled to know why they were being so hideously punished. One or two others swore that they must kill themselves if their sublime master disowned them in this way.

Others, Gauranga among them, objected more rationally: "Go about our business? But Lord, you have forbidden us our business!"

Murat looked at Carlo. Carlo looked back at him, waiting in happy expectancy, ready to be delighted with whatever his glorious Father should decide.

The Crown Prince closed his eyes for a moment, feeling a great weariness. In time, he repeated to himself, people tended to recover from what the Mindsword did to them. At least they recovered if they wanted to recover, if they were not exposed to the Sword's continued influence, if other pressures were in place to have some contrary effect on them.

He had no intention of ever drawing this particular damned Blade again. That being the case, he relented.

"Very well, those of you who want to follow me may do

so, for the time being. But sooner or later you must all go your own ways. I do not need your services."

Gauranga and his men looked sad on hearing this. Sad but determined, Murat decided. Some of them at least were certain to try to prove their worth as followers. And at least an immediate mass excommunication had been avoided.

FOUR

MURAT and his son, attended by their new retinue of ragged but faithful followers, continued their cross-country progress at a somewhat slower pace. As the hours passed, and time came to stop for the night, the Crown Prince came to find the presence of the bandits, or former bandits, less ominous and worrisome. It was, after all, pleasant to be able to fall asleep knowing that his life and his son's were guarded by sentinels of fanatical loyalty.

The next day Murat was able to obtain food—to almost everyone's surprise, he insisted on paying for it—from a village whose alarmed inhabitants were fortunate enough to enjoy a modest surplus. Murat intended to feed the former bandits, if he could, as long as they were with him, but beyond that he really felt no responsibility to them. After all, these men when in possession of their free will had been perfectly willing to kill him and his son. Nor was the Crown Prince willing to assume any responsibility, in his own mind, for what the current members of his armed escort might do after he eventually sent them away. Then they would be free men once more, and their conduct would be entirely up to them.

By afternoon of the second day of his escorted journey, Murat started to find some amusement in the robbers' continued adulation—they were often unintentionally entertaining, as drunken men or lunatics could sometimes be.

Chuckling, he commented on this fact to his son, who worshipfully agreed.

It was very fortunate, the Crown Prince thought to himself as they rode on, that he himself, instead of some raw youth—Carlo, for example, or almost anyone of Carlo's age—had recovered the Sword of Glory. Much better for such dangerous power to repose in the hands of one like himself, an experienced man of the world, someone able to take such things in stride. In happier times he as Crown Prince had already received—perhaps, he thought, sometimes even deserved—his share of adulation. A man in his position learned to accept praise and devotion graciously, and not to allow such things to warp his judgment.

As the odd group progressed southward the landscape grew hour by hour less barren, rugged, and desolate. More farms and villages appeared, and the trail they were following turned into a real road on which moved other travelers. These unanimously gave Murat and his rough escort a wide berth.

Near sunset of their third day on the road together, the Crown Prince and his retinue came upon a blind beggar sitting at the wayside, a pale abandoned-looking man, some fifty years of age to judge by appearances, who raised his thin voice in a moaning plea for alms. In the red evening light the beggar's clothes were gray as a pilgrim's, so worn and tattered that their material and original design were hard to discern. The wooden begging bowl at the wretch's side had nothing in it, as Murat saw when he reined near to toss in a small coin.

A grimy bandage covered the mendicant's eyes. His beard and curly hair might have been shiny black, just touched with gray, had they not been dull with dirt.

At the sounds of the coin clinking in his bowl, and of the hooves of a large party stopping, the beggar raised his sightless face and turned it from side to side, as if to hear better.

"Thank you, Master," croaked the beggar at last, hearing no more coins.

"I have not given you very much." Murat raised his head to glance ahead and behind along the almost deserted road. "And you seem to have chosen a spot where you can expect but little more."

Now words poured from the beggar rapidly; evidently he was eager to talk to anyone who'd listen. "You see before you, kind Master, a victim of malignant fate. A persecution almost beyond belief has toppled me from a position of great respect and brought me here."

In Murat's experience, most mendicants had some heart-rending story to tell, and some of their tales were doubtless true. But here was an oddity to intrigue the curiosity of the Crown Prince: this fellow's speech was that of an educated man, a rare attribute in one of his profession.

Meanwhile, the blind man was spinning out his tale of troubles. "Ah, if only my blessed mistress knew to what a state I have been reduced!"

"And who's your mistress, fellow?"

The answer came firmly, and without hesitation: "I was honored to be able to serve the glorious Princess Kristin, who still rules in Tasavalta—if only word of my plight could reach her!"

Murat paused, staring at the man. "I see—on good terms with royalty, are you?" A laugh went up from those of his armed retainers who were listening.

The wretch, as if he were truly capable of injured feelings, seemed to be trying to summon up his dignity. "Sir, for years I served faithfully the royal house of Tasavalta. You will not believe the old blind beggar, sir, and for that no one can blame you—but these hands have many a time held the little Princess, when she was only a child, and bounced her on this knee."

Murat paused again, longer this time, wondering.

"Are you lying to me, fellow?" he asked at last, in a quiet voice. "About knowing the Princess? If so, admit it now, and no harm shall come to you. I'll even give you another coin." He jingled his purse temptingly.

The blind man was silent for a moment; but then he had risen to his feet, and was lifting his angular face toward the Crown Prince, and shaking his head ever so slightly from side to side, as if he might be straining to use the sense that he no longer possessed.

At last he blurted out: "I am not lying, Lord. Great Lord, if you can bring me to the palace at Sarykam, blessed be your name, and granted be all your wishes." And with that he fell on his knees before Murat.

Murat turned to look at his son. But since his exposure to the Mindsword, Carlo had ceased to offer him any advice or argument. Now, whatever happened, Murat's son only waited worshipfully to see what his lord and master and father would decide.

Sighing, Murat turned to one of his new followers, and gave orders that the strange beggar be given food and drink, and one of the bandits' spare mounts.

Then he faced the trembling beggar again. "Fellow, I take it you are able to ride? Of course if I present you to the Princess, and she looks at you like the piece of rotten meat that you appear to be, and does not know you, I'll look quite a fool. If that proves to be the case, I'll see to it that you don't slip away forgotten."

But the fellow only raised his quivering arms, his repulsive face almost radiant with apparent joy. "A million blessings on you, glorious Master!"

Murat nodded absently. Already he half regretted his decision. "What is your name, by the way?"

"I was called Metaxas, Lord."

When a riding-beast was led to the fellow, he groped for saddle and stirrup and managed to get himself aboard. Meanwhile Murat had noticed one of the bandits picking the forgotten coin out of the bowl, and stuffing it away in his own pocket. Well, why not? thought the Crown Prince. The one wretch probably deserved it as much as the other.

"Ride on!" Murat commanded, and signaled the advance.

That night, while Murat's eager servants were making camp for him and Carlo, Murat strolled over to the former beggar, intending to question him further. But he was distracted from his questions by the fellow's greeting: "I see, Master, that you carry a great treasure with you. I see also that you have suffered much, but that in the future you will be rewarded as you deserve."

Murat was not impressed. He supposed that the man might well have overheard some talk among the bandits about the Sword. He said: "For one without eyes, you claim to see a great deal."

Metaxas only bowed in his new clothing—new to him— cheap worn stuff, but still a vast improvement.

The Crown Prince turned away from the beggar, but he had not gone far when he was approached, humbly, by Gauranga of the Mountains, the former leader and acting wizard of the bandit group.

"What is it?"

"Master," gray-mustached Gauranga whispered, "I sense something wrong about this ugly foundling."

"Wrong? In what way?"

"I don't know, Master." Gauranga shook his head. "But there's something I do not like. A bad smell, and I don't mean the kind of stink that can be removed by scrubbing. Beware of him!"

Murat cast a look over his shoulder at the beggar, who looked about as unthreatening as a man could look. "I will, my friend. Thank you for your warning. The old wretch seems harmless enough to me, but keep an eye on him just in case."

Again the Crown Prince walked on. A few minutes later, Carlo, frowning suspiciously in the direction of the blind man who was well out of hearing, approached his father and volunteered his first advice in days. "It would be good, I think, Father, to hear this beggar's history in more detail, to test if his claim is genuine."

The father shook his head. "I assumed at first that he was probably lying when he said he knew the Princess Kristin. But when I offered to bring him to Sarykam, he accepted at once, with what appeared to be unfeigned joy. Either he's an excellent actor, or he may be speaking the truth after all, in which case the Princess will be pleased to have me bring her an old family retainer I've rescued from disaster. Of course, it's still possible that our newest recruit has deluded himself with dreams of a happy past."

"That may be the answer, Father. And I was wondering, has it occurred to you . . .?"

"What?" Murat demanded impatiently.

"Well—that Woundhealer would have been used to cure him of his blindness, empty eyesockets or not, had he really been a favorite at the Tasavaltan court during the years when that Sword was there."

The older man frowned. "We'll see. Certainly we'll have to clean the fellow up further before we can bring him near the Princess. Remind me to have a couple of the men see to it tomorrow, when we reach running water somewhere."

"If you were to use your Sword now, Father, to make the blind man your loyal servant, then you could be sure of him at once."

Murat darted a sharp look at his son. "I told you that I am not going to use the Princess's Sword again."

Next day Murat took time to see that the blind man was cleaned up more thoroughly, dressed in somewhat better clothing, and his eyes—or rather the holes where his eyes had been—covered with a clean bandage. There could be at least no doubt about his blindness.

Within another day or two Murat, Carlo, and their crew of converted bandits, bringing with them Metaxas the sightless beggar, were closely approaching the frontier of Tasavalta. This boundary ran unmarked over vast stretches of country, but the robbers assured Murat they knew exactly where it lay.

"What will you do, Father," Carlo was asking now, "if Her Highness does not welcome you as a friend?"

"I thought I had explained that. I will talk to her. I believe she is as reasonable as she is beautiful, and she will listen."

"But suppose she doesn't?"

Murat looked steadily at his son. "I can assure you of this much. Whatever problem of credibility I might face when we reach Sarykam, there can be no question of my using the Sword to persuade Kristin to see me as a friend. Is that what you were going to suggest?"

"I wasn't planning to suggest that, Father. I was just—"

"Good."

Carlo was silent.

"This power," his father continued, thumping the black hilt, "is going to remain safely muffled in its sheath, until I can hand over the sheath and all to Princess Kristin. I wish to be fairly reconciled with the Princess, not win her over in a one-sided contest of magic."

Still, from time to time during the day, Carlo continued to express his doubts about his father's plan.

"I don't see, Father, why you are so reluctant to draw the Sword in her presence—or in anyone's. Now having experienced the effects for myself, I can testify that the Sword of Glory does not deceive—at least it doesn't when *you* are holding it. In your hands, it only enables the object of its influence to see the truth about its holder." After noting the way his father looked at him, the young man shook his head and dared to argue further. "It's true, Father! You really are a great man, and worthy of great devotion!"

The Crown Prince smiled, shook his head, and rode on.

Murat had heard that long stretches of the borders of Tasavalta were usually left not only unmarked but unguarded, so that more often that not it was possible to cross back and forth without being seen or challenged. Again, some of his magically reformed bandits confirmed this, though otherwise they had little good to say about the land they were about to enter.

But this time fortune decreed that they were not to achieve an unseen crossing. Scarcely had Murat's little party set foot inside the realm of Princess Kristin than it encountered a Tasavaltan cavalry patrol.

FIVE

THE land in the vicinity of the encounter was relatively flat and almost treeless; it was quite possible that the patrol had been a kilometer or more away when they caught sight of Murat's party crossing the border. However they had made the discovery, the Tasavaltans were now riding quickly to intercept the intruders.

"No doubt we are a suspicious-looking crew," muttered the Crown Prince to his son. "To the border patrol, we can hardly appear to be anything but bandits."

"What are we going to do, Father?"

"We are certainly not going to run away."

Ordering his followers not to flee, nor to begin a fight, Murat led them slowly forward. As the riders in green and blue drew near, the thuggish-looking members of Murat's escort closed ranks protectively about their leader and his son.

Sternly the Crown Prince ordered his bandit-escort to lower their weapons, and move into an open formation, so he could see the Tasavaltans and they would have a good view of him. Then he continued to ride forward, raising empty hands in a peaceful gesture. Carlo followed of his own accord, keeping a little behind his father.

When Murat had come within fifty or sixty meters of the patrol, some of the troopers began pointing toward him, and calling to their officer. The Crown Prince, when he thought about it, was not surprised; he supposed that probably the whole Tasavaltan army must have been alerted to watch for last year's most notorious villain, the foreign potentate who had been royally entertained by the Princess, and then had treacherously repaid Tasavaltan hospitality by stealing Woundhealer.

Finally the patrol's commanding officer shouted: "Ho, there! You are Crown Prince Murat of Culm?"

Murat reined his animal to a halt, and called back in a firm voice: "I am the man you name. I come in peace, Lieutenant, with my son beside me, to speak to your most honored Princess. I will require an escort to your capital, and I ask that you provide it."

The officer was very young, and his uniform impeccable, even after what must have been several days in the field. He glared at Murat in triumph. "As to the matter of escorts, you'll get one, all right. I have my orders as to what to do, should you ever be caught trespassing within our boundaries. And I intend to carry out my orders. If your son and the rest of your gang wish to depart now, they'll save themselves some trouble. I have no orders concerning them."

The officer, thought Murat, must have felt confident that the ragtag ruffians before him would take to their heels rather than confront regulars at equal odds, the moment he gave them leave to do so. But instead Murat's fanatical bandits, enraged at the very idea of their lord made captive, gripped their weapons and surged forward. Only the Crown Prince shouting at them made them stop.

Startled, the cavalry officer yelled commands at his men, quickly deploying them in readiness for combat. Then, his face reddening, he informed Murat that he and all his escort were prisoners, and that they had better throw down their arms at once.

Murat, struggling to control his restive riding-beast,

could feel his anger escalating and the situation slipping away from him. "I have told you that I come in peace—"

The patrol commander interrupted, ordering his archers to nock arrows.

Murat's fanatical defenders bristled; they were not disciplined troops, whom he would have been able to hold in check. His veteran judgment warned him that whatever sway he still held over the situation was rapidly disappearing. Now it seemed that everyone was shouting, so his own conciliatory words had no chance of being heard. A fight was on the verge of breaking out, in which his own life and Carlo's would be at stake. And if they were to kill Tasavaltan border guards, how could they approach the Princess afterward with a claim of peaceful intentions? But neither could Murat surrender and allow himself to be disarmed.

Once again, with a reluctance as great as on the first occasion, but now feeling a fatalistic acceptance also, he drew his Sword. Uppermost in Murat's mind as the dazzling steel cleared leather was the thought that he could not allow his own son to die in his defense.

This time the Crown Prince felt even less of the shock of unleashed magic than when he had first drawn this Sword. But this time, as on that first occasion, every other human being within a hundred meters was engulfed, overwhelmed by the Mindsword's influence.

In the matter of a few moments, the once-arrogant officer of the patrol had joined his men in abandoning their sworn duty without a qualm, and proclaiming their undying devotion to Murat. The Crown Prince, observing their behavior as disinterestedly as possible, thought the scene was very much like that of the bandits' conversion, except that this time the bandits were on hand to welcome their new comrades to the fold, and make them feel more comfortable with their new status.

And this time Murat found himself able to view the matter somewhat more calmly; true, Carlo had now been exposed twice to the Mindsword's power. But there was really no reason to think the experience would do him any harm.

The young lieutenant, as soon as he had regained control of himself, ceased groveling in the dust, brushed off his no-longer impeccable uniform, drew himself up stiffly at attention before the Crown Prince, introduced himself by name and rank, and asked his new lord's pardon for his inexcusable misbehavior of a few minutes ago, when in his confusion of mind he had actually dared to utter threats against his glorious master.

Murat, speaking in a distant voice, pardoned him freely. The Crown Prince, feeling suddenly depressed, was wondering to himself how he had managed, all unintentionally, to land himself in this situation.

One single pardon, in dry words, did not appear to be enough. The lieutenant, stumbling verbally, trying to control himself, and now, despite being forgiven, apparently on the verge of suicidal guilt and shame, explained that he and his men—he asked pardon for them also—had been unable to understand the situation clearly until the Sword was drawn. Its powerful magic had cleared their eyes and their minds.

Murat silently congratulated himself on the graciousness with which he listened to all this and once more granted absolution. This time he tried to sound more concerned, more human, even while concealing his mounting impatience.

Taking a swift visual inventory of all the men around him, the Crown Prince noted in passing that the old beggar, Metaxas, had evidently retreated to a safe distance in the rear at the first threat of combat. One of the bandits was now bringing the blind man forward again to rejoin the group.

Still more patience was required in soothing and forgiving the officer and his troopers. When the Crown Prince had finally convinced them of his forgiveness, he went on to assure them that he and those who followed him meant no harm to any of the Tasavaltan people, least of all the noble and deserving Princess. He, the Crown Prince—as he patiently explained once more—only wanted to be reconciled with Princess Kristin, and with that purpose in mind he was bringing her an impressive gift.

The Tasavaltan soldiers cheered this news—of course, Murat reminded himself, knowing the power of the Swords, these converts at the peak of their fresh-caught enthusiasm doubtless would have cheered their new master just as loudly and fervently had he announced his intention of raping and murdering their wives and sisters.

Eagerly, several of the frontier guards informed the Crown Prince that the Princess Kristin was not currently in residence in Sarykam, the capital city on the coast. Rather, she and her younger son, the only members of the royal family now in the country, were to be found at their summer retreat high in the mountains, some kilometers inland.

"Good! Very good!" Murat found the news pleasing. The difficulties brought on by encountering the patrol had given him pause, and started him worrying seriously about how he was going to approach the city. If the entire Tasavaltan army had standing orders to take him prisoner on sight— and the newly converted officer, reddening with shame, now confirmed that this was indeed the case—then he, Murat, could hardly expect to approach the capital without having to draw his Sword again, and very likely more than once.

But a summer retreat in the mountains was almost certain to be much more readily accessible. On his way there he and his escort would be able at least to avoid the larger population centers. Murat was about to call for a volunteer from among the guardsmen, to ride swiftly ahead carrying an important message to the Princess; but before doing so he had second thoughts.

Taking the Tasavaltan officer aside, Murat patiently explained the difficulty to him. "If I dispatch a man with a message for the Princess, and that man says he comes from me, and speaks only good of me, the Princess and those around her will certainly believe that I have some of their troops under a magical compulsion. Therefore they will credit nothing the messenger tells them. Instead they will dispatch their own messengers to the capital, to mobilize the entire land against me."

The young lieutenant blinked, trying to grasp a point of view he now found so inherently absurd.

"But that would be so foolish of them, Lord! We here, the men of my patrol, are under no compulsion. Quite the opposite. It is only that now our eyes have been opened to your true nobility." And he looked as if he might be considering breaking his stance at attention to make some obeisance, something on the order of casting himself at Murat's feet.

"Yes, of course, you are quite right. Their attitude is foolish," the Crown Prince murmured soothingly. "But send no message for the time being."

"As you wish, Lord."

Murat shook his head, seeing no way at the moment for him to communicate with the Princess credibly. I am one sane man, he thought, for the moment surrounded by those who cannot see straight or think straight. So I, at least, must retain my sanity. Because it is my responsibility to think for us all. And I must decide what will be best for Kristin and her people too.

Murat raised his voice: "We will all of us march together for the time being. Lead the way to her summer retreat."

The cavalry detachment, having been prudently provisioned for a long patrol, carried food enough to feed not only themselves, but the former bandits as well, adequately for the several days it would take for the combined group to approach Princess Kristin.

Further inquiries among his newest adherents gleaned for Murat a welcome confirmation that at least Prince Mark, whose presence might have complicated things immeasurably, was, as so often, out of the country. But Mark was expected back at any time now.

From certain things that the soldiers said, certain expressions that crossed some of their faces when Mark was mentioned, the Crown Prince got the idea that they might retain a high regard for Mark as a fair Prince and a capable soldier. But these indications of regard for Kristin's husband vanished as soon as the men learned that their new master's attitude toward Mark was less than cordial. From now on several of the men had only black looks and dark mutterings at any mention of their former commander. These, Murat decided, were probably men who had nursed some resentment against Mark even before they caught the vibrations of Murat's feelings toward him.

As for the Princess herself, all the troopers were glad to see and hear how highly Murat thought of her. They also continued to hold Kristin in great esteem.

Murat decided that he had learned all he needed to know for the time being.

"Let us march on," he ordered his combined force. "Toward the Princess, in her summer retreat."

SIX

FOLLOWING the surrender of the border patrol, the Crown Prince and his newly enlarged entourage enjoyed several days of almost uneventful travel. All during this time the Sword remained sheathed at Murat's side. As they traveled he observed his followers carefully, to see how and when the Mindsword's influence would begin to wear off—sooner or later, he knew, it probably would. And indeed, some of the men's behavior did change with the passage of hours and days. The Crown Prince thought that within two days three or four of the bandits and some half a dozen of the troopers had begun to have second thoughts about their quick conversion. The process, unlike that of their metamorphosis into his followers, was quite gradual, manifesting itself only in solemn faces and thoughtful stares; he had no fears of a sudden betrayal.

As the enduring effects of the shock of magic continued to weaken, the undisciplined bandits grew a trifle lax in obeying Murat's orders, and Carlo reported that some of the troopers were beginning to recall their broken oaths of fealty to Tasavalta's Princess. No dramatic event occurred to illustrate these changes, but small signs were visible to one who watched for them as the Crown Prince did. Quietly he asked his son's opinion on what was happening.

Carlo seemed dismayed at the thought of anyone who had once seen the light choosing to turn away from it again. He suggested that his father draw the Sword once more.

But Murat declined to do that. Instead, calling all his followers to attend him, he explained again, as openly and fairly as he could, his reasons for wanting to visit Princess Kristin. He maintained that his goals were just, and that reasonable people ought to be able to perceive them as such without the help of magic. Certainly he meant no harm to the Tasavaltans' beloved Princess or to any of her subjects. Just the opposite, in fact, or he would not be bringing her this great Sword as a gift. This was the first time many of his new followers had learned the nature of his intended gift, and he saw that it made a strong impression.

After he dismissed the meeting, the Crown Prince saw that Carlo was frowning again, and demanded to know what his son was thinking.

"Nothing you have not heard before, Father."

"Then tell me again."

"I am worried," Carlo said. "Worried by the idea of power such as the Mindsword's being simply given away. If someone other than yourself possessed it, such magic could easily convince people to follow the wrong leader."

"I'm sure it could. But Princess Kristin is hardly an evil leader. And the Sword is mine, to do with as I will."

"Yes, of course, Father. But is it in your best interest to have such a treasure pass completely out of the family? The ruling family of Tasavalta are practically strangers to us. And how do we know that they will always want to behave in a friendly way toward us in Culm? In the wrong hands, your Sword's magic might—thoroughly confuse people."

Murat took thought, and smiled. "Well, Carlo, as things have worked out, you and I are seldom in Culm anyway. I doubt that either of us has much future there. And I think what the Princess might choose to do with the Sword after she has it is beside the point. The point is that I owe her restitution for a great wrong, and I intend to give her this Sword to make up for the one I took away."

"As you say, Father," agreed Carlo dutifully.

But, once out of his father's sight, the son shook his head, still worrying. It did little good to keep telling himself that anything and everything his father did was right, and therefore Father must have a good reason for what he wanted to do with the Sword.

"Are you troubled, young Master Carlo?" The old blind man, sitting as usual on the fringe of the camp, raised his sightless face as Carlo approached. Evidently the beggar had sensed that something was wrong.

Carlo's feet slowed and stopped. He sighed, wondering if the beggar had recognized him by the sound of his footsteps. He wished he could confide in someone.

"Is there trouble, then, young Master, between you and your esteemed father?"

"I don't know," answered Carlo soberly. "I hope not. No, I don't really believe there's any trouble."

"Something, perhaps, concerning the Sword he carries?"

"Tell me, Metaxas—you say you have known the Princess—?"

"Years ago," returned the beggar cautiously.

"Tell me, what is she really like? What would she do with the Sword of Glory if she were to possess it?"

The old beggar heaved a wheezing sigh. Sounding worried, he suggested that it might be better if the Sword were not given to Kristin, nice lady though she was. Metaxas thought it would be much better, for all concerned, if the Crown Prince could be made to see that he should keep such a superb weapon for himself.

"As long as the Sword of Glory rests in the noble hands of the Crown Prince, we can all feel safe. Whereas, in any other hands . . ." Shaking his head, Metaxas let his words trail off.

"That is my own thought." Carlo sighed in turn. "But how can I persuade my father to do anything?"

"It is not for me to intrude between the two of you."

"Of course not. But . . ."

"But—sometimes—I feel it is my duty to make at least one small suggestion."

"Do so."

"It is just this. Blind agreement, blind obedience, is not always the greatest, truest loyalty."

"Blind—?"

"I mean, young man, that if there is some real danger to your father, and he is unable to see that danger clearly, it becomes your duty—and mine, of course, and all his followers—to help him. Even if what we say, or do, should anger him at first."

"I'm not sure I understand, Metaxas."

"Perhaps I have already said too much, young master. Anyway, it is my opinion that if your father feels he must give the Sword to someone, it should be you."

"Me!"

"That is not so surprising, is it? That such an inheritance should pass to a faithful, loyal son?"

"No—" said Carlo, then fell silent. Then he turned and walked away, not knowing if he was angry with the blind beggar or not. To have the Mindsword in his own hands . . . no, he told himself firmly. He did not wish for anything of the kind.

Later that night, with everyone but a pair of patrolling sentries fast asleep, Vilkata lay rolled in a borrowed blanket on the edge of camp. Choosing a time when both sentries were well out of earshot, he muttered certain antique words into his blanket, meanwhile holding the fingers of his left hand contorted into an unusual position.

Within the space of a few breaths he became aware of the

silent arrival of an intelligent presence, inhuman and invisible.

"What news, Master?" inquired the demon's voice. The dry leaves seemed to be swirling right in the Dark King's ear, but still they were barely audible.

Keeping his head three-quarters under the blanket's folds, and whispering, Vilkata reassured his partner that he still remained free of the Mindsword's influence. So far, using the demonic vision secretly provided by Akbar, he had managed to scramble out of range of the Mindsword's power each time that violence threatened. On the last occasion it had been close.

"I believe that most of these fools, if they take notice of me at all, think it only natural that a blind man should try to get himself out of danger when swords are drawn. At the same time they assume that the Mindsword must have caught me at some time, and that I am as loyal to their precious master as they are. I act the part, of course."

"And does the Crown Prince too assume you are his slave?"

"He is a fool like the others. I doubt he thinks of me at all, except as a surprise gift for his beloved Princess."

"Ah. Excellent. I have no doubt that you have managed to deceive them all. When will you seize the Sword, Dark Master?" The dry-leaves-and-bones voice of the demon nagged him eagerly. "Tell me, when?"

"I'll grab it from him as soon as I can, fool!" Vilkata in his frustration had to remind himself to keep his whisper low; mere subvocalization was more than ample for the demon to hear and understand. "I do not enjoy this game, as you can understand, but I must play it patiently. Any man who has worn a sword as long as our friend Murat, and faced as many treacherous enemies as he, is always on guard against being suddenly disarmed, just as he is always breathing. And if I should try to get the weapon from him, and fail, I'll get no second chance."

There was a silent pause.

"Of course, Master. Forgive any suggestion of disrespect that I may have given in my impatience."

"You are forgiven." The Dark King had no intention of offending his partner until he felt confident of being strong enough to exercise control.

Vilkata whispered on, venting his frustration, lamenting the fact that he had still been unable to find an opportunity to seize the Sword from Murat, even though in the Dark King's demon-powered perception Skulltwister loomed ever as a brilliant beacon.

He came near suggesting—though he stopped short of doing so—that Akbar have a go at snatching the Sword himself if he thought it would be so easy.

Then the man had a request. "Can you not make my human body younger, swifter, stronger? That would help."

"I assure you, Great Master, matters are not that simple. The man Murat is magician enough to detect any sudden magical alteration in your person. Magician enough to sense my presence should I come any nearer him than this. The instant he grows suspicious he will draw his Sword. Where should we both be then?"

Vilkata grumbled, but forbore to press his partner to give him more help, or to make an attempt to grab the Sword of Glory himself. He really had no wish to see the Sword in Akbar's hands.

Sounding as malleable and cowardly as ever, and repeatedly fretting about the dangers of discovery, Akbar wondered querulously if they were even safe from discovery here on the edge of camp, with almost everyone else asleep.

"There are no magicians here but me—certainly not the Crown Prince. No real magicians at all—well, there is one amateur who might conceivably be dangerous."

"Ah?"

"His name is Gauranga, the bandit with the gray mustache, and he posseses a sensitivity, if no real skill, in matters of magic. I am beginning to fear what he may detect."

"Yes, I see, Master. Such an individual could present a problem—let me try to solve it."

"I trust you will succeed. Without alarming anyone."

It was early on the morning after this conference that four of the converted Tasavaltan guardsmen approached the Crown Prince and asked his permission to speak.

"Permission granted."

Standing before Murat, the troopers informed him timidly, in one or two cases rather sullenly, that they wished to leave him and return to the service of the Princess.

Murat had begun to expect such a request from some of his men, and readily gave those who asked permission to leave his service. They looked somewhat relieved.

He raised a cautioning hand. "I would ask you, however, to delay your return to your former duties until after I have a chance to make contact with the Princess, which should be very soon now. Will you promise me that much?"

Standing as they were, confronting Murat directly, the troopers were unable to refuse him that much, although their Tasavaltan loyalties had obviously regained an ascendancy. The foundations of their conversion, Murat thought, had been built on nothing substantial in the mundane world, and were now eroding swiftly; in another day or two they might be capable of becoming his enemies once more.

The thought bothered him unreasonably.

"Wait another day," said Murat, "and I will put in a good word for you with the Princess. As soon as I have the opportunity."

He had thought that this gracious offer would relieve the men's remaining worry. But to his surprise the troopers looked more uneasy than before.

"Your pardon, sir, but . . ." Their spokesman hesitated.

"Well, what is it? Spit it out. Speak freely."

"To put it bluntly, sir, the Princess doesn't like you." The man hesitated, then plunged boldly on. "I mean, sir, in the case of someone like Princess Kristin, who doesn't really know you yet, who's never had the benefit of your Sword to clear her vision—well, in the light of what happened last year, isn't it natural that she at least *thinks* she doesn't like you?"

"What I believe you are trying to tell me, trooper, is that she won't listen to me, won't give me a chance to explain about last year. You believe that instead of my being able to put in a good word for others, I'm badly in need of one myself, as far as the Princess is concerned."

The soldier was relieved at not having to spell it out. "That's about it, sir. *We'd* be glad to put in a word for *you*, you've sure treated us handsomely. Only . . ."

"Only you will be regarded, at best, as deluded victims; at worst as deserters. Nothing you say will be believed. I understand." Murat paused. "But you are wrong."

"Sir?"

"Not about the kind of reception you may expect when you report back for duty; I'm afraid you're right about that. But you are mistaken about your Princess." The Crown Prince nodded for emphasis. "She'll listen to me. She'll be angry at me at first, over what happened last year, but she will still listen."

"Yes sir. If you say so, sir." And perhaps, Murat thought, the soldier was convinced.

Shortly afterward that man and the three other Tasavaltans who had chosen to return to their original loyalties rode away. Murat made no further effort to delay them; according to the best information his loyal people could give him, the Princess in her summer retreat was now no more than a few hours' ride away.

And scarcely were they out of sight than another small

delegation came to report to Murat that the bandit-magician Gauranga seemed to have been overtaken by an accident during the night. He had died of a plunge down a small cliff.

"Walked away in the darkness to relieve himself, it looks like, sir, and just walked a step too far."

The Crown Prince went to take a cursory look at the body. An odd incident indeed, but there was no evidence of foul play, and certainly nothing to connect Gauranga's death with the beggar. If any faint shadow of suspicion of the blind man crossed Murat's mind, he dismissed it in the next instant as preposterous.

That day Carlo reported to his father that one of the troopers who had chosen to remain with them was a veteran of that famous battle of fourteen years ago, when the armies of the Silver Queen and the Dark King had clashed in battle, each ruler armed with a different Sword.

That night, with most of the group sitting around a campfire some kilometers closer to where they might expect to find the Princess, Murat encouraged this soldier to speak to them of those days.

This veteran had served in the Silver Queen's victorious army, and told now how he had seen the great Lord Vilkata's soldiers overwhelmed by the Sword of Despair, many of them slaughtered on the field, but most taken prisoner while in a state of helplessness. There was no humor in the story, and no joy; it seemed that even the victors in that battle still bore the psychic scars of it.

At the beginning of the tale Vilkata had been crouched at the far end of the camp, alone and distant from the fire. But as the story progressed, the Dark King, seeing more than any of the others dreamed, gradually edged his way closer to the storyteller's fire, and listened unnoticed to this tale of events in which he had played one of the principal roles. The veteran, noticing at last the presence of the Eyeless One, remarked that he'd had an aversion to blind men ever since that day of battle, when he had glimpsed the Dark King from afar.

The blind man on hearing this smiled under his bandage, a sickly, unhealthy kind of smile. Several of the former bandits tittered. Murat smiled faintly, with the air of one whose thoughts are far away, but wished to share the general merriment.

A brief silence fell. When Carlo remarked that the Mindsword was the only one of the Twelve to be known under only a single name, Murat commented that he had also heard it called the Sword of Glory. Others in the fireside circle nodded to confirm this.

And the old veteran of that battle between Swords assured his new master and his comrades that the Sword now carried by Murat had indeed been given several other names by the common people in both armies.

Murat raised an eyebrow. "Indeed?"

"Perhaps you won't hear these other titles spoken in the palaces, sir, among the lords. But we used 'em in the ranks."

"We'll hear them now, then."

"Well, sir, there's Sword of Madness, Skulltwister, Brainchopper, and Mindmasher, that I can remember." The veteran frowned, not looking at Murat, seemingly unconscious that such terms applied to his master's source of power might be taken as offensive. "And there were others—let me see—"

Murat was not too pleased to hear his present source of salvation, his future gift to the Princess, called by such derogatory titles. "I think we've heard enough," he snapped.

"Aye, sir." The old soldier accepted the rebuke stoically and without question, as an old soldier should.

On the morning following that fireside discussion, Carlo had a second meaningful talk with Vilkata.

In the course of this conversation the Dark King worked again at planting the idea that it is sometimes necessary to disobey, even to deceive a lord—even a father—in order to serve him properly. He hardly knew himself what profit he might expect to gain from this intrigue; but he knew that time was passing, and he seemed to be getting no closer to his goal.

On that same morning, Murat was pleased to be able to estimate that even now, several days after he'd drawn the Sword for the last time, some four or five of his converts, from the ranks of both bandits and soldiers, and including the officer who commanded the patrol, still remained firmly devoted to him, if their behavior was not quite as fanatical as it had been immediately following their conversion. And the remainder of the men were still Murat's followers, perhaps as trustworthy as most soldiers in most armies.

The Crown Prince, philosophizing on these matters in conversation with his son, supposed that he and his Sword had happened to encounter these men at a time when they were ready to attach themselves fanatically to the first worthy cause that came along.

Carlo, still innocently fanatic himself, argued that on the contrary, these permanent-seeming conversions were a result of their master's own innate leadership and charisma.

The conversation was broken off when Murat noticed the beggar Metaxas hovering near, as if he would have liked to take part in it also. Repelled by the fellow, and yet reluctant to take any notice at all of his presence, the Crown Prince moved away.

Vilkata had been perfectly correct in what he had told the demon. Such was the disregard in which the Culmians held him that it had never yet occurred to either Murat or Carlo to wonder if the old beggar had really been caught by the Mindsword at all.

Murat only shook his head each time he received yet another round of fulsome praise from his most devoted followers. But he had to agree that he had not been without loyal followers at home in Culm, even when he was out of favor with the Queen and her consort.

His faithful Tasavaltans assured him again that the summer residence of their Princess was now only an hour or two ahead.

Now in his own mind Murat began to rehearse in detail the explanations he meant to offer for his conduct on his last visit, the strong arguments that he was going to present—with great gentleness, of course—to Kristin as soon as he saw her.

He sighed, reminding himself that the Princess might well be angry with him at first sight. Yes, her anger was practically certain. Given how he'd offended her, nothing else could be expected. But at the same time, he had faith in Kristin's fairness and justice. She would listen to him when he approached her, deferentially yet boldly, with his apology. With calm speech and concise reasoning the Crown Prince meant to convince that loveliest of women that he had not really invaded her territory with the intention of subverting her army. Despite what the old soldier had said—what did such men, worthy and loyal as they were, know of princesses?—Murat really had no doubt that he'd be able to persuade her when the time came.

He had another discussion with Carlo on this point. But Murat broke off the talk in irritation when Carlo still seemed doubtful—and when, once again, the old beggar hovered near.

And anyway, the Crown Prince was beginning to think it

not all that surprising that a number of people, including some of the more worthy Tasavaltans, should really want to follow him from now on, even after their minds were cleared of magic. If that was what they wanted, it would be unjust of him to prevent their doing so.

His mind was running on such thoughts when his confrontation with the Princess came, at least an hour before he expected it. The meeting was sudden, and startling on both sides.

SEVEN

ALONG the east side of the mountains, on the long slopes facing the distant sea, it was a day of low clouds, mist, cool winds, and occasional sunlight. The scenery here tended toward the spectacularly beautiful, with meadows and scraps of forest alternating with stark mountain crags. Small streams tumbled and frothed, pausing for rest in green-fringed pools. This was the land of Kristin's own childhood, to which she retreated whenever possible.

Early this morning she had ridden out from her summer residence for a long ride, accompanied by her younger son, eleven-year-old Stephen, and a small handful of attendants. The party was nominally engaged in hunting, but none of its members cared much if game were taken or not. For Kristin the joy of this kind of hunting consisted chiefly in being able to observe the grace and speed of the high-flying hybrid winged creatures, raptors bred to kill small game for their masters, or track larger prey for mounted humans to pursue.

Whatever degree of success the flying creatures might have today, the Princess knew an aftertaste of bitter envy as she watched them soar in freedom.

She was recalled from useless pondering upon her fate

when her son rode close to speak to her. Stephen was a sturdy eleven year old, his once-blond hair now turning darker, becoming a good match for that of his absent father. These days, the boy was looking forward to his father's imminent return from another in the long series of journeys and pilgrimages Mark had undertaken in an effort to serve the Emperor.

"Father will be home soon, won't he? In a few more days?"

"I don't know." Then Stephen's mother regretted the shortness of her reply and the sound of indifference in it. She was not indifferent. "Do you miss your father very much?"

"Of course. Don't you miss him?"

Kristin hesitated, brought up short by the sudden look of wonder in her son's eyes. "Naturally I do," she said at last. "I wish he wouldn't go away so much."

"Why does he have to go away so much?"

It was not the first time Kristin had heard that question from one of her sons, and it grew no easier to answer.

"Because he feels he must," was her reply this time.

"Because he wants to help the Emperor; I know that. But why does he do it so often?"

"Because that's what your father feels he must do."

The boy did not reply at once. Then he said: "Father wants to help Grandfather against his enemies."

"Yes. Something like that." Kristin did not doubt that the Emperor's enemies existed, and that they were evil; she could have named a goodly number of them offhand. But more and more it seemed to her that those scoundrels claimed a much larger portion of her husband's thoughts and actions than she did, and more and more she questioned the need for that.

For a short time mother and son had been quite alone, but now a couple of attendants, one of them armed, appeared riding nearby. These days, the summer retreat and its environs were but lightly guarded by troops and magic. One squadron of cavalry had been detailed for protection, and at the moment was supposedly keeping just out of sight of the hunting party; there was no particular reason to expect any hostile incursion.

Meanwhile, young Stephen, as he did with increasing frequency these days, began questioning his mother about his mysterious grandfather the Emperor, and expressing his hopes of being able to meet him someday. The boy sounded keen on the idea, like someone looking forward to a challenge. Part of Stephen's problem, his mother knew, was that his brother Adrian, only two years older, had already met the Emperor, and had even engaged—more or less on the Emperor's behalf—in difficult and dangerous adventures far from home. There was of course some rivalry between the brothers, and Stephen was the one who seemed by temperament more fitted for high adventure.

"When is Adrian coming home?"

That was not a new question either. "Whenever he reaches a point in his studies when his teachers decide he should have a vacation. Magic is a difficult subject, if you're going to do it properly. Even for someone as talented as Adrian."

"Then it could be years."

"Possibly. I know you miss your brother too."

Stephen was silent, while their mounts carried them a hundred meters. Then he announced: "I'm going up on the hill, Mother. Maybe I can see the flyers better from there."

"Bring me back some interesting news, if possible."

Kristin's son turned his mount, and dug in his heels. In moments he was almost out of hearing, and still riding swiftly.

The Princess watched him go. She was now left for the moment practically unaccompanied, the two attendants who were in sight riding at a distance of some forty or fifty meters.

Moments later, in the process of following a tenuous trail around the steep base of a house-sized boulder, Kristin came face to face with Murat, who was riding just ahead of a small advance guard of his followers.

For a long, long moment there was silence. It was Murat who recovered himself and spoke first. "Do not be afraid, my lady. You need never be afraid of me."

"Treacherous villain!" Even as Kristin gasped those words, she took note of the young man riding a few paces behind Murat, who somewhat resembled him; and of the uniformed Tasavaltan troopers just a few meters farther back. These soldiers were not of the troop assigned to protect the summer residence; and the attitude of these men, looking expectantly toward Murat as if for orders, crushed any momentary hope that this hateful intruder was their prisoner.

Princess Kristin's next thought was that the Tasavaltan uniforms must be a trick, and that these were the villain's own men dressed for more Culmian treachery.

But the troopers, seeing their beloved Princess confronting their master, hastened to close in on the pair, showing her every sign of courtesy and respect, and trying to explain. The explanations at first made no sense at all to Kristin, but she could no longer doubt that these were Tasavaltans.

Murat silenced them with a gesture. Urging his riding-beast a little closer to the Princess, he assured her confidently: "You will have no cause to abuse me this time, my lady. I come in peace."

But now a very different-looking crew, a stretched-out file of six or eight men who looked very much like bandits, were coming in sight behind Murat's mysterious

Tasavaltan escort. And far in the rear, one last rider, a man who appeared to have a bandage on his eyes, dawdled on a mount led on a long rope by the last bandit.

These matters were of small interest just now. Immediately on Kristin's left, almost close enough for her to touch, was the huge boulder around which circled the path she had been following. The way was open to her right, where at a distance of some thirty meters a screen of lesser rocks and stunted trees blocked the view. In the middle distance there loomed slopes and crags, at the moment looking utterly unpopulated. Nowhere was there any sign of help.

But still the Princess had not yet begun to be afraid; her outrage had not left her time for fear.

Facing Murat, she declared: "This time, I see, you have come as a bandit leader—a more open and therefore less dishonorable appearance than last year, when you posed as a diplomat."

But even as she spoke, fear was beginning to take its place beside her anger; she struggled to keep the change from showing. The most urgent of her silent worries was for her son: Had Stephen managed to get safely away? And where was Captain Marsaci and his troop? For the moment Kristin could do no more than hope that help might be at no very great distance.

Several of Murat's Tasavaltan converts, still innocently wearing their uniforms of blue and green, were unable to keep silent despite their new master's order. Now some of these men burst out with fresh importunings of their Princess, telling her what a great man the Crown Prince was, and how it would be a grave mistake, even a great sin, for her to delay in placing her whole realm at his disposal.

Murat saw her turn pale under her tan on hearing this lunatic advice offered in such a reasonable tone. But a moment later Kristin felt something like relief as the most logical explanation for these defections crossed her mind.

And from the first thought of magic it was only a step to the strong suspicion that the Mindsword must be involved.

Now one of the young Tasavaltan soldiers, on seeing the Princess's expression change again, thought with relief that she was on the point of being converted to Murat's cause. At once the youth began explaining earnestly that all the fuss last year about Woundhealer being stolen must have been only a misunderstanding.

One of the trooper's comrades interrupted to remind him, rather hotly, that, after all, if Crown Prince Murat wanted that Sword, or anything else, he had a perfect right to take it. Didn't he?

A word from Murat was needed to put down the incipient quarrel; but that word was instantly effective.

"And do you believe that you have such rights?" Princess Kristin demanded of him. Her only real hope, she had decided, was to stall for time; but nevertheless, she found that she could not contain her bitterness. She was surprised by the depth of hatred the sight of Murat evoked within her. "What have you come to steal from us this time?"

When the Crown Prince, obviously stung by her words and attitude, started to reply, she interrupted him: "You robber, I never thought to see you cross our borders again of your own free will! You must be as mad as these underlings, these traitors, who follow you."

Murat, though he glared at her momentarily, chose his words carefully and kept his voice soft. "I am not insane, Princess, believe me. True, for a long time I despaired of ever being able to enter your lands again. But here I am, and I bring good news."

"The only good news I can imagine hearing from you is that you are departing more swiftly than you came. And this time going empty-handed." *Where is my son? And where my loyal cavalry?*

The man confronting the Princess mastered his own

anger and pressed on. "Last year, in the casino where I helped to rescue your older son—"

Kristin knew it was important for her to be clever, to play for time. She knew that she ought to hear out his absurd argument, whatever it might be, with an appearance of patience. But her emotions kept her from doing that.

"You speak of my son Adrian? You, of all people, claim to have *rescued* him? Your thieving treachery only contributed to the danger that he faced!"

Despite the many times the Crown Prince had rehearsed this encounter in his own mind, nothing about it was going as he had planned and hoped. Instead, matters were taking a sharper turn for the worse than he had ever feared. He had expected anger from the Princess, but somehow he had never envisioned such a depth of enduring bitterness. And her last accusation, thought Murat, was completely unfair. He could feel righteous anger at this injustice reddening his face, but still he did not argue. His own real responsibility for this lady's unhappiness was too shamefully clear in his mind to allow him to do that.

Feeling proud of his ability to continue speaking calmly and fairly under these conditions, he replied, "Nevertheless, dear lady, there was a point in Sha's casino when I was trying to help the lad, and I was fortunate enough to have some measure of success. But the point I am trying to explain now is that during that scene of great confusion at the gambling house, the Sword Coinspinner fell into my hands. With such help I was able to get away, bringing Coinspinner with me."

"And I suppose it is the Sword of Chance you wear at your belt now?" Coinspinner's overwhelming good luck, thought Kristin, might account for this villain's having encountered a patrol of cavalry who for some reason were ready to defect.

"Not so, my lady." The Crown Prince paused for a

moment, his own resentment ebbing away helplessly as he gazed at the angry face before him. Kristin's blue eyes were even lovelier than he had remembered. To him, this woman at this moment looked no older than eighteen, though he knew that she must be over thirty. And her beauty was not the deceptive glamour some women were able to achieve by means of magic. Murat felt confident of always being able to sense that particular deception, and he detected no trace of it now.

She asked him crisply: "Then are you bringing back the Sword you stole from us?"

"My lady, if ever again I have Woundhealer in my possession I'll bring it back at once. But unfortunately I do not have it now."

"Then what is your business here?" Kristin demanded icily.

"I have come to bring you a gift," the Crown Prince said, and felt profoundly unhappy when his words seemed to make no impression whatsoever upon his hearer.

He continued doggedly, speaking into the strained silence: "Coinspinner eventually took itself away from me, as the Sword of Chance is wont to take itself from anyone who holds it. But before vanishing, it showed me clues by which I might be able to possess a certain other Sword. That is the Sword I am wearing now. It is the Sword I wish to give to you, to make amends in some small measure for my behavior of a year ago." Murat bowed in his saddle, at the same time frowning lightly to himself. Somehow his speech had not come out as abjectly apologetic as he had earlier imagined it would be.

But he thought that Kristin relaxed slightly. He did not know that she had caught a momentary glimpse of blue and green and armor, not far to her right, just behind the screen of rocks and stunted trees. More bewitched defectors? She was going to gamble that they were not.

A moment later, with an abrupt effort that took Murat

and his escort by surprise, she was reining her mount sharply, spurring away from them. From the screen of rocks and bushes twenty meters away erupted a rush of cavalry in blue and green, Captain Marsaci and his force, howling in a charge upon Murat and his men. The Princess had not, after all, been caught completely unprotected.

EIGHT

EVEN as Princess Kristin, crouching low over the animal's neck, spurred her mount away from Murat, she was shouting orders to her attacking troops. Carlo thought he heard her cry out a command to take the Crown Prince alive. But whatever her order might have been, it came too late to have any immediate effect upon the line of charging mounted men who had now burst out of cover.

Carlo had drawn his own sword and was shouting also, knowing that his words too were useless even as he cried out a superfluous warning to his father. In the next instant he saw his father struck by a slung stone. But the Prince managed to remain in his saddle, and a moment later he had drawn the Sword of Glory again.

A moment after that, the attack by the blue-green guardsmen was aborted. Their charge ended in plunging, rearing confusion, men and animals swallowed in the dust cloud raised by twenty riders simultaneously reining in their mounts.

But the defensive reaction that charge had provoked among Murat's guardians went on for a few seconds longer; it did not stop until the Crown Prince had shouted orders to his men, and in that brief period more than one of the attackers were struck down.

Carlo rode quickly to his father's side. Murat, his face

pale, was managing to control his riding-beast with one hand.

"Father—where were you hit?"

"Right thigh. I'm all right. A glancing blow, no more."

Carlo sheathed his own sword and watched the immediate effects of the enemy's conversion. He thrilled with triumphant pride as once more the Mindsword's intervention produced its inevitable result; soon the largest harvest yet of new followers, their weapons discarded, were arrayed around Murat in attitudes of prayer and submission, begging forgiveness from their new master for not having seen him clearly a few minutes ago, for having committed the unthinkable crime of daring to attack him.

Murat, despite his repeated insistence that he was not much hurt, needed help in dismounting. Carefully slitting his right trouser leg with the point of his dagger, he disclosed a great bruise swelling on the outside of the thigh. He could stand on the leg, though at the cost of some pain; it seemed that no bone had been broken.

Obviously the Crown Prince was angrier this time than on the two earlier occasions when he'd drawn the Sword.

A murmur spread swiftly among the men gathering around him. The slinger who had inflicted the injury had just used his dagger on himself, his last breath leaving his throat in a scream of remorse.

Carlo felt a sense of loss; he'd been looking forward to seeing the unfortunate cavalryman cut up into little bits.

But Murat paid little attention to his attacker's fate; even before the attack on him had come to an end in confused, abject, and horrified surrender, he was already looking around for Kristin.

The sight of her mount, running riderless, gave the Crown Prince a sickening moment. But then he beheld his beloved Princess, physically quite safe, kneeling in front of him, her head thrown back, tears in her eyes and on her cheeks. Murat needed a moment to make sure that they were tears of joy.

Sheathing his Sword, and leaning on Carlo, the Crown Prince hobbled to her as quickly as he could.

As he approached she said, in a breaking voice: "My lord Murat, I am now able to see you for the first time as you really are. You must forgive me, I beg you, for what I have done against you in the past, and what I was saying about you—only a few minutes ago. Could it have been only minutes? It seems to me a much longer time, because when I said such horrible things about you I did not understand. I had to be born again to understand."

Murat wanted to kneel down facing her, but his injured leg screamed pain at him. For the moment he could only lean on Carlo. "Princess! Kristin? I beg of you—get up!"

In a moment the lady had sprung up nimbly to her feet. "As you wish, my lord Murat. Whatever you wish, from now on. I am yours forever. Do with me what you will—but you are hurt! Gods, let it not be serious! Say that it is not!"

"It is nothing. I will not die of a bruise." Then, taking both of his beloved's hands in one of his, Murat tried to frame some reply in accordance with what honor and duty demanded. But the shouting celebration which surrounded Kristin and himself made it difficult to think.

Half an hour after Kristin's conversion, she and Murat were sitting together in front of a newly made small fire, while their armed guardians, now a band some thirty strong under the command of Captain Marsaci, saw to their comfort and safety. Marsaci had guards patrolling a perimeter surrounding the royal couple at a distance of thirty or forty meters.

There was no physician in the Crown Prince's newly enlarged retinue, but several of the troopers were veterans with experience in all kinds of battle damage, and they agreed with Murat's own assessment of his injury: walking and riding would be difficult for several days, but the wound was no more than a bruise, and with rest it would heal.

When Murat at last commanded the circle of worshipful, worried gawkers to stand back, he happened to catch sight of the blind man Metaxas, standing in the background. Impulsively announcing to the Princess that he had a surprise for her, he ordered the former beggar brought forward.

"Do you know this man, beloved?" Murat asked, when the ugly fellow was standing immediately before them.

"No, my lord," Kristin answered promptly. But a moment later a shadow crossed her face, and she shook her head. "No . . . that is, I do not remember."

As soon as she had spoken, Metaxas knelt before her. "I know the voice of my beloved Princess," he murmured, his own voice almost inaudible.

Kristin still hesitated. "I—I don't know." But she seemed upset.

Murat gestured the fellow away, and burly troopers took him by the arms. "Never mind now, my lady. Later we can talk of him, if there is any need. Now there are more pressing problems that must be faced."

"You mean the reaction of my people, when I tell them how my eyes have been opened to your true nature."

"I—yes, that is a good way to put it, I suppose. How can we avert a conflict?"

"I will speak to them. I am their Princess, and they honor me and will listen to me."

"Let us hope so." Murat turned to his son who was standing nearby. "Carlo, take half a dozen men and reconnoiter. See if we are under observation, if you can; at least discover if more Tasavaltan forces are in the vicinity."

Kristin shook her head. "I should doubt that very much, my lord. But by all means send out your scouts. I pray there will be no more unnecessary fighting."

"I share your feelings," said Murat fervently. Then he nodded to Carlo. "Go!"

At midday, Murat was still sitting in almost the same spot, for he had to avoid putting weight on his leg as much as possible. He was now saying to the Princess, for what seemed to him the hundredth time since he had found her: "But I want to help you. I have come here to help you."

Kristin was sitting on the grass a little apart from the Crown Prince now, and gazing at him adoringly. "Help me? But you have already transformed my life. From now on, my lord, I live only to help you."

Perhaps, Murat thought to himself, it was hopeless to try to explain his position to his beloved now. No doubt he would do better to wait until the effects of the Mindsword wore off, or at least moderated to some extent, as he thought they were bound to do. But with Kristin before him, hanging on his every word, her every expression one of perfect trust and contentment to be with him, he was compelled to keep trying to explain.

"Kristin, what I wanted to do was . . . ever since we met for the first time, I have hoped someday to win your love."

The Princess glowed. "Do you mean it?" she whispered softly.

"Yes, of course I mean it. Now I can—I must—openly acknowledge that was my secret purpose in coming here. But—I never wanted it to happen like this! I do not want you as a slave."

The lovely woman drew back. To Murat's astonishment it was almost as if he had slapped her face. She said in a much different voice: "You may call it slavery or not, as you choose. I only know that all the love I have to give is yours. I am sorry if there is something in the situation that does not please you."

He leaned forward, forgetting his injured leg, provoking a sharp twinge of pain. "Don't weep! I beg of you do not weep!"

Moved by the sincerity in her lover's tone and manner, the beautiful young woman ceased to cry. Tentatively she essayed a smile.

But Murat, shaking his head, could not force a smile in return. He could only mutter once again: "I did not want it to be like this."

Kristin's smile lingered. "But this is the way I am, my lord, and this is how things are. I rejoice to hear that you have wanted me for a long time, and I am overjoyed that you want me still; only the thought that one day you might cease to want me brings utter desolation."

Murat opened his mouth and closed it again, remembering how some of his first converts had been ready to kill themselves at the mere suggestion that he was leaving them. He was not going to suggest anything of the kind to this beloved woman. Nor was he going to take advantage of her in her present enchanted condition.

Presently a call from a lookout informed the camp that Carlo and his scouting party were returning. Getting to his feet with an effort, his weight on his left leg, Murat waited for his son's report.

It was brief and to the point. The reconnaissance patrol had discovered no signs of fresh Tasavaltan activity.

As if the sight of Carlo had reminded her of something, Kristin began to look around, her gaze sweeping the distant hills and meadows.

"What is it, Kristin?"

"My son Stephen was somewhere around. . . ."

"Was he—within a hundred meters, when we met?"

"A hundred meters?" Kristin did not appear to grasp the significance of the distance. "No, I don't think so. He may have ridden back to our summer house, before—before you and I met."

The Crown Prince sat down again, with a grunt of relief. "I remember Stephen. He'll be a year older since I saw him—a likely lad, well able to take care of himself, I'd say." But Murat called his own son to him again, and shortly a cavalry patrol was scouring the area for the boy, with orders to bring Stephen to his mother if that could be accomplished without using force.

While the search was in progress, Murat gave orders to set up camp where they were, and maintain a perimeter patrol, to give warning of anyone approaching.

Murat's leg needed rest; even more desperately, he decided, he needed time to think. Where was he to take the Princess now, where to lead his augmented force of fanatical followers? He asked her who else was at the summer lodge, and found there was only a minimum staff.

He also learned from Kristin that she and her party were not expected back there until late in the afternoon, and no one at the lodge would be really concerned about them until nightfall. Probably not until tomorrow would there be any thought of sending out a search party.

Hours passed, and the patrol dispatched to search for Stephen did not return. Again Kristin expressed some vague concern about her son—"He'll think something terrible has happened to me"—but everyone assured her that there was really no reason to be worried about the lad.

"If he did observe our meeting, and saw how you—came to join me, and if he is now raising an alarm—well, in any case, my Princess, someone will do that, sooner or later, when you do not return to your summer house. What are we to do now, Princess?" The Crown Prince was shaking his head. "What am I to do? Believe me, I had no intention of coming here and making you my prisoner by magic."

Kristin blinked at him, and seemed to have trouble

grasping the idea. In fact she could hardly believe her ears. "Your *prisoner?* My lord! Am I a prisoner now?" She laughed at the idea.

"Of course you are not." Murat paused. "I mean that is certainly not my intention. I want you to be completely free, my dear one, and you are, you shall be, as free as I can make you . . . but I'm afraid that your people, those who remain outside my Sword's influence, are not going to see the matter in that light."

Kristin was almost indignant. "If any of my people should come out from the city against us, my lord, or if more units of my army appear, be assured that I am their Princess. They will listen to me when I tell them that nothing at all is wrong." She paused, smiling. "I have formed a new . . . alliance. That is all."

"Yes, no doubt they will listen to you, for a time, at least. But as soon as they learn that you have been exposed to the Mindsword's powers they will react differently. . . . Where is your husband now?"

A cloud crossed Kristin's brow. "Mark is where he usually is. Out of the country. Somewhere."

Murat could all too readily imagine Mark's reaction when the news reached him of what had happened to his wife.

The Crown Prince raised both hands to run tense fingers through his hair. "Let me think. I must have time to think."

Everyone respected his wishes.

Limping away to a little distance from the others, he sat on a rock and nursed his wounded leg and tried to think. The Sword in its sheath seemed to weigh heavily at his side.

His latest mass conversion had caught a beastmaster among the Tasavaltan troopers, who had with him a pair of small winged messengers. So it would be possible to send a written warning to whatever authority remained in Sarykam with the Princess gone. . . . Murat tried in his mind, without success, to frame a message—from himself? from the Princess? signed by them both?—which would keep that authority from trying to interfere.

Next he turned over in his mind the idea of sending Carlo on to Sarykam bearing a flag of truce, perhaps with a few converted soldiers, perhaps alone, to explain how matters stood. If he, Murat, were to go there himself, with or without the Princess, he would only be forced to draw the Sword again, and probably more than once. And if Kristin were to go alone, her people—with good reason—would think her possessed, enchanted, and they would keep her there by force.

And naturally he, Murat, would not be able to allow that.

He thought he could visualize the ensuing chain of events, as stronger and stronger forces were sent against him, to be converted in turn; and he as an experienced soldier knew how to force battle if an enemy did not wish to give it.

Could it really be that easy for one man, with the help of the gods' Sword-magic, to bring a whole kingdom to its knees?

The Crown Prince was beginning to think it could. But perhaps the conquest would have a chance of becoming permanent only if the people of the kingdom were in fact dissatisfied with the rulers they now had, and ready to be conquered. Was Tasavalta—perhaps—in that condition?

With a mental shudder the Crown Prince put such temptations from him. He hadn't come here as a conqueror, but to make amends to the woman he loved, and then to try to win her freely given love.

While Murat had sought to be alone temporarily, he had not actually forbidden Kristin to approach him, and it was soon apparent that she had no intention of remaining at a distance. Tentatively approaching her new lord now, she saw from Murat's slumped posture and woeful expression that he appeared to be deriving no benefit from his interval of silent thought.

Advancing more briskly, she broke silence and resumed her efforts to soothe him. "I will go back to our summer lodge alone, my lord, and explain everything to my people there."

Her beloved smiled at her mirthlessly. "But don't you see, Kristin? Your people love you, and some of them would die for you, but they won't accept your explanations for such a sudden change in your behavior."

"I can lie to them about the Mindsword. Say only that I experienced a sudden change of heart."

"I do not want you to lie to them. They wouldn't believe you anyway. And in any case your magicians would soon detect the touch of magic on you."

She sat at his feet. "Then tell me what to do, my lord Murat. I will be happy to do whatever will satisfy you."

The Crown Prince started to stand up, grimaced, and sank back on the rock.

Then with a decisive gesture he began to unbuckle his swordbelt. He said: "Then I will simply do what I came here for. I want you to accept a gift."

The man who now called himself Metaxas was twenty meters away, watching with demon-vision, easily observing all that happened from behind his bandaged, empty sockets. Now he held his breath. Was the Mindsword about to be drawn yet again? He was on the verge of hobbling away from the couple and their treasure at a speed that would certainly raise suspicions.

And where was his precious demon, who ought to be ready to whisk him from the scene?

"What are you doing?" The Princess seemed alarmed at Murat's actions.

"I am giving you this Sword."

Springing to her feet, she recoiled. "My lord! I will be

pleased and honored to carry your Mindsword sheathed for you, if that is what you wish. But I will never draw it, never. Not even if you should order me to do so."

He who called himself Metaxas, watching from a distance, began with a hoarse cough to breathe again.

Murat could only ask her, feebly: "Why not?"

"Because, my lord, I could never draw or hold that Sword. I should be terrified of putting you into a situation where you might worship me. I am all unworthy, and such a thing would be utterly unthinkable. Utterly!"

Murat, holding the weighty unfastened swordbelt in his hand, posed slumped on his rock like the statue of a rejected lover, no longer able to think of what to do or say.

The Princess continued, "And besides, my lord Murat, there are practical reasons why you had better continue to carry your Sword yourself. Very likely you are going to need to use it again, perhaps quite soon, for your own safety. It pains me to say it, but having thought the matter over I must admit that here in Tasavalta you are still surrounded by real and potential enemies, some of whom will think I am bewitched and refuse to listen to me. It would be good for you to convince them all as soon as possible of the truth."

The Crown Prince said in a tired voice: "I had hoped that would not be necessary."

"Happily we can still hope, Lord Murat. My people love me, and usually they accept my judgment. It is I, and not my husband, who has inherited the throne."

"I think your husband," said the Crown Prince, "is not the man to accept the loss of his position in meek silence."

Kristin frowned. "No," she said thoughtfully. "No, Mark will not do that. He is basically a good man, you know. I owe him my life, for on the day we met he saved me from the Dark King."

"Someday I must thank him for that," said Murat, dryly but seriously.

"I fear him now," said Kristin suddenly. "Not for myself. I fear what he might do to you."

"As to that, I have a long history of being able to protect myself." Still, Murat was more concerned than he allowed himself to sound. He had nothing against Mark, and no wish to hurt the man, but still less would he care to be destroyed by him.

By mid-afternoon, Carlo and his scouting party had returned from their latest effort, and there was still no word of Stephen. Murat, trying to ignore the undiminished pain in his leg, was sitting by himself, staring at his sheathed Sword, and thinking.

An hour ago, when he had tried again to denounce his own behavior of a year ago, none of these faithful people around him would listen. Respectfully they insisted on howling in protest. And in fact Murat's apologies were now beginning to sound mechanical in his own ears. All these Tasavaltans, from Princess down to private soldier, now saw the matter of Woundhealer's removal from the realm in a much different light. They could marshal arguments that seemed convincing. A year ago the Crown Prince of Culm had only been following his Queen's orders, and had shown commendable loyalty by so doing. He had wanted and needed the Sword of Love only to heal the intolerable difficulties in his own royal house.

Once the subject had been raised, Kristin quickly proclaimed that last year's difficulties over another Sword had been her own fault, and not at all Murat's. There was no excuse, she insisted, for her not allowing this admirable Prince to have Woundhealer, when he had come asking so decently only to borrow it!

The same Crown Prince today was slow to reply. At length he nodded. "I think I must agree with you there, my lady—even if it is only Sword-magic that now compels you to view the matter in so favorable a light." Murat held up a hand, forestalling her objections. "Not that I was right in stealing the Sword when you refused me, but—"

"Please, my lord, don't call what you did stealing! Of course you were right to take the Sword when I so stubbornly refused to lend it. What else could you have done?"

He sighed. "At the time it seemed to me that I was dealing with a bad situation in the best available way. Later, of course, I came to repent my choice."

There was another chorus of objections. Kristin and her compatriots all repeatedly assured the Crown Prince that last year's difficulties were not his fault but hers; she had been very wrong in not letting him have the Sword. Of course she should never have denied him anything he wanted!

Near sunset there came another moment when Murat and the Princess were more or less alone. She took this opportunity to ask him softly: "Is it true that my lord wants me?"

The look in her eyes made it very plain to Murat that he had not mistaken her meaning. When he tried to frame a reply, he found himself stumbling and stuttering like an inexperienced youth.

"I—how could I ever possibly answer no to that?"

Happiness glowed in Kristin's eyes. "Then I am yours. Completely. I hereby divorce my husband."

The Crown Prince looked bewildered on hearing this; but Captain Marsaci and some of the other Tasavaltan soldiers, near enough to the couple to have heard at least part of what Kristin said, were quick to rejoice. They also joined their Princess in explaining to Murat a certain provision in the ancient traditional law of Tasavalta.

By this custom it was in the power of any reigning

monarch, be it king, queen, prince, or princess, to achieve a very quick, legal and formal separation from a spouse. The provision had been invoked only two or three times in recorded history, and its use required certain conditions. As Kristin saw the current situation, these conditions now obtained.

Prolonged absence from the realm by the unwanted spouse was one of the conditions.

On every level of his being, Murat was greatly pleased that this woman he loved was ready to abandon everything for him, even though he knew it was the irresistible magic of the gods which made her do so.

But, as an honorable and practical man, he was horrified at the idea of her invoking this old law now. He saw a bloody civil war looming as a distinct possibility.

A new thought struck Kristin now, and she dared to question Murat indirectly, about his own wife. "Lord, does there exist in Culm any obstacle to our union?"

Struggling with the feeling that events were moving too fast, the Crown Prince experienced a certain relief as he explained that he was still married. He hastened to assure Kristin that his wife no longer meant anything to him. They had not truly lived together for many years.

Carlo, who had recently joined the other listeners, was looking very thoughtful now.

Murat said gently to Kristin, "The Queen and those around her have been angry with me for a long time. For various reasons. And our adventure last year did not help matters. You know, I suppose, that after all my efforts, Woundhealer never reached Culm?"

"We have heard as much in Tasavalta—but few details of the failure reached us."

The Crown Prince could not provide many details either. Last year someone else, troops serving a power still unidentified, had ambushed Murat's troops who were carrying Woundhealer toward Culm. The Sword of Mercy had been stolen en route from those who had stolen it from Tasavalta.

"And so," added Murat now, with assumed lightness, "it would seem that all the treachery I practiced here was quite in vain."

"Treachery!" Kristin was truly outraged, really appalled. "I will not hear that word applied, not even by you, to your behavior, to anything you've ever done. Treachery, indeed! Who dares to call it so?"

Not long ago she herself had been using that word, and others just as bad, quite freely. But he was not going to remind her of that fact now.

The Princess also expressed her outrage against the unknown aggressors who had taken the Sword of Love from the Culmians. "We shall see about them! We shall hunt them down, and retrieve your property."

Even as Murat pondered the futility of arguing with Kristin in her present enchanted condition, it crossed his mind—perhaps not for the first time, but for the first time of which he was fully aware—that his own wisest course might be, after all, to retain the Sword of Glory for a short while to use it at home. Kristin would only be the better pleased if he kept possession of the weapon long enough to obtain justice for himself in his own house and his own country. Besides, his position now in Tasavalta looked intolerable; something like a full-scale war seemed inevitable if he were to remain.

And now, as if he'd spoken his thought aloud, the woman he loved began to insist that the wrongs her lord had suffered in his own country took precedence—they must be righted before he and she turned their attention to anything else.

She spoke with an air of simple practicality. "I see now, my dear, how it must be. We—if you agree, of course—

will at once proceed together to Culm. There you will straighten out matters with your family, and settle any difficulties that may arise with anyone else whose opinion and goodwill you consider important. You will be appearing among your own people as the new Prince of Tasavalta," Kristin added complacently, "and I think such an accession of territory and population cannot fail to help them see things your way."

Once more Murat stared at the black hilt at his side. Now he began to see the possibility of good fortune in the fact that he'd been unable to go through with his original plan of handing the Sword over to Kristin at their first meeting. For the first time the Crown Prince had to admit to himself that there might be definite advantages in going about things differently.

For one thing, it was plain that Tasavalta could know no peace as long as he was here with the Sword. His presence in their land, and the fact that he had the Princess with him, could not long remain a secret from most of the people. Either he had to leave Tasavalta for the time being, or else prepare to convert the bulk of the population to his cause—and he still shrank from such a conquest. So far he'd used the Sword only in self-defense, and he'd not go a step beyond that if he could help it. He wanted no allegiance that had to be bought with magic.

No, the best thing to do was withdraw from this land, for a time, until Kristin had recovered her own will, and could make her own decisions freely—meanwhile doing his best to make sure that she would still look on him favorably when that happened.

"One day I *will* give you the Sword, Kristin. As you know, it was my intention to do so as soon as we met, but—"

"Please, my lord. If you love me, do not try to force me to accept that gift."

It was more than Murat could do to keep from blurting out how much he loved this beautiful, devoted woman. Loudly he proclaimed that he was as much enthralled by her as she was by the Sword.

"It is not your Sword, my love, that enthralls me. What is the Sword, after all? It is only an incident."

The Crown Prince gave a wild laugh, and made an extravagant gesture with both arms. "How will I ever be able to leave you?"

The Princess reacted with alarm. "Do not speak of such a thing, my beloved. Not even in jest!"

"I will not! I'm sorry, I promise, I will not!"

Trying to ignore the pain in his leg, hoping to get to sleep in his lonely blanket roll, Murat tried to picture to himself their arrival in Culm. He thought the pair of them ought to rate a reasonable welcome—at least he hoped so. With even a minimum of good luck he ought to be able to live there for a time without having to draw the Sword again. There, in his homeland, he ought to be able to keep it sheathed.

In the morning they would have to ride, whether his leg still galled him or not. He did not intend to be in Tasavalta when Prince Mark returned.

Murat was on the verge of sleep when his attention was caught by a figure standing nearby, almost motionless in the light between two dying fires. It was the blind man, Metaxas.

The Crown Prince sat up, conscious of the weighty presence of the sheathed Sword, snugly almost beneath him, as it always was these days when he lay down.

"What do you want, beggar?" he demanded, hearing the words come out more roughly than he had intended. More mildly he added: "Be careful, you'll walk into a fire."

"I thank the great master for his concern, but it is not

necessary; I can sense the heat. The truth is that I remembered something that I feared my lord might have forgotten."

"And what is that?"

"Only," said Metaxas, "only that there are still three other Swords, forged by the gods, in the royal Tasavaltan armory in Sarykam."

NINE

IN the morning, when Murat reminded Kristin of the existence of three more Swords in the Tasavaltan armory, she eagerly confirmed the presence there of such weapons, and blamed herself for not having thought of them before.

When the Crown Prince mentioned the blind man's visit to him during the night, her face clouded, though at first she made no comment.

"Do you remember him now?" Murat asked her. "From your childhood?"

"No. Though there were many servants about when I was a girl, and I cannot be sure. I suppose he had his eyes then?"

"I had assumed so, though I never asked him. Shall we have the fellow here now and question him?"

"Not for my sake," Kristin answered quickly. "I do not like him. The Dark King was eyeless too, and I still sometimes encounter him in my nightmares. The way he looked at me—I know he could see me somehow—while his magicians were—causing me pain."

"I would do anything," Murat told her softly, "rather than cause you pain again."

Kristin gave her beloved an adoring smile. Then, becoming businesslike, she urged the Crown Prince to issue marching orders. If possible they ought to seize the three Swords in the armory quickly, to prevent their falling into the hands of Mark or some other potential enemy. "Of course it may be too late already. But I think that we must try."

Grimacing, Murat thought the matter over. He had hoped to avoid entering the capital, but . . .

He asked: "Which Swords are there?"

"There are Dragonslicer, Stonecutter—and, most important, Sightblinder."

"Then the blind beggar told me the truth."

"Who controls the first two may make little practical difference to us in our situation, but the Sword of Stealth could be a deadly weapon against you—indeed, against anyone."

"How well I know it!" Murat closed his eyes for a moment, wishing for a chance to rest. Events were rushing him into territory he had not planned to enter. Still, that was a common enough situation for a soldier, and no protracted deliberation was necessary.

"No doubt you are right," he said. "We must try to bring that one with us."

Opening his eyes, he added: "I am surprised that Mark did not take Sightblinder with him on his latest journey, wherever he may have gone."

The Princess hesitated before answering, and again a shadow crossed her face. At last she said: "Mark has good qualities. I suppose he thought that Sword might be needed at home, to defend the realm."

Murat grunted something; he did not care to hear about the good qualities of the man who, he had every reason to expect, would soon be trying to do his best to murder him.

Then, turning, the Crown Prince issued orders to all his followers that they prepare to move quickly on Sarykam. In his own mind he proposed to deal with his leg wound by ignoring it—that was a common tactic for a soldier, and in the past it had served Murat well.

Next he addressed the Princess once more. "I had hoped to avoid entering the city, but I must try to get Sightblinder."

"A wise decision, Father," Carlo approved.

An early morning patrol sent out to take a last look around for Stephen returned, before camp was broken, with nothing to report. But the Princess no longer appeared particularly worried about her son.

"He'll be all right. Frightened, I suppose, poor child, that his mother should be missing overnight—but there's no help for that just now. We may find him at the palace in Sarykam."

The Crown Prince shook his head, and his hand touched the black hilt at his side. "I had no wish to draw this weapon before, and I've less inclination to employ it now. But if the alarm's been spread, by Stephen or anyone else, I suppose I'll have to use it at least once more when we reach the city."

"Murat, my love, I fear you are too scrupulous. It is not as if you are hurting anyone when you draw that beautiful blade—I think it should be called the Sword of Truth as long as it is in your hands. While you have it, it will not harm my son, or any of my people, any more than it has harmed me."

The Crown Prince said nothing in reply. Though he had assistance in mounting, it still cost him an effort not to cry out with the pain in his leg. But then he was in the saddle, and he found that he could ride, at least at a moderate pace. In a few minutes everything was ready, and the march to the city got under way, Carlo riding at Murat's left side and Kristin at his right.

Once on looking back, during the morning's ride, Murat noticed absently that the blind beggar was riding in the rear as usual, his mount dutifully following the animal ahead.

The man represented a minor mystery to be sometime resolved.

In this way the small procession proceeded for some time, Murat riding in thoughtful silence. As soon as Kristin saw that he wanted to be alone for a time, she dutifully dropped a few meters behind.

As he rode, the Crown Prince was meditating on the Swords. It was true that Dragonslicer and Stonecutter each had very impressive powers, but they were also very specialized, and under present circumstances he did not see that either of those Swords was likely to be of much benefit to him if he should gain it, or much harm to his cause in the hands of an enemy. Nevertheless, Murat determined to take both of those Swords with him if he could, on the grounds that they were really Kristin's, and the general principle that it was almost always better to possess any Sword than not to have it.

But Sightblinder was a different matter, and the more Murat thought of that Blade the larger it loomed in his calculations. The Sword of Stealth could render even an otherwise negligible opponent deadly dangerous; and Prince Mark was anything but negligible. In fact Murat knew him to be strong, clever, ruthless, and determined, and of all human beings perhaps the most familiar with the Twelve Swords' powers. In Mark's hands Sightblinder might well pose a murderous threat, even to one as well armed, experienced, and wary as Murat.

Sarykam, as Kristin assured him, was nearly a full day's ride away, and Murat had no wish to arrive there at night or with tired men and exhausted riding-beasts. Therefore at sunset he called a halt, went through the painful process of dismounting, and ordered his followers to make camp. Murat saw to it that Kristin was provided with her own small tent, one that the troopers had been carrying; he and Carlo lay nearby, under the stars.

The Crown Prince had much to think about before he slept. When he said good night to Kristin, and made it plain that he did not intend to join her in her tent, she had asked him what was wrong.

In answering Murat chose his words slowly, and his voice was grim. "There is no difficulty that we cannot overcome in time. Princess—there is nothing I want more in this world than to embrace you. And, when you have been three days free of the Sword's power, I intend with all my heart to do so."

"Foolish man," she whispered fondly. "Do you still believe that your Sword there has enslaved me? Is there some magical significance in a period of three days? What I feel for you is not going to change in three years, or in three centuries."

"I'll not wait as long as three years, I assure you. But grant me the three days, for my conscience. It seems a reasonable interval."

"Of course." The Princess smiled, and looked around their little camp. Everyone seemed to be studiously avoiding watching them. "By then, perhaps, we will have found a place where we can be more completely alone." And, leaning forward, she swiftly kissed Murat on the cheek. A moment later she had disappeared into her little tent.

Next morning at dawn, the Crown Prince, his escort, and his close companions resumed their march. Murat tried to convince himself that his leg at least felt no worse than before.

As the city came into view in the distance, then grew closer and bit by bit more distinct, Murat became more intensely alert, and steadily more suspicious. These roads near the capital, which at this hour ought to have been at least moderately busy with all kinds of traffic, were ominously deserted.

Kristin, too, frowned on observing all these empty fields

and highways, and spoke of her concern to her lover, who was riding at her side.

Murat only shrugged fatalistically. "I suppose we ought to have expected it. No doubt someone has spread word of what has happened—that you have joined me." His hand was already resting upon the Mindsword's hilt.

Kristin tossed her glorious hair, and smiled with a determined optimism that Murat decided he had not yet—quite—begun to find irritating. She said: "All of my people are going to learn the truth sooner or later anyway; our love cannot remain a secret."

"Of course not."

"Poor Murat. I see your conscience is still bothering you unnecessarily."

The inhabitants were still totally and ominously absent when Murat and his group reached the city wall. The broad gate which normally allowed access to and from the high road was tightly closed. No sentries appeared on the high wall, and only a distant barking dog responded when the Tasavaltans escorting the Crown Prince and Princess tried to hail their countrymen.

At Kristin's order several of her soldiers pushed and pulled on the massive timbers of the gate, but evidently it had been barred on the inside. The obstacle caused only a short delay; a couple of soldiers with a rope, working unopposed, made short work of getting atop the wall, and moments later were able to open the gate from inside.

One of the two troopers, on emerging from the gate, reported to Murat in a puzzled voice: "It looks deserted inside the walls, sir. How can my people fear you that much?"

Murat did not attempt an answer. He only commented to the Princess: "I fear we may find the armory already emptied of what we would like to find in it."

"I share your fear," said Kristin in a subdued and

troubled voice. "Are they all in hiding, or in ambush? What can they be thinking of?"

Alertly, the party advanced toward the city's center, traversing one street after another normally thronged with people, but this morning as deserted as the country roads had been. Certainly, Murat thought, someone had assumed leadership within the city, and had acted decisively and effectively during the night. Stout stone-built houses looked down in utter silence on the visitors. Were the folk who lived here all hiding behind their closed shutters and doors, or had they evacuated the city? Murat, riding the eerily quiet street, could not tell which course the populace had taken, and did not particularly care. Well, he could easily understand why these people were fleeing him and his Sword as if he were the plague. But even so, such a welcome was annoying.

The great square in front of the palace was as deserted as the broad streets. Again, somewhere in the background a single dog was barking, a forlorn and frantic sound. The stout doors of the armory, adjacent to the palace, were closed and locked just as the city gate had been, but Kristin was in possession of the keys, both mechanical and magical, that would enable her to enter here.

No human guards had been posted outside or inside the armory. Not one additional recruit, it seemed, was to be left for the Mindsword to enlist in an intruder's cause. But the strong spells of protection woven by old Karel, Kristin's magician-uncle, were still in place, and Kristin warned Murat and his son as well as the converted troopers against trying to enter. Only the Princess herself approached the doorway, through which she was able to pass freely.

The Crown Prince waited nervously, but he had not long to wait. In a matter of moments Kristin emerged again, her expression grim.

"My lord Murat, all three of the Swords are gone."

Under his breath Murat blasphemed various of the long-departed gods. Beyond that there was not much to be said. No doubt someone—whether it was young Stephen or not made no difference—had reached the city long hours ago, bringing an eyewitness account, or perhaps some garbled version of one, telling what had happened to the Princess. Whoever had taken charge here on receipt of that news had issued orders swiftly and forcefully.

"Neatly done," Murat commented. "But I wonder where they can all have disappeared to?"

"To no great distance, I suppose," said Kristin, sadly. She was obviously hurt that her people had run out on her, without waiting to hear what she might have to say to them. "But it doesn't really matter. I'll explain to them."

Finding pen and paper in the deserted office of the armory, she announced her intention to quickly write out several messages, some addressed to various individuals, others to her people in general. Then she would dispatch runners to leave these notes in prominent places within the city where they could not fail to be discovered.

Standing in the doorway of the little office, watching Kristin as she began to write the messages, Murat smiled fondly at her. "What exactly are you telling your people?"

"Simply that I am going to be their Princess, as before— but no, not quite as before. There will be certain changes in the realm, but only for the better, because from now on I will serve in the name of the most glorious Crown Prince of Culm, who is soon to be Prince of Tasavalta also—and tomorrow, perhaps, the Emperor of the World!"

Murat sighed gently. "I think it will be better, my dearest, more conducive to peace, if you do not claim any thrones for me just yet."

The Princess hesitated. "Very well—I suppose you're right." She crumpled a paper and threw it away, picked up a fresh sheet and began again.

Minutes later, the letters having been hastily distributed nearby, the Crown Prince, Princess Kristin, and their entourage were on their way out of Sarykam.

When the city was an hour's ride behind them, the Crown Prince began to see Tasavaltan cavalry in the distance, but so far the uniforms of blue and green were only scouting, warily maintaining a prudent interval of several hundred meters.

Presently there also appeared a few high-flying winged scouts, keeping track of Murat's small moving column from above.

Murat had cursed energetically on learning that Sightblinder was already gone. But the full implications of his failure to seize that Sword were only now becoming apparent to him. The Sword of Stealth in the hands of a determined enemy meant that from now on, he'd have to be agonizingly suspicious every time he saw someone he loved approaching him—and doubly fearful if ever he saw a being he feared too much to face in combat. Not that, in Murat's case, there were many human or inhuman entities who'd fit either category.

Ah, if only he'd been able to get Sightblinder into his own hands! Then he might have been able to enforce peace. That weapon and the Mindsword might well have formed a practically irresistible combination for controlling minds. Besides providing its possessor with deceptive concealment, Sightblinder also allowed him or her a better perception of the true nature of other folk.

Yes, he was going to have to take the most careful precautions against the great and subtle Sword of Stealth.

And not, perhaps, only against that one. To the best of the Crown Prince's knowledge, six more of the Twelve Swords forged by the god Vulcan were still scattered about the world.

Murat had passed almost his entire life not being in

possession of any of the Swords, and in that state had never spent much time worrying over what might happen if one were used against him. But on those rare occasions when he had got his hands on one of the Twelve Blades, he always found himself suddenly much concerned about the others.

Of course, anyone having one Sword became a much more likely target for whoever controlled the rest. The titular Crown Prince of Culm as an itinerant and landless nobleman was one thing, and the same man as a Sword-holder was quite another. It was as if the acquisition automatically thrust him, willy-nilly, into some great, only vaguely defined game, whose players had each as his object the domination of the world.

The Crown Prince carefully corrected his thought. The other players, perhaps, had such an objective. His own ambitions remained much more modest.

Now moving briskly along toward the frontier that he and Carlo and Kristin must cross on their way to Culm, Murat considered what he knew of each of the other Swords still in existence. The strongest was probably Shieldbreaker, which immunized its bearer completely against the Mindsword's power, or indeed against the action of any other Sword or lesser weapon, whether material or magic. Only an unarmed opponent could— and almost certainly would—prevail against the holder of the Sword of Force.

The great and evil magician Wood had grasped that fact, certainly, a year ago when he had been forced to cast away the Sword of Force to save himself in Sha's casino. Some-one else must have picked up Shieldbreaker there. But who had done so, and who might hold that tremendous weapon now, were unanswerable questions to Murat. Nor was it likely that anyone in Tasavalta had the answers, as his new ally the Princess had already assured him.

Next on the list, somewhere out there in the world, was Wayfinder. The Sword of Wisdom could help its owner avoid fatal traps, doubtless including the Mindsword's sphere of influence, and could indicate to him or her the proper path to any goal. Wayfinder's use entailed certain drawbacks, however, usually increasing its owner's risks.

Kristin, who shared much of her husband's extensive knowledge of the Swords, had confirmed that no one knew what had happened to Wayfinder either. At least neither she nor her husband had heard anything new of the Sword of Wisdom since it had vanished from the body of the dead god Hermes, some eighteen years ago.

. . . The Mindsword's sphere of influence, yes. What factors set its limits, exactly? Murat had observed that the effective distance seemed to vary slightly from one use to the next, but what caused the expansion or contraction he did not know. Whatever the causes, he knew that his Sword's influence extended throughout a space of about a hundred meters in every direction from the Sword itself.

And what an influence! All along Murat had known, in a theoretical way, what he might expect the Mindsword to do for him, because he knew what it had done for others who'd possessed it in the past. But the actual experience of drawing and using such a weapon had been beyond his power to foresee. He wondered if the previous owners of the Sword of Glory had felt the same way. Who had they been? The most famous of them, of course, was Vilkata, the Dark King whose image still haunted Kristin's nightmares, a man Murat had never met, now missing for fourteen years and presumed dead.

After checking with Carlo on their line of march, the Crown Prince proceeded with his mental inventory of Swords. There was of course Soulcutter—Murat experienced a faint internal shudder at the mere thought of that Sword, though he had never seen it in action, even from a safe distance. He'd heard that the Silver Queen, who'd used it once, had spent most of her years since then on one religious pilgrimage after another.

Murat knew that Soulcutter had beaten the Mindsword at least once before. But on that occasion, an open confrontation between armies, the two Blades had never been brought into actual physical opposition. The Crown Prince had no idea which might prevail if that were to happen.

—And Coinspinner, which had so recently been his, might one day be his again. That Sword came and went as if by its own random preference, and no human being, it seemed, could do anything to keep it once it chose to leave. The Sword of Chance would probably provide anyone who held it with the good luck necessary to stay out of the Mindsword's sphere of influence; and Coinspinner was also capable of inflicting bad luck, sometimes disastrously bad, upon its owner's enemies.

The Sword of Mercy could give protection against injury or death to anyone who held it. And it could heal even the wounds, otherwise practically incurable, inflicted by the Mindsword when it was used as a physical weapon.

The last of the six Swords still somewhere out there in the world was Farslayer. Enough to say of the Sword of Vengeance that it could unerringly strike the Mindsword's holder, or any other target, when thrown from any distance. No defense was effective—except of course that provided by Shieldbreaker. Neither Kristin not Murat could guess who now held Farslayer.

Keeping an eye out for more Tasavaltan cavalry, Murat urged his steed to a faster pace. He and his followers still had a considerable distance to go to reach the boundaries of Culm.

TEN

PRINCE Mark and his single companion were still some hours' ride west of the Tasavaltan border when the small winged messenger from Sarykam, having located the Prince, came spiraling and crying down toward him, a tiny black omen falling out of a vast gray sky.

The Prince reined in.

"Ben!" he called in a cautious voice. At the same time he held out his left arm to make a perch for the small courier.

The huge man who had been riding a few meters ahead of Mark along the narrow trail turned at the call, then tugged his own mount to a halt and watched the messenger descend.

Of the two riders, both still under forty, the Prince was slightly younger, somewhat taller, and much less massive, though certainly robust enough by any ordinary standard. Both men had time to dismount before the spiraling, skittish messenger ceased to fly in circles and came to perch upon the Prince's wrist.

Having alighted at last, the small feathered creature stuttered in its inhuman, birdlike voice that it was carrying a written communication to the Prince from the wizard Karel.

"Mark, Mark, are you Mark?" it demanded boldly of the man who stroked its head, as if it might even now be able to withhold its burden from an impostor.

"I am Mark—you know it, wretched beast—you must have seen me around the palace since you were a hatchling. Hold still and let me have the message!"

And the Prince of Tasavalta reached for the tiny leather pouch and slipped its belt off over the creature's head.

Ben made no comment, but lumbered closer, openly positioning himself to look over the Prince's shoulder and read the message as soon as it should be unfolded.

The written words, in old Karel's familiar script, were few. Mark's magician-uncle urgently and tersely urged him to abandon all other projects, whatever they might be, and get home as soon as possible. The phrasing hinted at tragic happenings in Tasavalta, though clearly reassuring Mark that there had been no death in the royal family. What had actually gone wrong was not spelled out, against the possibility that the message might fall into the wrong hands.

Ben, having read the message, grunted and said nothing.

Mark made no comment either, but folded the paper briskly and stuck it in his pocket. Then he tossed the winged creature back into the air, calling after it: "Tell the old one I am coming, as quickly as I can."

"Pardon, Prince, but I must rest!" the winged one squawked.

"Come back and rest, then, on my saddle, or behind me if you can. It seems that I must ride." And Mark swung himself up into the saddle again. Moving homeward once more, no faster than before upon a mount already tired, he absently dug out food and water from his saddlebags for the messenger.

Ben, silent and gloomy, was now riding close beside him once again.

In half an hour, the messenger suddenly took wing again,

squawked a brief farewell, and soon vanished over a hill ahead.

Ben and Mark maintained a steady pace, each man looking ahead to try to spot some source of water and forage for their animals. Their journey, like some others they'd undertaken, had been long and hard but had brought no visible reward.

Now at last the two men began to discuss the message, and Mark speculated on what exactly might have happened to cause Karel to send it.

Ben offered such comments as he could think of that might be helpful; they were not long, or many.

The Prince, his mood growing blacker the more he thought about Karel's note, finally made a bald admission. "Ben, I have long neglected my wife and family."

"Ha. So have I; not that Barbara any longer cares much what I do."

"It's my fault if you have. What have we accomplished on all these journeys?"

Ben could find only a vaguely encouraging answer to that. Which under the circumstances wasn't much.

Next day, as the weary pair were nearing the Tasavaltan border, they were met by a mounted party, including Karel himself, hastening out to meet them. The old wizard had already received Mark's answer and, relieved that he was already so near, had ridden to intercept him. Having the advantage of winged scouts, the magician and his companions had felt confident of being able to locate the returning pair efficiently.

Mark, on first catching sight of the approaching search party, stared intently, shading his eyes with a broad hand, at the figure in its lead.

When he spoke, the relief in his voice was evident. "Thank all the gods, Kristin's well. She's ridden out herself to meet me."

Ben opened his mouth, but then said nothing. At the head of the approaching party he beheld not Princess Kristin but a certain red-haired girl. Even at the distance he had no trouble recognizing her, as strong and young and vitally alive as she had remained for many years now in his memory.

Realization of the truth followed only a moment later, though too late to dull the renewed pang of loss. The figure they were looking at was of course neither that of the Princess nor Ben's old love. It was someone else, and whoever it was was carrying Sightblinder.

Mark was not so quick to come to this conclusion—after all, he had good reason to believe that Kristin was still alive.

"Yes, it's Kristin, all right," the Prince announced. Then he glanced at his old friend, away, and back again.

"Why are you looking like that?"

"Because that's not who I see."

The Prince swung back to face the approaching party. "Kristin, certainly. Or . . ." He looked at Ben again, and in a moment understanding came. "Yes . . . yes, of course."

Actually it was stout Karel himself riding at the head of the welcoming delegation, with the Princeling Stephen close behind him. The old magician entrusted his Sword to an aide as he approached, turning a young officer temporarily into a figure of fantasy whom the others present, all more or less inured to Sightblinder's effects, generally managed to ignore.

Stephen, spurring his mount forward, was the first of the approaching party to reach his father. Clinging to Mark's arm, the lad began at once to pour out a tale of magical horror and outrage.

Reporting loyally to Mark in turn, Karel confirmed the bitter story, adding some details. Then he informed his

Prince that General Rostov had already taken one of the other Swords, Stonecutter, from the armory into the southern mountains, where an effort was under way to cut off the road that would offer Murat his most direct route back to Culm.

"Then there can be no doubt it is Murat again."

"There can be no doubt."

Next Karel and Stephen between them related, more or less efficiently, more details of what had happened to Kristin.

The Princeling in a strained voice told his father once more what he'd seen with his own eyes: his mother encountering that evil man who'd been here last year, the Crown Prince of Culm, who had turned out to be such a thief and traitor.

Stephen, watching that encounter from a distant hill, had been too far away to be sure of the stranger's identity at first. He had seen the blue-green uniforms riding with the unknown man, and so had not taken alarm immediately. He'd watched with curiosity, thinking that possibly a squad of cavalry was bringing in a prisoner, or else escorting some visitor of importance.

And then, riding a little closer to see better, Stephen thought he had recognized the evil Crown Prince. He had seen the man drawing a Sword, and had observed by its effects the otherwise invisible wash of magic from that weapon, felling or stunning everyone within about a hundred meters.

Mark was staring intently at his son, hanging on his every word. "And your mother? What more of her could you see?"

"She did not fall from her mount, Father, but she dismounted of her own accord. And then a moment after that, the villain dismounted too—I think he was hurt when our men charged, because he needed help afterward to get off his riding-beast—and then it seemed to me that Mother went with him willingly after that." Stephen's voice faded almost to inaudibility on the last words, and he bit his lip.

It all sounded very convincing, and Karel, looking as grim as Mark had ever seen him, could do little more than confirm the essentials of Stephen's story. Murat of Culm, at the head of a small armed party—but nothing like a real invasion force—had ridden into Tasavalta carrying the Mindsword. First he had ensorcelled a whole patrol of cavalry, and then had taken Princess Kristin hostage— Karel's own arts now told him that she was thoroughly under the Sword's spell. If there were any doubt remaining, she had left written messages proving as much.

The Prince, listening, felt numb and hollow, an empty man going through motions because it was his duty. "Messages?"

Karel dug into a pocket and pulled out a folded sheet of paper, which he handed over to Mark.

"This one is addressed to you, sir."

Hastily Mark broke the little seal, unfolded the paper and read it, first silently and then aloud. There, in what was undeniably his wife's familiar handwriting, were words telling him that he had been divorced and deposed as Prince. The message concluded with good wishes for his future welfare. It read, thought the Prince, rather as if he were some senior official being nudged firmly into retirement.

Mark started to crumple the paper to hurl it from him, then thought better of the gesture and instead handed the document back to Karel's reaching hand. Any token from Kristin might possibly give a great wizard some magical advantage when the contest for her will was fought—as it was going to be—and in the circumstances every possible advantage would be needed.

"But she is physically unharmed?" The Prince marveled at how calm his own voice sounded.

The magician bowed his head slightly. "So it would seem, sir." Everyone else was gravely silent.

"Then we must do our best to see that she stays that way. Where are they now?"

Karel described the place where Murat and his enthralled followers were currently encamped, then detailed the military and magical steps he and General Rostov had already taken. Besides dispatching a force to cut the southern road, Rostov was deploying chosen units of his army on the home front, while a reserve of troops had been mobilized and stood ready for the Prince's orders.

Mark, listening, put aside grief and fear and began to grapple mentally with the practical difficulties of attacking an opponent armed with the Mindsword.

"Any word from Murat himself? Is he asking for negotiations?"

"No, sir."

"Then we'll not give him the satisfaction of asking for them either."

Quickly making decisions, the Prince formally assumed command, then sent a small detachment of men under Ben to take over the efforts being made with Stonecutter to close the mountain passes and high trails leading toward Culm. Rostov, once relieved from duty there, would be free to oversee a general mobilization.

Having dismounted to sketch a couple of crude maps in the dust, Mark wiped them out again with his boot, and climbed back into the saddle, this time on one of the fresh mounts brought out from the city by the welcoming party.

He announced: "We'll concentrate first on keeping the villain in our country, until we can plan how best to attack him."

Ben saluted and rode off quickly on a fresh mount,

taking with him a few picked men from the small escort of troops who had come out with Karel.

Everyone else soon set off at a brisk pace, in a different direction. On Karel's advice the Prince was leading them in the general direction of Sarykam.

Mark as he rode soon issued more orders. A messenger was dispatched to his older son Adrian, giving the facts of the incursion and kidnapping, and such scanty reassurances as were possible. Karel had been reluctant to send word to Adrian until he could talk to Mark.

Mark was anxious to take the field against Murat, but Karel thought it would be best for the Prince to meet first with the Tasavaltan Council. That body was already in session, considering whether to depose Kristin at least temporarily as Princess, since she had demonstrably taken leave of her senses.

"What good will that do us? The point is that we must get her back, do you not agree?"

"Wholeheartedly, Prince. But the Council is involved. If they should depose the Princess Kristin, it would become the duty of your son Adrian to assume the throne. And I fear your own formal authority as Prince Consort might be undermined as well."

"My friend, if I have any authority in my adopted land at all, it is only because you and the other Tasavaltan leaders choose to give it to me. Our son Adrian is still too young to rule, and in any case he's too far distant to be brought home in a few days. The Council must see that the problem can't wait for that."

Karel, announcing confidently that he was able to speak for Rostov and the other military officers, confirmed that they wanted no one but Mark as their Prince.

Mark doubted that the sentiment was quite as unanimous as Kristin's uncle made it sound; but he could not worry about that now.

"Then let us send a messenger ahead, to try to stop the Council from taking action until we talk to them. Or let them send some representative to meet us in the field."

Hurrying eastward, the Prince of Tasavalta made plans for his attack on Murat.

ELEVEN

A T twilight on the second day after the conversion of the Princess, as Murat's party halted to make camp, he again dispatched his son, along with a few chosen troopers, on a scouting mission to see what Tasavaltan forces might be in the vicinity. The Crown Prince was sure that Karel and other enemies had his party under surveillance now, and it was only to be expected that they were planning some kind of counterstroke. The reconnaissance ordered by Murat was a routine precaution.

Carlo, full of unhappy presentiments before riding out of camp, grumbled to his father about Fate.

After a full day in the saddle, the Crown Prince's leg was aching like a broken tooth. His response to his son's philosophical bitterness was not sympathetic.

"Let us create a new fate if we do not like the one that confronts us. Anyway, to me, our current situation does not appear so bad."

But at the last moment, struck by a foreboding of his own, Murat called his son back and handed him the sheathed Mindsword.

"I need not tell you that you must use it only to defend your life, and those of your men."

Carlo accepted the gift automatically from his father's

hands, then paused, holding the heavy weapon gingerly, as if he were on the verge of refusing the loan.

"Take it," Murat urged him tersely.

"Thank you, Father," Carlo acknowledged quietly. In a moment he had buckled on the gods' Blade, on the opposite side of his belt from his own sword.

As soon as the scouting party had ridden out of sight, Murat entered his tent, seeking such privacy as he could manage, and did his best to assess his situation.

Though he had no real belief in Fate, he had to admit that a number of factors seemed to be conspiring to keep him from getting his band of followers out of Tasavalta as quickly as he'd planned.

To begin with, there was his wound, which was not improving as he'd hoped it would. Forcing himself to ride had only made matters worse. The injured muscles in the limb had stiffened, the swelling was refusing to go down, and the pain had if anything grown worse. Sharp knifeblade pangs ran from knee to hip whenever the Crown Prince tried to move in certain ways, or alternately if he held the leg in the same position for any great length of time. The few troopers in his band who claimed some knowledge of healing could only shake their heads and offer the opinion that perhaps a nerve had been damaged by the unlucky slinger's hit.

Riding for another full day with such an injury might well prove impossible, and he had the feeling, perhaps irrational, that it might cripple him permanently as well. When he made an announcement to this effect, some talk sprang up among the master's worried devotees of rigging a litter in which he could be transported. But the Crown Prince refused categorically to consider using any such device. He wasn't dying, he snapped at his subordinates, nor was he helpless; after a day or two of rest, he should be ready to ride on. Meanwhile, alertness by all hands, com-

bined with his enemies' knowledge that he possessed the
Mindsword, ought to render the camp secure against
attack.

It was well after dark when Carlo and his men returned
from their scouting trip, which had proven uneventful.
They had seen no Tasavaltan military people anywhere,
though several flying scouts had been observed. Carlo
dutifully handed the unused Sword back to his father.

Next morning at first light, Murat on peering out of his
tent was slightly surprised to discover the familiar, repulsive figure of Metaxas squatting patiently nearby, at a little
distance from the nearest sentry. The Crown Prince ignored the beggar's presence at first, but as the day wore on
the visitor continued to hover in the vicinity of the injured
man. Murat had the impression that Metaxas managed to
grope his way a little nearer, and again a little nearer,
whenever a likely opportunity arose. Drawing almost no
attention to himself, and managing somehow to keep out
of everyone else's way, the blind man appeared determined
to maintain his presence near Murat.

But Kristin, who arrived at Murat's tent at dawn to
spend her time with the Crown Prince, trying to do
something for his wound, soon became irritated by what
she considered the beggar's intrusive presence, and told the
fellow to take himself away.

Metaxas at once obediently arose, turned, and started to
move off, tapping his way with a crude cane someone had
provided for him. But before he had gone half a dozen
steps he turned back, pleading.

"Your pardon, my lady. Pardon me, Great Lord. But in
my youth I possessed some small skill in the healing arts."

Murat and Kristin both looked at him doubtfully, then
at each other. Nothing else was doing the injury any good.

Evidently encouraged by silence, the beggar made the

most of his chance. "With your permission, I would like to try to alleviate Your Worship's pain, to make it sooner possible for Your Worship to ride again, and lead us where you will."

"What manner of treatment do you have in mind?" Murat rasped at him, his voice half-suspicious, half-contemptuous.

Metaxas launched into an excited plea. "Oh, the master need not be concerned! I will not ask for hair, or finger-nails, or any substance proceeding from the great lord's body. Not a scrap of his clothing will I require, nor even a pinch of dirt from his footprint. It should be enough, with your permission, for me to chant a few words from afar."

Murat stared doubtfully at the wretch for a few moments, then shrugged. "Chant, then," he agreed. "Preferably from the greatest possible distance that will allow you to remain within the camp. Or go farther, if you will; suit yourself about that."

The eyeless man bowed, muttering words of gratitude. By this time a pair of half-suspicious Tasavaltan guards, taking their cue from their master's attitude and tone, had come to flank Metaxas, and they guided him in his withdrawal to the other side of camp.

Murat engaged once more in conversation with Kristin, and promptly forgot about the former beggar. But a few minutes later the Crown Prince, happening to move his leg, noted that the pain was much diminished. The improvement had occurred with magical suddenness.

Soon he had to admit to himself that Metaxas had demonstrated his ability to work a minor healing spell, even while not being allowed to touch the patient.

When Murat called Kristin's attention to this fact, she was delighted at the improvement, but at first unwilling to give credit to the eyeless man. Murat, however, insisted that he knew the touch of healing magic when he felt it, and the Princess was forced to admit that the great bruise on his leg now looked better. The swelling in his thigh had clearly started to diminish, though the leg was still too painful for him to consider riding except in the most immediate emergency.

Despite Kristin's continued antipathy to the begger, Murat had him summoned again and thanked him. Then, in response to a pleading look from the Princess, he banished his benefactor once more to the far side of camp.

Even had Murat been ready to ride at once, still there would have been delay in getting on the road to Culm today. The men in charge of the riding-beasts and loadbeasts came to report a newly discovered problem. A swarm of mice, which everyone was sure must have been produced or at least mobilized by Karel's magic, had appeared overnight to devour and scatter much of the grain in camp. Feed would have to be carried for the animals on a trip across the badlands. It would be folly to trust to forage on the journey; there were certain to be long barren stretches where the grazing was inadequate.

Nor were mice the only new difficulty. Harness kept breaking, every second or third time an animal was saddled or loaded. And the sky to the south was leaden, shot through by flickers of distant lightning, indicating that a savage storm was brewing.

Murat was well aware of Karel's reputation, and had had no wish to make an enemy of such a powerful magician. But, as he reflected in conversation with Carlo and Kristin, events had swept him along, and there had really been no alternative.

His listeners slavishly agreed.

The rest of the day passed fairly uneventfully. During the following night, Vilkata as usual stretched out at full length on the earth beyond the firelight, at the extreme edge of camp. Lying so, and mumbling into his blanket, he was soon engaged in another secret conference with his inhuman partner.

As soon as the demon arrived, it began lamenting—almost silently—Vilkata's continued failure to seize the Sword.

In a whisper almost choked with anger, the man sternly ordered his subordinate partner to stop whining. He, Vilkata, could now report that he seemed to be gaining the Crown Prince's favor, and could look forward to playing a larger and larger role in service as Murat's magician—since the removal of Gauranga, there was no one else among the converted bandits or soldiers remotely qualified to play that part. But patience was essential; he, Vilkata, might have, could have, done better with the healing had he been granted the boon of hair or fingernails or spittle. But the royal couple were still suspicious of him, and he had not dared to seem to want such powerful tokens.

"And were you, Master, able to make the injury worse from a distance, before you promised to try to make it better?"

"Actually I was. You see, the fellow continues to assume that I have been caught in his Sword-magic, like all the other members of his entourage."

Akbar rejoiced fawningly in his master's success, and praised his farsighted wisdom. He, the demon, devoutly wished that he had been able to do more for their common cause. But alas, Fate as yet had not seen fit to decree him any opportunities.

Vilkata delivered a cold judgment. "You and the young Prince both seem to believe in Fate."

"Alas, it may be that we are both seeking to avoid responsibility. Master?"

"Yes?"

"If I may dare to ask—what *are* the prospects for your snatching the Sword?"

The Dark King sighed. "As I have said before, I am waiting for a good chance, in fact an excellent chance. Because I am unlikely to be granted a second one should the first effort fail. And while we are on the subject," Vilkata added, "let me say that the eyesight you have given me seems not altogether reliable in imaging the Sword itself. When I can get a clear look at the weapon at all, the shape of the handle seems obscure."

"I am doing the best I can, Master."

"Try and do better," Vilkata snapped—or came as close as he could to snapping without speaking the words aloud.

"I will try." Akbar sounded exceedingly timid, if not actually frightened.

"And more than that is going to be required of you. I will have to rely heavily on your help to make me look good as a magician. My own powers are still weak, although with exercise, and with your help, my faithful Akbar, they are beginning to revive."

"Of course, Master! Call upon me at any time for assistance. Does your vision continue to be satisfactory, other than the difficulty with the Sword?"

"In the main, satisfactory, I suppose. Somewhat less garish colors would be preferable. And the difficulty with the Sword, as you put it, threatens to undermine our entire plan."

"That is too bad. I can only do what I can. No doubt the trouble arises because of Skulltwister's own powerful magic."

"Perhaps. In the old days, with others of your kind assisting me, I never had any trouble seeing this Sword or any other."

"I will do what I can."

By the time another day had dawned, Murat's leg felt almost well enough to let him ride. But experience counseled another day of rest. Once more Carlo, again carrying the Sword on loan, took a few men and went out scouting.

The pair of winged scouts were sent out also; and in a couple of hours came back to their Tasavaltan-defector handler with the unwelcome news that the main road leading toward Culm, really little more than a trail, had been cut.

"From what the beasts tell me, the road's completely gone, sir," the converted beastmaster reported.

"Gone! An entire road?"

"Wiped out, at a couple of really narrow places, in the passes. Lord Murat, from the description my little flyers give me, it looks like some heavy magic's been worked against us there. Something's cut away limestone and even granite there, like so much cheese."

"Stonecutter's work."

"I should say so, sir. Very likely."

By now Murat's three days, his self-imposed waiting period before he should accept Kristin's love, had passed. But he found himself making no move to enter her tent. It was as if he were really waiting for something else—perhaps, he thought, a time when they could be truly alone with each other, and at peace. The Princess gazed at him lovingly, and was content to accept what he decided.

With the benefit of Metaxas's healing efforts—the beggar made sure to claim credit at every opportunity—Murat's wound continued slowly to improve. But though this afternoon he was able to walk with only a slight limp, and ride almost normally, he was hardly conscious of relief. The Sword of Stealth was looming ever larger in his thoughts. His fear of that weapon and of Mark's revenge was increasing.

Vilkata, observing the behavior of the Crown Prince intently, and keeping mental notes of all that happened in camp, made a shrewd guess at what these fears were, and considered exerting subtle efforts to exacerbate them. The Dark King wanted the conflict with Mark to go on. Ideally Murat, instead of retreating peacefully to Culm, would stay here until he had enslaved or defeated the Emperor's son. But still Vilkata kept silent on the subject, fearing that any effort he made to influence the decisions of Murat and Kristin might have the opposite effect.

And Vilkata wondered how much longer it would be before the woman recognized him, despite his altered appearance. He discussed this point with the demon when they had another conference.

Still the Dark King feared at every moment to be caught by the Sword's spell if Murat should once more draw it suddenly; some provocation might arise at any time. For this reason Vilkata welcomed the intervals when Carlo took the Mindsword with him on patrol. On these occasions Akbar, taking no chances, continued to spend almost all his time at a safe distance.

During each of his clandestine conferences with Akbar, Vilkata reminded his demon to be ready to whisk him away to safety at a moment's notice.

"I shall certainly do so, Master," the dry voice always soothed him. "Have no fear on that account."

Vilkata even considered trying to browbeat the demon into attempting to seize the Sword—but the man shuddered and again rejected the idea, whose success would be worse than failure. He could not bring himself to contemplate a future in which he would be required, without hope of release, to offer lifelong worship and obedience to a demon. That was one of the most hideous fates that he as an experienced torturer was able to imagine.

During the remainder of the day Murat limped about his camp—the last increments of pain and injury in his leg were stubborn—alternately trying to use and then discarding a cane whittled for him by the cunning fingers of the eyeless man—who else? In the course of his restless movement the Crown Prince reminded his perimeter guards at frequent intervals that they must challenge anyone, no matter who it might appear to be, who approached the camp from outside. Murat also saw to it that everyone in his band was thoroughly briefed on Sightblinder's powers, and made them all swear solemnly that they would allow no outsider into camp without their master's approval.

For the past several days Carlo had been watching and listening to his father with growing fear and dismay. The Crown Prince, rather than looking better with the healing of his wound, now appeared haggard, with dark circles under his eyes. Over and over Murat declared his determination not to be swayed from his planned course of action whether by fear of his enemies, bad luck, or Karel's magic. He meant to take the Sword of Glory on with him to Culm, and there to utilize it—as sparingly as possible, of course—to regain his rightful place in his own land.

Murat vowed that Kristin, who would stand beside him from now on, deserved no less than a new kingdom in addition to her own.

Several times he assured Kristin that, once having accomplished his own rehabilitation in his own land, he would present the Sword of Glory to her, and from that moment he, Murat, would be her faithful servant—as well as her lover, if she would still have him.

She answered quietly: "I already worship you, my love. I think no magic is capable of changing that."

Murat was too deeply moved to reply in words.

And the Princess Kristin, also silent now, vowed to herself that if her lord ever forced her to accept the Sword as hers, she'd only keep it for him, undrawn, until he someday had need of it again.

TWELVE

TOWARD the middle of the night, Kristin, unable to sleep, was wandering restlessly around the camp, wrapped in a soldier's borrowed cloak. The mind of the Princess was in turmoil, seeking some way to help Murat, and at the same time struggling against the sadness that engulfed her with every thought of her lost children and her estranged people.

In her pacing she frequently passed the tent wherein Murat was resting. Each time the sentry looked at her with sympathy.

"He sleeps?" she asked the man quietly, pausing for a moment.

"I do believe so, Princess." The reply was almost in a whisper; no one wanted to disturb the great lord, to deprive him of a moment of his well-earned rest.

The Princess took another turn around the camp. As she was considering whether to try once more to sleep, she heard a sentry call, and a quick answer; it was Carlo and the men of his patrol, returning to the camp at last.

The Princeling, looking tired, rode slowly straight into the center of camp and dismounted near the small watchfire, where he spoke a few words with Captain Marsaci. Then Carlo turned and walked toward Kristin, who stood between him and his father's tent.

Only now did it register in Kristin's consciousness that one or two members of the patrol appeared to be missing, and another had been slightly wounded.

"What happened?" she asked Carlo hesitantly as he was about to pass her. The Princess was well aware that this young man had no great liking for her.

The look Carlo gave Kristin as he paused confirmed that idea. Coldly he said: "A skirmish. Such things happen in war. Don't worry, the precious Sword's all right."

Then the Princeling moved on, muttering over his shoulder: "I must report to Father." Carrying the unbuckled Mindsword in its sheath, he went into his father's tent.

Kristin, following slowly, was able to see past the young man through the open flap. Inside, Murat was dimly visible, stirring uneasily on his simple roll of blankets.

Leaving the tent flap open, Carlo put the Sword down gently at Murat's side, and started to shake the older man.

"Father! Wake up!"

Suddenly Murat started up. His eyes glittering in firelight, he stared at Carlo for a moment as if he did not recognize him.

And then, before anyone could utter a word of caution, or otherwise react, the Crown Prince had grabbed the black-hilted Sword and drawn it from its sheath.

The faint firelight entering the tent through the open doorway fell upon that bright steel and rebounded, striking the eye like an explosion of live steam. Carlo, inside the tent, fell to his knees, covering his eyes. Kristin, standing just outside, heard herself cry out the name of her beloved.

From all the other men in the encampment, sleeping or waking, a muttering went up, a sound compounded of joy and resignation.

Inside the tent, the Crown Prince had leaped to his feet beside his blanket roll, newly drawn Sword once more in hand. His clothing was disarranged, the expression on his face wild and confused.

Then he bent uncertainly over his kneeling son. "Carlo—is it indeed you?"

A pale, drawn face turned up to him. "I'm here, Father. It's really me."

"Then who intruded?" Murat looked bewildered.

"Intruded, Father?"

"Someone was here . . . just now."

The eye of the Crown Prince fell on the smiling figure of Kristin, waiting outside the door, and terrible suspicion overcame him.

"Is it Mark, then—?" Murat murmured. In another moment, feeling himself hampered in the awkward space of the little tent, he hurled the scanty camp furniture aside, and waved the Mindsword at her as if in exorcism. Then, pushing his son aside, he leaped out toward the Princess, getting within striking distance, raising the keen, heavy blade.

The face of the cloak-wrapped apparition before him paled. The slender figure confronting Murat recoiled from the bright steel, as that god-forged Blade flashed in the air.

A voice indistinguishable from Kristin's burst from her shrinking image, pleading: "My lord—what is wrong?"

Knowing only an inner certainty of treachery and betrayal, Murat raised the weapon in a two-handed grip. The Crown Prince shouted at the one who now faced him: "If you, whoever you are, are carrying Sightblinder, I command you to throw it down immediately!"

He stared expectantly, but no other Sword appeared, and the woman's image did not change in the slightest. Other figures, in the background, were huddling in frightened silence.

Slowly the realization came that he had been dreaming of horror and betrayal. It was only Kristin, the real Kristin, who faced him now. Kristin, empty-handed, white-faced, wrapped in some soldier's cloak, her slender body trembling with the knowledge of how close she had come to being slain by her lover.

All around them, the camp was silent. Somewhere in the distance a nightbird called.

Murat, fully awake now and suddenly stricken, stumbled a step closer to the Princess on his wounded leg. "Oh—my dear—my love—I was afraid that it was Mark. I feared to let him come near you—"

Kristin raised her eyes. Wistfully, fearfully, she said: "I do not think that Mark would ever hurt me."

By now a newer and uglier murmur of noise was going around the camp. Men were glaring at one another in mutual suspicion. Their lord had mentioned Sightblinder. Had someone entered the camp by means of the Sword of Stealth? Rumors, challenges, and speculation flew back and forth, hands gripped weapons, and several fights were only narrowly averted.

Suddenly a new noise rose above the rest. It was the eyeless man, screaming unintelligibly about something. For the time being everyone ignored him.

Murat began shouting orders. In the matter of a few moments, fights had been averted, something like calm had been restored, and Carlo could begin to give the report for which he had awakened his father. For this purpose the two men reentered the tent.

The Princeling, setting up the small folding table that had been knocked over, reported in a distant voice that his patrol had been forced to fight a skirmish with a small Tasavaltan patrol. The fight had been brief but savage, and the enemy had withdrawn before Carlo had been compelled to resort to the Mindsword.

Murat was now fastening the sheathed Blade at his own side again, and trying to concentrate on what his son was saying, even as he listened with half an ear to the screams and moans of the blind beggar in the middle distance.

Someone was shouting threats at the wretch to shut him up, and the Crown Prince devoutly hoped that they succeeded.

He said to Carlo: "Would that you had used the Sword. I gave it to you for your protection."

"I realize that, Father. But I did not need the Sword of Glory to survive. And I could not in any case have saved our two men who fell, the fight began so quickly."

"Very well, I'm sure you did the best you could."

After answering a few more questions, Carlo left the tent. As he pushed aside the flap to go out, Murat was moved by the sight of Kristin, her slender figure still muffled in a cloak, waiting just outside.

She came in, without waiting for an invitation, as the young man left. The tent flap closed her in, with darkness and her lover.

At first no words were exchanged. For once casting his own Sword carelessly aside, the Crown Prince for the first time embraced his beloved unrestrainedly.

Kristin responded with passion.

For the time being they were secure against sudden interruption; there was a sentry just outside the tent to see to that. Murat's lips sought Kristin's mouth, and then her throat. His hands explored her body freely. Somewhere in the back of his mind, almost obscured by the rising torrent of madness in his blood, was the thought that if he took her now, just after he had once more exposed her to the Sword, he would be violating his own self-imposed pledge. But just now one more broken promise more or less did not seem of great importance.

He had lifted the maddening, enchanting woman in his arms and was on the point of lowering her to his humble bed, when they were, in spite of sentries, interrupted.

It was the eyeless Metaxas, struggling now with the guards at the very doorway of the tent. The man was still screaming, or trying to scream though he was almost out of breath. Between his howls of sheer emotion he pleaded with the men who held him back and threatened him. He begged that someone must hear his confession, and his words had a coherence and an urgency that made it impossible to simply banish or ignore him; the soldiers were arguing among themselves now as to whether they should disturb the Lord Murat.

With a groan he set down Kristin on her feet, and turned to deal with this disturbance.

As Murat appeared in the doorway of the tent, Vilkata tried to throw himself on the ground before his new master. The Crown Prince signed to the soldiers to release his arms.

"Great Lord Murat!" the beggar wailed, from the dust.

"What is it, man?"

"Can you possibly be merciful to me? I am the most wretched, treacherous—"

There was no mercy in Murat's voice. "Get hold of yourself! Speak plainly, and be brief, or by all the gods, I'll—"

Some of the soldiers standing by voiced their readiness to kill this confessed traitor out of hand.

Murat ordered them to wait until they had heard what the fellow had to say.

Meanwhile, he who had been called Metaxas rolled on the earth, still beating his breast and proclaiming his guilt, tears running down his bearded cheeks.

"Forgive me, Lord! I would destroy myself now, to expiate my sins—except that now you truly have terrible need of help, help that only I can give you!"

The Crown Prince, losing his temper, savagely kicked the prostrate form before him. The impact sent waves of renewed pain up through his own leg, but at the moment he scarcely noticed.

"Are you going to tell me what the matter is, or not?"

"Yes, Lord! I am—I must confess that from the beginning I have been in your camp under false pretenses. Even before we met, I was plotting to do you harm."

Kristin had now quietly emerged from the tent, her borrowed cloak discarded, garbed in the dress that she had worn beneath it. She was staring past Murat at the eyeless man, and her face was frozen in an expression of horrified fascination.

"Oh?" Murat, bringing his concentration back to Vilkata, could not at first take seriously such a confession from such a source. "You? Plotting how, against me? With whom?"

"With Akbar—does Your Lordship know that name?"

The Crown Prince stared at the strange figure huddled on the earth before him. "Akbar? No. I have heard no one in this camp called that. Is he a Tasavaltan?"

Once more Vilkata screamed in remorse, even more terribly than before. "Alas! Lord Murat, it is not the name of a man!—but of a demon." And with those words he melted entirely into sobs.

THIRTEEN

A demon," Murat repeated in a whisper. On legs suddenly gone weak he retreated, one step, two steps, getting out of reach of the shaking, pale-skinned, black-haired hands that would have clutched his ankles seeking forgiveness. The Crown Prince knew a sensation as if a lump of ice had suddenly, by some enemy magic, been made to materialize inside his stomach.

Clinging with one hand to the tent pole just inside the open flap, Murat bent forward, eyes fixed on the crumpled figure before him.

"Who are you, then?" he demanded, in a terrible whisper.

In the course of the eyeless man's convulsions of repentance, the bandage that had covered the upper portion of his face had fallen off, and as he sat up he turned his horrible empty sockets toward the Princess.

"I am Vilkata," he rasped. "I was once the Dark King."

Kristin screamed.

The wretch who huddled on the ground before her shrank back. His speech failed him completely for the moment, and he confirmed his confession with a spasmodic nod.

The Princess slumped, and might have fallen had not

Murat quickly moved to support her. Lifting her tenderly, he turned and carried her back into the tent.

He was out again in a moment, ignoring the small gathering crowd of puzzled troopers and converted bandits. Bending down to seize the helpless, hapless Vilkata by the front of his garments, the Crown Prince hauled him to his feet.

"A demon, you say." This time the word was heard by most of the onlookers, and an abrupt silence fell among them.

"Alas, sire, yes—"

"Where is this alleged demon now?"

Vilkata swore he was ignorant of the whereabouts of Akbar. "But I do know, Master, the trick of summoning the foul thing."

"You know the trick? You tell me that a demon is under your control? Or are you babbling, old man, are you utterly mad?"

The Dark King screamed again. "Alas, no, my master, I am not mad. Would that I were!"

Controlling himself with a great effort, he who had been calling himself Metaxas went on to explain.

"Until a few minutes ago, my lord, I had managed to avoid the power of illuminating, healing magic in the Blade you carry. Wretch that I am, I deceived you, having in mind only my own advantage. I only pretended to be convinced of your perfection—I only feigned loyalty, while at the same time Akbar and I were plotting to seize Skulltwister as soon as a good chance should present itself."

Murat's interior lump of ice was, if anything, growing larger and colder. His hopes that the eyeless man was no worse than mad were fading rapidly.

"We'll deal later with whatever crimes you may have committed. Are you telling me the truth now, you offspring of diseased demons?" And again Murat seized the hapless villain, this time brandishing the Sword right under his victim's nose. Again the Blade glowed with unnatural brightness in the muted firelight. "I want the truth!"

Utterly collapsing, the beggar swore over and over that he was now telling the complete truth. The demon had provided for him, was still providing, a kind of vision that functioned despite his lack of eyes; the demon and he had plotted together to do the master harm.

Under the circumstances, with the man subjected now to the full glowing power of the Mindsword, the Crown Prince at last was forced to believe him. Conviction in the matter of demonic vision was reinforced by an impromptu test; when Murat silently brought his Sword-point close to the eyeless face, the cowering one tried to draw away, as if in fact he could see the danger.

After ordering several troopers to keep a strict watch over the confessed partner of demons, Murat drew Carlo a little aside to confer with him.

Murat started to speak to his son, then paused, staring at the weapon still gripped in his own fist. Then he demanded: "You say there was a skirmish, but you did not draw the Mindsword? Did I hear you truly? Or were sleep and nightmares still ruling my brain, when you came in to report?"

Carlo stared at him. "Yes, Father, that's what I told you. We had to fight a skirmish."

"Good. Good, then I can trust my memory. In these last few days there have been times when my life seems to be turning into the stuff of dreams. Or nightmares." The Crown Prince heaved a great sigh. "I'll hear the story of your skirmish in detail later. Tell me now, what are we to do with this ragged wretch who claims to be a king, and own a demon? Do you believe his tale?"

Carlo gestured helplessly. "I cannot doubt that the man

is now telling the truth. Or at least that he believes his own story. But I don't know what to advise you, how best to deal with him."

"Let us be rid of him, as quickly as we can." This came, in a quiet voice, from Kristin, emerging from the tent. The Princess looked pale, but had otherwise recovered from her faint.

"A demon," Murat repeated distantly. Now something in the two words seemed to grip his imagination in an unhealthy way, almost to paralyze him.

"Be rid of him, I say," Kristin repeated urgently. "What other choice is there?"

And Carlo, overcoming his own indecision, seconded her advice. "I agree with the Princess, we must be rid of him, and of his demon."

Murat, shaking his head as if to clear it of some unwanted presence, had to agree with their point of view.

"Yes, I suppose we must. But first there are some things that I must find out. I'll see if he's able to summon this demon before us, and make sure of the truth of the matter."

"No." Kristin shook her head.

"This Blade I hold will protect me during the summoning, and no one else need be present. For your safety we—this beggar—or king—and I—will go outside the camp to do what we must."

Carlo looked agonized, but he had learned to tell when arguing with his father was certain to be futile.

Kristin said to Murat: "I see you are determined."

"I am."

"Then promise me at least one thing, my lord—do not sheathe your Sword again, at least not until you are safely out of Tasavalta. And free of demons."

Murat looked at the Sword, and back at his beloved. Once again, for a moment, he seemed afraid.

The Princess went on. "Your safety, my Lord Murat, is

the most important consideration for all of us. And for you to keep the Sword of Glory always in hand is now the best way—nay, the only way—to ensure your welfare."

The Crown Prince nodded slowly. "You are all depending upon me now. I know that."

The Princess took him by the arm. "One more thing—I'm sure that man is the Dark King."

"Sure?"

"I recognize him now, from the day long ago when—when he almost killed me. And I pray you to get rid of him, because I fear him now just as terribly as I did then."

"I have the Sword, and—"

"Even so, Sword or no Sword, what I most dread now is that this evil counselor's presence will be harmful to my most great lord. I would not trust the man the thickness of a knifeblade, regardless of any magical protection. Regardless of how he may swear, and protest, and what he may do to demonstrate his loyalty."

"Father," said Carlo, swallowing. "Let me repeat, I think the Princess is right."

The Crown Prince looked at them both, then at his Sword once more.

He said: "I like the idea very little. But—as a temporary measure only, until we have reached a place of reasonable safety—I'll carry this tool with me naked, and even sleep with it at night."

For a moment it seemed that Murat would say more. But his next thought, unspoken, only hung in the air as he looked at Kristin. And she thought that she could read it: *That means that for the time being, no one is going to share my bed.*

The low-voiced conference among the three was at an end. Now, determined to test the eyeless man's confession by having him attempt to summon the demon, the Crown Prince, with Carlo and the Princess looking on in horrified fascination, once more confronted the wretch who had called himself Metaxas.

The beggar's eye bandage had been restored to its proper place, and he squatted on the ground under the suspicious stares of a pair of guards, standing over him with weapons ready. Other men nearby had equipped themselves with torches.

No, the crouching man admitted, he had never bounced the Princess of Tasavalta on his knee—that had been only a near-blasphemous pretense. Yes, he had once been the Dark King, and yes, the horrible accusation hurled at him by the blessed Princess was quite true—he had once been prepared to torture her to death in an effort to increase his own magic powers. Only the interference of the man who was later to become Prince Mark had kept him from committing that hideous crime.

Murat's anger blazed at the bald admission. Caught up in a holy, murderous fury, the Crown Prince extended the naked Sword in his strong arm toward his victim's throat, until another centimeter's thrust would have drawn blood.

"I'd kill you at once, swine. But I mean to extract more information from you before you die."

This time Vilkata had not cringed away from the Blade. "Certainly I deserve death, Lord. But there are secrets I can tell you first, information I can provide that you must have."

"It seems we are in agreement on that much." Murat pulled back his Sword-point slightly. "And where is your demon partner now? If he indeed exists?"

Before Vilkata could answer, there came a murmur among the onlookers. Kristin, tough lady that she was, could no longer bear this continued confrontation with her former torturer. On the verge of fainting again, she pleaded with her new lord: "Send him away! Or kill him!"

Lowering his Sword, Murat spoke to her in soothing

tones. "My love, will you go back to the tent now? Carlo, escort her."

"Let me remain, my lord," the Princess pleaded, "to see the demon if it comes. I want to share your peril if you are determined to face the foul beast, and it should somehow be able to avoid or even overcome the Sword's power."

"Go back to your tent, I say. Carlo, escort her."

Gently but firmly the young man took the Princess by the arm, and led her away. She made no further protest.

As soon as Kristin and his son were out of sight, Murat, after a word to Captain Marsaci, ordered his newly acquired magician to stand and walk. Then he directed the eyeless man, who proved his ability to get around without special guidance, some fifty meters or so beyond the fringe of the camp. There the two came to a secluded hollow in an angle between hedgerows. This was a spot where, Murat decided, any bizarre demonic manifestations would likely remain unobserved by anyone at the distance of the camp.

Vilkata, who for the last few minutes had regarded all his previous schemes with utter loathing, had been examining his conscience to see what additional offenses he might be required to accuse himself of.

He was now on the brink of confessing that he had some days ago made Murat's leg injury worse by means of magic; but before he blurted out another crime, it occurred to him that Murat would be better off without being required to hear such a confession. Indeed, a moment's reflection made the Dark King think that he ought not to have confessed as much as he already had. True, he deserved to die many times over for the harm he had inflicted upon the lord Murat, and upon the woman who had now become valuable and useful to the lord. But confession now would not help that. Above all, Vilkata's death would not help

Murat in his present difficulties, but hurt him instead. It was clear to the Dark King that his new master was likely to need all the help he could get in the days ahead.

The master must be brought to trust, rather than hate, his most recently enlisted and cleverest adviser.

A few moments later, in the hollow between hedgerows, Vilkata, muttering and gesturing, went through his brief ritual of summoning Akbar.

Murat, naked Sword in hand, was standing at a little distance from the wizard, inside an elaborated pentacle of magical protection which Vilkata had hastily sketched out on the ground. Not that Vilkata had much faith in the efficacy of such devices against demons, certainly not compared with the protective value of the Mindsword; but he was now determined to take no avoidable chances with his master's safety.

Scarcely had the magician's fingers ceased to move in the gestures of the ritual of summoning, when the creature materialized, startling even Vilkata with its promptness. An androgynous human form, wrapped in dark garments, appeared out of nowhere, standing between the men. The manifestation was accompanied by a drumming or banging sound, which in a few moments trailed away into silence.

Murat, controlling a sudden surge of fear and loathing, firmly stood his ground inside his pentacle, brandishing the Mindsword in front of him.

The demon turned a blank, pale face in the direction of the Crown Prince, then recoiled with a scream of rage when it found itself gripped by the power of the weapon nestled in Murat's right hand. But even demonic rage could not endure the Mindsword's force. A moment after it screamed, the foul quasimaterial beast had assumed a dog-like shape, and a moment after that Akbar had thrown himself down, brutally fawning and cringing, near Murat's feet.

The dog shape did not persist for long. Looking as helpless as any mere converted human, Akbar groveled before his new lord and master, presenting himself in a series of suitably humble and would-be disarming images, some human and some animal. Babies, old women, cuddly pets, appeared and disappeared in swift succession.

Murat, feeling a tremendous disgust, and at the same time exulting in the establishment of his authority, drew back a few paces. Now he felt confident that his safety was assured by the Sword of Glory, and did not depend at all upon the merely human magic embodied in the diagram scratched in the earth.

As in his earlier confrontation with Vilkata, the Crown Prince was holding the Sword level, pointed at the demon, as if he might be required to skewer an enemy physically upon the blade. But this time he felt less of an urge to kill, and greater physical loathing. In fact he felt sick to the point of nausea. Akbar's current display of sniveling cowardice and self-abasement was if anything more repugnant to him than the show of demonic arrogance he had unconsciously been expecting.

Vilkata was watching with great vigilance. Now he made a prearranged gesture to Murat, signifying that the demon was safely Murat's to command.

The Crown Prince called out in a sharp voice: "Foul demon! Your name is Akbar."

"Yes, Master." The demon's voice was unlike any sound that Murat had ever heard before.

"I order you to choose some coherent shape, and remain in it, so a man can look at you at least."

At once the demon assumed a distinct human form, youthful, plump, and eunuchoid. It sat there smiling at its master timidly.

Murat, finding this shape particularly repugnant, quickly commanded Akbar to change to something else. In a moment the eunuch had become a comely maiden, dressed simply and with a fair amount of modesty.

The Crown Prince, even more than most people, had always feared and loathed demons. But tonight, to his great satisfaction, he found himself quickly able to master his natural sentiments and adopt a businesslike attitude.

The demon seemed to sense almost immediately that the worst of the Crown Prince's fear and disgust had passed. The maiden rose lithely to her feet, her peasant skirt swirling lightly, and said in a clear voice: "I am at your service, glorious Master! What are your commands?"

Murat drew a breath of satisfaction. "My first demand upon you—and upon the unfortunate human who admits to having been your partner—is to be told all the details of the plot that you hatched between you."

Both offenders bowed in reverence.

"First, I command you to tell me: Is any other plotter, human or otherwise, implicated?"

Both villains at once began to blubber in unison—even the demon's image seemed to cry. With one voice, speaking with tearful vehemence, they assured their new master that no other conspirators had been involved.

"Very well. I'll take your word on that—for the time being. Next, tell me, what exactly was the object of your conspiracy?"

Akbar stuttered, doing an excellent imitation of an appealing maiden in distress. Vilkata confessed that they had been plotting, of course, to get their hands on Murat's Sword. Both partners wept—Vilkata could still weep, it seemed—and tore their hair—or seemed to tear it—at the mere thought of having contemplated such a crime.

But after a few moments of this demonstration, Vilkata pulled himself together.

"I was—I am—the Dark King." This much was no

longer a confession, but had become a proclamation, made with a certain pride. "Like other players in the great game, I wanted to eventually possess all the Swords. Like others, I wanted to rule the world with them."

The Crown Prince glared at him. "And now? What are you now, fallen king, failed wizard? No longer a player in the great game, as you call it. What do you now want?"

"I am—I devoutly hope to be—Your Lordship's magician, and faithful counselor. Certainly I would still be glad to have a Sword, or many Swords. But now, I would want them only as effective tools, that I might be better able to serve my lord."

"Well answered—I suppose." The Crown Prince nodded judicially. "And the demon?"

Akbar, both he and his fellow plotter agreed, was to have been content with the role of second in command when his master Vilkata had succeeded in winning his way back to power.

Murat, suddenly feeling tired almost to exhaustion, lowered his Sword and thought for a moment. Then he made a gesture that was not quite one of dismissal.

"All right, enough. You may spare me the vile details." But his curiosity on other subjects was still unsated, and a moment later he was questioning the scoundrels again.

The next thing the Crown Prince wanted to know was the location of Akbar's life. Everyone knew that the only absolutely sure way of controlling any demon was to have in one's control the object wherein its life was hidden.

Vilkata swore that he had no idea where Akbar's life might be concealed—that was naturally the last thing that any demon wanted to reveal. He turned to his former partner expectantly.

Akbar, who unlike the man seemed to remain in a state of abject surrender—the maiden's head drooped pitiably —proclaimed himself unable to withhold anything from his new master.

"Well, then?"

The demon's slender maiden's arm stretched out, fore-finger pointed at Murat's right hand.

Her tender voice murmured: "My life is hidden in the Mindsword itself."

Vilkata's jaw dropped, in what appeared to be genuine surprise. But the wizard-king said nothing for the moment.

Murat gazed at the Blade in his own hand, first with astonishment and then with new calculation. He swished the god-forged steel several times through the air.

At last he looked back at Akbar. "So! Very clever of you, beast. How did you happen to be able to accomplish such a feat of concealment? But never mind, I can hear that tale later."

"At any time my master wishes."

The look of calculation had not left Murat's face. Suddenly he turned to the human magician and ordered him to make fire.

Vilkata blinked at his master. "Sir?"

"It's a simple enough command. I want you to create fire for me, a small flame, here and now. Right here on the ground in front of me. Surely, as you claim to be a mighty wizard, such a feat is not beyond your powers? It seems to me that it might serve as a test for some low-level magical apprentice."

"I fear, my lord, that I can no longer claim to be a mighty wizard. But—you are quite right. Fire ought to be simple enough."

Creeping about on all fours, Vilkata with unsteady hands gathered dried grass and twigs from the fringes of the hedgerows, heaping his harvest into a little pile before Murat. The magician muttered words into his dark beard. A moment later, a small tongue of flame danced forth atop the pile.

Another moment, and the Crown Prince was holding the

Mindsword's blade directly in the fire. At the first touch of the live flames the demon emitted a scream of torment. In another moment Akbar was thrashing about on the ground, the demure maiden gone, the creature's apparent body contorting madly as it changed into a bewildering variety of shapes.

The Crown Prince kept at his roasting for a little while, confident that a little heat was not going to hurt his Sword. Rare indeed, he thought, would be the human being who felt any compunction about putting any demon to the torment, for whatever reason; and he himself could feel none now. But for the moment, being under the necessity of holding rational discourse with the thing, he ceased to punish it.

"Very clever," he remarked, when the Blade had cooled somewhat, and Akbar had ceased to scream, now lying huddled and twitching on the sand much as a broken human being might have done. "Very clever, choosing one of the Twelve Swords in which to hide your miserable life. Since the Swords are all but indestructible, there would seem to be no practical way for your life to be destroyed; therefore I cannot reasonably threaten you with extinction. But as we have just seen, your existence can be made hell; and I promise you it will be, if you disobey me."

The demon raised its face enough to peer at him with one clear human-looking eye. "Never again will I even think of disobedience, Lord! Never! My only wish now is to serve you faithfully!"

"See that you do not forget it!"

In fact Murat no longer had the least doubt of the loyalty of either of his new slaves. Before dismissing the demon and his human partner, he formally placed them in charge of the magical defenses of the camp, warning them that they would be held responsible for any enemy success. Let there be no more mice, or other tricks. The pair responded with effusive expressions of gratitude and loyalty, vowing their determination that Karel would be frustrated.

The Crown Prince also ordered his newly allied occult experts to take the offensive as soon as possible against his enemies, Prince Mark in particular. The partners agreed enthusiastically with this objective.

Then, with a gesture of disgust, Murat ordered them both out of his sight for the time being.

In moments they were gone, the demon vanishing as abruptly as it had come, Vilkata trudging back to camp. Finding himself alone in the little hollow, the Crown Prince sat down in the sandy soil beside the dying fire, and threw on some twigs to keep it going.

Bleakly Murat tried to understand the new situation in which he now found himself. At the moment his chief worry was just how he would ever be able to free himself of this demon when the time came, as it inevitably would, to do so.

No matter the degree of loyalty to which Akbar might now be constrained, as soon as the Sword's overwhelming power had been removed from him for a while—a matter of a few days at most—the demon could be expected to strike back at its former master and tormentor more readily, and with a more terrible effect, than even the most revengeful human. In the case of a demon, Murat could see no chance of a conversion becoming permanent, as happened in a certain proportion of the human ones.

Presently Murat, moving tiredly, also made his way back to camp. There he rejoined Kristin and his son, who both expressed great relief that he had come through the ordeal unscathed, and bombarded him with questions about the demon.

Kristin, as soon as she had heard the story of the summoning and confrontation just passed, protested mightily against any alliance with demons, or with the Dark King, who she described as a demon in human form.

But right now Murat felt disinclined to heed her objections on this point.

He returned to his tent, where, alone as before, he tried to get some sleep before dawn.

At dawn some enterprising Tasavaltan commander dispatched winged creatures, not couriers but larger raptors, trained for hunting, in a surprise attack on Murat's camp. These flyers were all but mindless and so all but immune to the Mindsword's power. Their objective, which had obviously been firmly impressed upon them, was to drive off the loadbeasts and riding-beasts from Murat's camp.

The convert troopers standing guard duty at the time, and the remainder who were quickly wakened, sent up a barrage of arrows and rocks, wounding several of the attackers and driving the others off, before the four-footed targets could be stampeded.

Vilkata was at Murat's side almost as soon as the Crown Prince came running out of his tent. The wizard hastened to assure his master that new magical defenses would be promptly put in place, to squelch any future flying assaults effectively.

"Akbar, Your Highness, ought to be particularly good at that."

"So he ought. But perhaps we ought to take some other measures as well."

Murat and his followers had long been aware of the existence, somewhat less than a kilometer from their present camp, of a sturdy farmhouse and its outbuildings. Murat and Marsaci had expected this farm to be occupied as an observation post by Tasavaltan reconnaissance units —or that it would be so occupied if there were any such observers so close to Murat's camp.

Now those well-built walls and roofs were beginning to look inviting, for bad weather was now setting in, summer thunderstorms and hail marching closer from the western horizon. The Crown Prince decided to take a look at the place, and if no disadvantages became apparent, occupy it himself.

Holding his Sword still continuously drawn, and riding at the head of his small force, Murat advanced at a deliberate pace toward the comfortable-looking farmstead.

The farmer and his family could be seen fleeing, mounted on loadbeasts, before the invaders came within two hundred meters. No Tasavaltan troops appeared anywhere, and Murat began to think that they had not after all been using the place as a post for observation or command.

Occupation of the hastily abandoned farm was accomplished without further incident, and provided a bonus. Besides shelter, Murat's party had now come into possession of a great number of fowl, and a dozen or so four-legged beasts that could be killed for food, or put to carrying burdens. Such luxuries as eggs and milk were suddenly available. A good supply of rich cheeses was discovered in the cellar, along with a good stock of salted and dried provender.

An hour after his decision to move camp, Murat sat musing with Kristin in the new comfort of the farmhouse.

"Not a palace, my Princess. But in the course of time we'll come to live in palaces."

"I have had palaces, and I do not need them. All that I need, my lord, is you."

"You will have me into eternity. I swear that."

Murat leaned back and closed his eyes, feeling for the first time in days almost at rest. When he opened his eyes again he admired the construction of the house that they were in, and wondered that mere farmers could afford, or cared about, such pleasant decorations.

The Princess murmured that this was little more than

the typical Tasavaltan farmhouse. She mentioned that of course they would leave gold when they departed, or find some other means to pay the farmer for the use of his property and the supplies consumed.

For some reason Kristin's proposal irritated Murat. He was short of ready cash, and doubted that any of the rest of his loyal party had much money with them either.

But the Princess persisted. "They are my people, Lord. It is our custom here to compensate our people, when possible, for losses suffered in time of war." It sounded almost like a rebuke.

"A worthy custom," the Crown Prince said, trying to be agreeable. And in fact he did sympathize to some degree with the abused and evicted peasants; yet he remained irritated. "I have not declared war on these householders, or attacked them. Of course they might have stayed at home and welcomed us; you know, don't you, that I'd have seen the farmer and his people came to no harm at my men's hands?"

"I know that, my lord." The Princess smiled her beautiful smile for him.

"The truth is, Kristin, that I do sympathize with your farmers, and I would like to pay them if I could. But I sympathize even more with my own faithful followers. I think it not entirely Sword-magic that now binds them to my cause."

"Indeed, my lord, I'm sure that it is not."

Murat nodded. "They are, and will be, hard-pressed by the enemy, and I am not about to stop them from eating this farmer's food, or enjoying the shelter of these buildings. Anyway, you are these farmers' rightful monarch, are you not? Surely they ought not to begrudge you and your escort some hospitality."

Kristin meekly bowed her head.

"Anyway," the Crown Prince continued, "I also find it irritating that Tasavaltans like these peasants should not only willfully refuse to hear our case, but actually decline to obey orders given them in the name of their rightful Princess. Remember the messages you were at such pains to distribute? I am beginning to think that it might serve some of these people right if they do suffer a little abuse."

Suddenly the Princess was trying to keep from weeping. But for the time being her lover did not notice.

"Yes," said Murat, "let some of these fat farmers try going on short rations for a while, as our loyal folk have been pleased to do willingly in our service—as even you, my dear, might be compelled to do before we finally succeed in establishing ourselves in Culm."

And why should his beloved Princess and he himself go hungry when these rascal oafs had more than enough for themselves, and no thought of sharing willingly?

So matters stood, or very nearly, when another day dawned. Kristin had spent her first night in the farmhouse in a bedroom alone, and Murat had slept, Sword in hand, in the upstairs hallway just outside her door.

By now Murat's leg had recovered almost entirely; he was even considering that if he should be wounded again, he might allow the magician Vilkata some personal tokens of himself, that the healing spells should be more effective.

He now felt perfectly able to ride again. He decided he was well, and there was probably no more need for Vilkata's healing magic. In this decision the former Dark King now willingly concurred.

The Crown Prince considered taking his Sword and galloping out with a few troopers on a swift reconnaissance, trying to see if a certain alternate route to Culm was clear, or if that way too had been blocked.

But he hesitated. In fact he was coming around to the idea that it would be better after all, in fact it might be necessary, to stay in Tasavalta and conquer it.

FOURTEEN

MARK, after crossing the Tasavaltan border, had changed his original plan and decided to delay his return to the capital—the Council and its decisions would have to wait. Instead he rode directly with Karel and a small escort to join Rostov at the general's field headquarters, hastily established in a farming district four or five kilometers from Murat's encampment.

On reaching Rostov's headquarters, amid a confusion of gathering troops, arriving supplies, and hurrying messengers, Mark learned that Ben had arrived there some hours earlier, and had already gone out with Stonecutter and a small squad of cavalry, to see what additional barriers might be created between the intruder and his native Culm.

Ben returned from his expedition somewhat earlier than expected, only a few hours after Mark's arrival in the headquarters camp. At least some of the Tasavaltan soldiers who had gone out with Ben were missing, and Mark's old friend reported they had been lost in an unplanned skirmish against a patrol of defectors led by Prince Carlo.

The Prince only nodded; skirmishes had to be expected. "Any hope of carving some new barriers with Stonecutter?"

"I don't think so. The terrain doesn't lend itself to that."
Ben's huge frame was slumped in a creaking camp chair, as
if he were inordinately tired.

Mark nodded. "We've had no indication until now, have
we, that Murat's son is with him?"

Rostov and Karel both confirmed this opinion.

"How'd you make the identification, Ben?"

Mark had to repeat the question before the big man
seemed to hear him. Then Ben shifted his weight in the
chair. "I heard one of our renegade Tasavaltans call him
Prince Carlo. Also he was wearing a Sword."

"He wore the Mindsword in a skirmish but he didn't
draw it?"

"I couldn't swear it was that particular Sword, but if
Murat and his people have others at their disposal, we'd
probably have heard about it. And I suppose I might even
be wrong about the hilt—there are black hilts in plenty.
Still, as you know, the real thing has a certain look about
it. . . ."

"I know," said Mark.

"The Princeling and I both came on the scene a little
late, after the fight had started. I got my people out of there
as quickly as I could once I saw how he was armed."

"Wise decision."

Ben rubbed his eyes. No, he told Mark, he hadn't seen
anything of Murat himself, nor, of course, of Kristin.

After answering a few more questions from Rostov and
Karel, Ben, who looked worn out, was sent to get some rest.
Mark remarked that his old friend didn't seem quite right.
Well, losing people in a fight was always a wearing experi-
ence.

That night the moon was full and bright, the weather no
worse than partly cloudy.

After the Prince of Tasavalta had tried to rest for an hour

or two, he was up again, unable to be quiet while Kristin was so near and at the same time so completely out of reach.

Someone had just escorted into camp the displaced and outraged family whose home had just been occupied by Murat, and Mark spoke eagerly to these people, learning what little he could about the enemy disposition. He also had the farmer sketch out for him the floor plan of their house, though at the moment the knowledge seemed unlikely to have any useful application.

After ordering the family to be sheltered in tents for the time being, Mark abruptly decided to ride out by night to take a look at the commandeered farmhouse, accompanied only by Karel.

Mark, as he rode with the ageless magician at his side and Sightblinder sheathed at his belt, turned over in his mind several possible schemes for rescuing his wife. In none of them, at the moment, could he see any reasonable chance of success.

Silently, the Prince recalled how once, years ago, this same Sword that he now carried had been able to protect him to some degree against the Mindsword's force. On that day, too, he had ridden toward an enemy camp in which Kristin was held prisoner, and which was dominated by the Sword of Glory in a villain's hands.

That day marked the first time Mark had met the woman who was to become his wife, and on that day he had saved Kristin from a most horrible and painful death. But, on that distant, marvelous, and terrifying day, Mark's enemy the Dark King had not been holding the Mindsword continually drawn, as Murat was now. And when Vilkata had finally drawn the Blade, Mark had been able to resist its power only partially; and he had realized that he would not have been able to do that much without the Sword of Stealth in his own hand.

Sightblinder's gifts: his eyes are keen
His nature is disguised.

On that far-off day, possessing Sightblinder had made resistance possible—barely possible. Mark was sure that in no very great length of time the Sword of Glory, performing its prime function, would have overcome Sightblinder's secondary attribute of giving its holder enhanced perception.

The Mindsword spun in the dawn's gray light
And men and demons knelt down before.
The Mindsword flashed in the midday bright
Gods joined the dance, and the march to war.
It spun in the twilight dim as well
And gods and men marched off to hell.

Now, as the two men quietly covered the moonlit distance between their own camp and the enemy's, Karel thought the time appropriate to deliver to his Prince a new report, concerning the latest results of his days-long struggle to create and extend a magical domination over Murat's encampment and the people in it.

An early phase of that assault, the plague of mice, had succeeded admirably, but later efforts were having less and less success.

"And during the last few hours the reason has become plain, my Prince. My task has been complicated considerably by a real wizard's opposition."

Mark turned in his saddle. "A real wizard? Whom has he converted now?"

"The news is not good, my Prince. Though there may be some good to come from it in the end—"

"Who?"

Karel told him.

"Why didn't you tell me this at once?"

"I did not want the news to get around our own camp. I am sorry if that was wrong."

Mark drew several deep breaths. "No," he said at last. "You were right. Though of course the troops must be told eventually. When we've had time to prepare them. So, the old bastard's not dead after all."

"Unfortunately he is not." After giving his sovereign a few more breaths in which to digest the disturbing information, the wizard added: "And there is more to tell, almost as bad."

"Then tell it."

"We now face a demon also. Let me hasten to add that Kristin seems to be in no immediate danger from the thing."

Mark, on recovering somewhat from this second shock, felt confident that he could readily drive the demon away if it confronted him directly—at least he had always been able to master such creatures in this way before, through the power of the Emperor's name, though understanding of this power eluded him. But the demon perhaps realized this as well as Mark did, and it might be avoiding him, retreating whenever it sensed the Prince of Tasavalta was approaching.

After a brief discussion of the problem posed by the demon, the two men rode on in silence for a little distance, each busy with his own thoughts.

At last the Prince asked: "I suppose there's no doubt?"

"There is no doubt, sir, that both the Dark King and the demon are now allied with the Crown Prince. But neither Vilkata nor the demon is in command. Rather they seem to be as completely enthralled by the Mindsword as any of the others who now surround Murat."

"Can you overcome them?"

"As for Vilkata, I can, and will, and have, though to beat

him thoroughly will take time. His strength in the art is not what it was in the old days; and even then he excelled mainly in the control of demons. Only one of that tribe is in his service now, and that one—its name is Akbar—I consider even more cowardly than most."

"Cowardly, but powerful, I suppose."

The magician nodded. "Formidable, even for a demon. But Akbar I will leave to you, should the foul thing ever dare to confront us directly."

Prince and wizard approached Murat's defended camp warily, climbing the far side of a long hill from which they would be able to overlook the occupied farm. When, extending their view cautiously over the hilltop, they had the house and barn in view below, Karel by his art was able to let Mark see just how far they were from the boundary of the Mindsword's magic. Touching his fingers lightly to his Prince's eyes, the magician rendered that field of force visible to Mark, in the form of an eerie, transparent blue glow in the atmosphere.

"And now, magician? Is there something else that you can achieve in this situation?"

"I can but try, Prince. I am going to try to put everyone in Murat's encampment sound asleep. If that succeeds, we may be able to try something more. Let me have a few moments for silent concentration."

Standing guard while Karel concentrated, cautiously peering over the very top of the hill, Mark gazed down at the buildings and smoldering watchfires of Murat's camp, where a few huddled human figures were discernible in the bright moonlight. The faint bluish haze of Sword-power, visible to his eyes and presumably to Karel's, was centered on the upper floor of the farmhouse, and extended to about twenty meters from where Mark and Karel now sat their riding-beasts. At that point the blue haze faded out abruptly.

Some minutes passed. Then Karel, who had looked as if he were dozing in his saddle, roused himself to whisper encouraging words to his sovereign. The magician's efforts to put everyone in the camp asleep by magic were on the verge of almost complete success.

Mark murmured back: "I don't suppose our friend is likely to sheathe his Sword before he dozes off?"

"I don't suppose so, Prince. But we can hope."

Soon Karel announced that the sleep-pall was even now taking full effect upon all the people in and around the farmhouse. But unfortunately, as Mark was able to see for himself, the Mindsword's influence continued unabated.

"He grasps the weapon tightly even in his sleep, my Prince. Therefore you must not dream of trying to enter the camp to bring Kristin out. We must seek some other way."

Mark was not so easily discouraged. "I have Sightblinder. If I were to try the fringes of this blue haze, test it first with only an arm or leg, and see what—"

Karel was uncharacteristically vehement. "No, you must not attempt it, Prince! Sightblinder will not serve to protect you. At this moment she is still unharmed, except for the spell cast on her by the Sword. We will find another way."

"With a demon hovering near her? We can't wait!"

"I tell you, you must wait! The demon is not near her now. Not anywhere near here—it may have retreated when it sensed the Emperor's son approaching. You'll be no good to her or anyone if you become Murat's slave."

Mark, reluctantly acknowledging the wisdom of Karel's advice, and seeing no other choice, gave in.

In a few more moments Karel was able to assure him that the pall of sleep he had been gradually weaving over the enemy had now indeed taken full effect. The charm had worked so subtly that none of the victims, even Vilkata, had realized that they were being enchanted. To work such magic was comparatively easy at night, because most of the subjects, or victims, would be expecting to go to sleep anyway.

The Prince thought it would be far less easy than Karel made it sound. Then Mark was struck by a sudden hope.

"If I cannot go down to her, can you get Kristin to come out?"

Karel closed his eyes. "The possibility had already crossed my mind. I will do what I can to call her here. But what I can do will probably be insufficient, unless she believes, even in the Sword's enchantment, that she has a reason to come."

Kristin, rousing from a light sleep, had the distinct sensation that someone had just called her name—one of her parents, perhaps, though both her mother and father were long dead. It had been only a dream, then . . . or had it?

She sat up in the unfamiliar farmhouse bed—there was no difficulty in remembering how she had come here—and pulled aside a window curtain. The casement behind stood open to the summer night, and moonlight flooded into the small, neat room which Murat had assigned her. Though small, it was the biggest bedchamber in the house, and the best furnished, with table and chest of drawers and even a little mirror on the wall.

Looking out of the window, Kristin could see a pair of watchfires in the farmyard below, smoldering and dying. There were dim motionless forms of troopers and bandits slumping and lying around them.

It was none of these who had called her.

Raising her eyes and gazing into the moonlit middle distance, the Princess beheld two mounted figures at the top of a long, grassy hill.

Her sense of wonder grew at the strangeness of the

awakening call. Unsure at first whether she might not be still asleep and dreaming, the Princess arose from her bed and groped with her feet until she found her shoes. Otherwise she had lain down fully dressed. Opening her bedroom door, she went out into the hallway, partially lit by moonlight filtering through the oiled-paper window at one end. The white walls and coved ceiling, here in the hallway as in the rooms, were neatly plastered as in many prosperous homes in Tasavalta.

Kristin's feeling that she might still be dreaming faded at the sight of Murat, who lay sleeping on the floor just outside her bedroom door. She had to step over him to leave her room. His face was shadowed. The Princess paused to look adoringly at her new lover, who moaned almost inaudibly in his slumber. The Crown Prince was sleeping of course with the Sword in his hand, and she drew in her breath with sudden fear that he might turn over in his sleep and gash himself on that Blade. The Princess knew from old and bitter experience that the Mindsword made terrible physical wounds, almost impossible to heal. Briefly she considered moving the Sword a little, for her lover's safety, but then decided against making the attempt. Tonight Lord Murat might well need the protection offered by that black hilt in his hand, even at the risk of a sore wound.

And besides, she feared to wake her lord just now, lest he prevent her doing something that she had decided must be done—for his sake.

Scarcely had Kristin started down the hall than she stopped again, with a sharp intake of breath. Vilkata was sleeping only two or three meters away, on the floor near the head of the stairs. To her disgust, Kristin found herself compelled to step over his loathsome body as well; and as she did so she considered killing him—for Murat's sake.

The Princess had left her hunting knife back in the

bedroom, but there was a dagger in the demon-master's belt that might be snatched away and plunged into his heart. Only two thoughts stayed her hand: this fiend was now sealed in loyalty to Murat, and the possibility was all too real that her beloved might soon be in need of every ally he had. Even this one.

Kristin let the wizard go on living. Stealing downstairs as quietly as possible, she encountered a few more sleeping bodies in parlor and kitchen, but to her surprise no one was awake and on guard. Surely some of these men should be faithfully on duty?

Perhaps, she thought, her lord in his wisdom had stationed the real sentries outside.

Still nagged by the feeling that someone had wakened her by calling her name, but more and more convinced that she had dreamt that much, the Princess went outside, through the kitchen and back door.

The pair of smoldering watchfires in the farmyard seemed to be burning even lower now than when she had glimpsed them from upstairs. Fires or not, there must certainly have been sentries posted out here; but Kristin saw to her surprise that they too, or at least the individuals who might have been sentries, were also fast asleep.

She took one of these men by the arm and tried, without success, to wake him.

Abandoning the attempt, the Princess turned. Peering uphill, into an alternation of darkness and moonlight created by the passage of some clouds, she could again make out the two dim human figures at a distance of something over a hundred meters. Up there on the summit two men were sitting their riding-beasts, at a distance Kristin judged to be somewhat beyond the limits of the Mindsword's invisible power.

It struck her that she was able to see one of those men remarkably well, considering the conditions. Something about the figure's clothing suggested a military uniform, though in the moonlight and at this distance it was really impossible to determine colors. The Princess was suddenly quite certain, without any conscious logic having entered into her discovery, that the man who seemed to be in uniform was a simple military messenger, come under a flag of truce to bring her word of her husband's death in some remote place. In a moment he would ride down the hill toward her, his face grim, shoulders slumped under his tragic burden—

—but wherever the thing had happened, Mark was dead, slain in some stupid combat, or dead in some pointless accident, on one of his hopeless missions attempting to serve the Emperor. And this rider, the anonymous messenger she had feared with all her heart and soul for years, was on the verge of cantering downhill to bring her the word that she had dreaded for so long—

Kristin, knowing in her heart that her doom had come upon her, and moving in a sick, dreamlike calm, observed a path that led out of the farmyard and up the hill. A moment later she was following the path, climbing the hill.

Just as she was leaving the farmyard she took note of a man who ought to have been a sentry, sprawled sleeping at what must have been his post, just inside the fence beside the path. The man moved slightly as she passed him, but the eyes in the upturned face were closed—rather, almost closed—and he snored faintly.

Kristin went on her way. Looking uphill again, she thought that the second man on the hilltop, the one who sat his mount beside the messenger's, looked very much like her uncle Karel.

Mark, straining his eyes, and gripping the hilt of Sightblinder tightly in an effort to enhance his own perception as much as possible, bit back an outcry. He recognized his wife by moonlight almost as soon as she stepped out of the shadows of the farmhouse doorway more than a hundred meters below.

Murat, after stretching himself out on the floor of the upstairs hall in the farmhouse, had taken no alarm when he began to grow heavily, deliciously sleepy. Such sensations were only natural, considering that his various concerns and responsibilities, together with the slowly diminishing pain of his wound, had allowed him but little rest on several successive nights before this one. He had welcomed the chance to lay his body down, with the black hilt of his drawn Sword still clutched in his right hand, upon a folded rug in front of Kristin's door.

Only in the last few moments before the Crown Prince dozed off did certain unwelcome thoughts enter his mind. Since making his decision to keep the Mindsword continually unsheathed, he had found himself growing more rather than less afraid of Mark. The nets of defensive magic that Murat had woven about his own person with the Sword, and with Vilkata's and the demon's help, was bringing him no increased feeling of security.

Rather the reverse.

And then there was Kristin, and her all-too-justifiable unhappiness caused by Murat's toleration of the foul wizard-king Vilkata. Perhaps worse, in her view, was his new reliance upon an actual demon. Kristin, tender-minded and basically innocent, was unable to face the fact that he, Murat, must now depend upon such creatures.

Well, Vilkata was—or had been—a foul villain indeed, and under other conditions Murat would not have delayed in putting the eyeless man to a horrible death, in payment for what he had once done to Murat's beloved bride-to-be. But the purifying power of the Sword had transformed the foul, treacherous torturer and beggar into a trustworthy servant, at least for the time being. And the fact was that Kristin's own welfare, perhaps her very survival, now required Murat to seek help wherever he could.

That was the last thought of which the Crown Prince was conscious before he fell asleep.

As Kristin climbed the hill, mounting closer and closer to the two men who seemed to be waiting for her at the top, logic suddenly awoke to remind her that Sightblinder, in someone else's hands, might be the cause of her perception of a dreadful messenger. But logic could offer only cold and fragile comfort against the inner certainty of that waiting figure's identity, and the nature of his message. These were horrors that had formed the core of her worst dreams over the past few years. Fatalistically, she climbed on.

Mark had been sitting motionless in his saddle, gazing downhill with fierce intensity, hardly taking his eyes from that small figure as it approached. He had seen his wife, as if in response to the sheer power of his will, leave the unattainable camp below and come deliberately walking up the hill toward him. Now the Prince feared to move or speak or even breathe, lest he break whatever beneficent spell was granting him his most fervent wish.

Karel, waiting beside the Prince, was silent too, and almost motionless.

Breathing softly now, Mark dared to move, to dismount. Once on his feet he did nothing but stand and wait, while Kristin in the course of her next few steps emerged from the eerily visible haze of the Mindsword's influence. Then, approaching in deliberate silence, she came to stop some four meters from her husband.

At that point she spoke. "Mark? I feel it is really you before me, and not the form I see."

The Prince unbuckled Sightblinder from his belt, then

handed the weapon, sheath and all, up to Karel, who still sat mounted. In the next moment the Prince turned and took a swift step forward, meaning to enfold his wife in his arms.

But Kristin stepped back quickly, avoiding Mark's embrace; and as she moved she uttered a strange gasp, partly of relief and partly of something else.

Mark halted himself in mid-stride, reminding himself that the Mindsword's spell could not be so easily dissolved. Considerable time and loving care would be needed to heal Kristin of its effects, even after she had emerged from the field of its direct influence.

There would be no point in beginning with an impassioned declaration of love. "What form did you just see?" he asked his wife, in as calm a voice as he could manage.

She tossed her hair. Her voice was almost bright. "Some anonymous courier, come to tell me that you were dead."

"Kristin!" Again Mark spread his arms, and started to move forward.

Again with a swift, lithe movement she maintained the distance between them. "Mark, I have come up here to tell you, face to face, that from now on you must allow me to go my own way."

Mark managed to edge a half-step closer without provoking a reaction. Silently he cursed all Swords; he cursed Murat. He could see now that he was probably going to have to seize Kris bodily, if he could, to keep her from darting back into the Mindsword's sphere of magic. He could see the blue haze flickering almost at her heels.

Of course he should be subtle; but at the moment he could not.

"Kris, that Sword, *his* Sword, is making you go away from me."

"No!" Her denial, though forceful, was calm and matter-of-fact. "The Mindsword shocked me at first, but—no. Do not think, my former husband, that I am its slave. Or Prince Murat's."

"I am your husband, now and forever—but later we can talk about that. Right now—"

"We must talk about it now. Or rather, I must convince you now that our marriage is at an end. You no longer have any right to command my people, my armies—or my magicians."

Here she swung her gaze abruptly toward Karel. And Mark could see her pause, as if in renewed horror, at whatever image she saw in her familiar uncle's place.

Since Kristin's arrival the old wizard had waited in his saddle, silently and patiently. He was holding Sightblinder now, and when Mark glanced his way he saw instead a second image of Kristin, this one mounted, gazing reproachfully back at him.

When Karel spoke, he did not respond to what Kristin had just said to him. Instead he said: "Holding the Sword of Stealth, I can see more than I did. I see the two of you—"

His words broke off.

"Well?" Mark cried impatiently, at his wife's mounted image. "What is it, old man?"

Kristin too was staring at her uncle, but Mark could not guess who or what she might be seeing in his place.

"Never mind," said Karel at last. For Mark, his voice was Kristin's too. "Never mind. Let us finish our business here."

For Mark, it was, as usual, easier not to look at whoever was holding the Sword of Stealth.

And it was foolish, thought Mark, as he faced back to Kristin, for him to stand here arguing—because he was arguing not with his wife, but with the powers of Murat's Sword. Kris in her present state was no more than a puppet, compelled to say these awful things.

As if determined to prove that the bond between the two of them might after all, when put to the test, be stronger than all magic, the Prince extended a hand toward his wife.

"Come with me, Kris."

Without moving, she gazed back at him. Her expression, clear in the moonlight, was one of calm, patient rationality that chilled him more than any rage or venom might have done.

After a brief pause Kristin spoke. "I tell you, Mark, that you are my husband no longer. Do not blame the Sword, or any magic. That only helped me to see the truth. And the truth is that, even if no one had brought the Sword of Glory near me, I was ready to leave you anyway."

Kristin glanced toward her uncle once more, and this time recoiled noticeably, closing her eyes for a moment. Evidently this time she had seen the old man as someone or something very terrible. When her eyes opened again, her gaze stayed averted from him.

Then with an effort she said: "Uncle, I know that it is you."

"My Princess," said the wizard heavily, while Mark, glancing sideways, now saw him as Murat, with half a dozen Swords hung from his saddle. "My Princess, you are not yourself."

At that Kristin dared to look back at Karel again. "But I am myself, Uncle. More so now than—"

Mark broke in. "Kris, no one in the world outside that camp behind you really believes that we two have been divorced. Our children certainly don't believe it. Nor does anyone imagine that I have really been deposed as Prince of Tasavalta."

For the first time since she had climbed the hill, Kristin seemed shocked. "The messages I left in Sarykam—"

"Have all been read. Everyone understands that you were not in your right mind when you set them down."

"I was completely in possession of myself."

Kristin had raised her voice a little now. She still spoke with a deadly certainty, her eyes locked on Mark's. "And every word I wrote in those notes was true." Now she turned to cast a quick glance back over her shoulder, into the great web of the Mindsword's magic, still invisible to her, at whose center Murat was sleeping deeply.

Then, once more meeting Mark's gaze firmly, his dear wife said to him: "The simple truth is that I have found one who matters much more to me than you do."

The Prince could feel his scalp crawl with shock and anger, though at this stage the words should have come as no surprise. He said in a weak voice: "Kris?"

Her fists were clenched. "I tell you, Mark, that the Sword in my Lord Murat's hand really had very little effect on me. It provided only a momentary shock, a stimulus to help me see things as they really were. Only Murat himself do I now see in a new way; it did not make me see anything new about you at all—"

"It is useless for the two of you to argue these matters now," broke in Karel in a dull voice, this time recognizably his own. Perhaps, thought Mark, the old man, feeling secure in the knowledge that the three of them were quite alone, had dropped Sightblinder to the ground.

Mark edged another half-step closer to his wife.

"You say that Murat's control over you is not absolute?"

She shook her head impatiently. "You persist in misunderstanding, despite all your knowledge of the Swords. Murat does not control anyone—except by being the glorious person that he is, so anyone who sees him for what he really is must serve him faithfully from that moment on. He does not know that I am here now, talking to you, and he would certainly not approve—but I have come here anyway, because I hope that I can serve his interests, by persuading you to let us alone."

Karel grunted as if with satisfaction. "I did not expect that his followers would necessarily obey his every wish—

as long as they are convinced that by disobeying, they can more truly serve him. Well, that is reassuring."

Mark, ignoring the magician's comments, said to his wife: "Our son is waiting in my camp to see you."

A shadow that might have been guilt crossed Kristin's face. "Then Stephen is safe. Very good. I was sure he'd be able to take care of himself under the circumstances."

"He saw what happened to you." Another half-step closer. "He was not happy about that."

"He did not understand."

"Oh yes he did. That's why it was so terrible."

Mark's last half-step had been too much. Kristin let out a small cry and turned to dash back into the Mindsword's zone of domination.

But the Prince, who had been shifting his weight forward and making every other subtle preparation he could contrive, was a shade too fast for her. He had no need to turn before he pounced. His left hand caught her by the arm in a crushing grip, and yanked her back from the fringes of blue haze.

Kristin, who had come unarmed, tried to bite, and screamed, and struggled, but her husband held her now in both arms and swung her off her feet, toward his waiting mount. Karel, having wisely maneuvered himself into the exact place where he was needed, leaned from his saddle, Swordless, wheezing, recognizably himself. The wizard's large right hand, pale and gemmed with rings, moved out to palm Kristin's forehead softly. In the next instant she went limp.

Murat was awakened by the sounds of distant screaming. Not quickly awakened, for it seemed to him that he spent endless time struggling toward consciousness from a slough of oblivion. But at last he was conscious, sitting upright on the floor of the upstairs hall in the expropriated farmhouse, the Mindsword's hilt still grasped in his right hand.

He shouted for Vilkata, but at first only a sleepy mumbling answered. In any case it was now too late. He needed no wizard or demon to tell him that Kristin had somehow fled or been snatched away.

FIFTEEN

KRISTIN came drifting upward out of oblivion, joyfully cradled in a small canoe wrought from the stuff of dreams, borne by this craft with no volition of her own into a beautiful dim grotto that reminded her of someplace, sometime long ago. This was a condition of great happiness but it proved transitory. The Princess yearned for the enchanted canoe to stop at this point but it would not, instead carrying her along a stream that flowed with increasing swiftness.

And then her canoe jolted against reality, and turned abruptly into a plain field cot. With the sudden arrival of full wakefulness the blessed environment of watery dim stream and grotto transformed itself into the dim interior of a military field tent, where a single candle on a map table was all that held back darkness.

And Kristin knew that something horrible had happened. . . .

Her eyes wide open now, the Princess lay without moving on the field cot, covered by a brown army blanket. The desolate rush of returning memory confirmed her fears; Mark and her uncle had captured her, seized her violently just outside Murat's encampment. They had dragged her away by force, detached her from the one being in the universe who now meant more to her than all the rest. . . .

Yet her separation from Murat was not the mortal pang it might have been. A pleasant haze of dulled perception, relaxed indifference, kept her from feeling the full pain that ought to have come with such a loss.

Turning her head, Kristin saw that she was almost alone inside the tent. A woman soldier of the Tasavaltan army, uniformed in blue and green, was dozing, her head nodding, in a camp chair almost within arm's reach of the cot. The woman in the chair roused herself as soon as Kristin stirred, and a moment later had hurried to the doorway and was passing word to someone outside the tent that the Princess had awakened.

Kristin remained inert, trying to marshal her strength, for what kind of effort she was not sure. After the passage of an interval, which to the Princess seemed neither short nor long, her uncle Karel's face appeared above her, swimming dimly in a pleasant haze of lethargy; and soon, beside it, the familiar countenance of Mark.

Speaking tenderly, and as calmly as they could, the two men took turns explaining to Kristin that she was safe and secure in Mark's camp, surrounded by her own loyal soldiers.

Looking from one face to the other, she asked in a small voice: "Loyal to whom?"

The two men exchanged glances. Then he who had once been her husband said quietly: "To their land, and to their Princess."

"Is Rostov here?"

"He is."

"Then kindly convey my compliments to the general, and tell him that I wish to see him."

Another interval went by in the dim tent without looming faces; when they returned, Rostov's steel-stubbled black countenance was there between the other two.

"General, I have orders for you," Kristin murmured sleepily. Somehow she was having trouble calling any authority into her voice.

Rostov nodded. It had never been his fault to waste much breath in unnecessary speech.

"You are to accept no further orders from this man"— the Princess indicated Mark—"who was formerly my husband. Instead you are to send messengers to the Lord Murat, and place yourself and your armies entirely at his disposal. Is that clear?"

The general must have been warned, before he came into the tent, to expect something of the kind. He only bowed lightly, and responded calmly enough.

"As I love you, my Princess, and as I would serve you, I cannot accept such orders from you now."

Mark was silent, but Kristin's uncle standing on the other side of Rostove said to her: "Your soldiers will obey you gladly and most lovingly, Madam, as will I, once you are thinking clearly again."

She shook her head, back and forth on the flat pillow. "I am thinking very clearly now—or I was, until you befuddled me tonight with your magic, Uncle. What kind of enchanted existence have you condemned me to?"

With an effort the Princess sat up, shaking her head some more and trying to clear it. She saw when the blanket fell back that she was still wearing the clothes in which she had joined Murat two days ago—could it have been only two days, or was it longer? For a moment the grief of separation threatened to overwhelm her.

Karel said: "I am sorry to befuddle you, as you put it, Princess. But you must be allowed a chance to rest." And the wizard made another magical pass or two.

The Prince realized that Karel was allowing Kristin to drift up slowly out of her enchanted sleep. But the old magician did not allow the young woman to return all the way to full awareness, holding her rather in a state of soothed tranquility, numbed enough so that her sadness at being separated from her new lord was quiet and gentle; not the violence of rage and hate that, as he had assured Mark, it would otherwise have been.

Mark, in whom strong feelings of relief and rage contended each time he looked at Kristin, now had a new idea. Drawing Karel away from the cot for a moment, he whispered to the old wizard that they might try giving his wife Sightblinder to hold, in hopes that she would be enabled that way to perceive the true state of affairs.

Karel, after some hesitation, agreed.

Mark sent for the Sword of Stealth, which one of his officers was now guarding. While they were waiting for Sightblinder to arrive, Rostov excused himself and left the tent.

When the black hilt was at last presented to Kristin, she refused to touch it, withdrawing her hands under the blanket.

Mark had reclaimed the Sword Sightblinder, and was about to leave the tent with Karel when, to his surprise and momentary delight, Kristin called him back.

She gazed at him, her eyes luminous with the haze of Karel's relaxing magic. But there was urgency in her voice. "There is something that I must tell you."

"What?" Putting the Sword of Stealth aside again, Mark knelt beside the bed. He reached automatically for Kristin's hand, but she pulled it away from him.

Shuddering, the woman on the cot said: "In—in Murat's camp—there is now a demon. And also a man—if you can call him that—who is the demon's master. The Dark King himself. I saw him."

Mark and Karel exchanged glances. "We know about the demon, and the magician," said the Prince, trying to make his voice confident and soothing. He paused. "Did either of them harm you?"

The luminous blue eyes flickered. "Harm me? No, they

would not have dared do that. My gracious Lord Murat has ordered all his followers to honor and serve me. But—for *his* sake I must warn you about the demon, and about its keeper. Because I fear that in the end such servants and counselors will destroy him."

Mark paused. "I will destroy the demon," he said, "if I can. Or I'll send it hurtling to the ends of the earth." Then he patted Kristin's hand gently, touched her hair once, and got to his feet. Then impulsively he started to bend over her, meaning to kiss her on the cheek. But again she shrank away.

He straightened up.

"As for the Crown Prince Murat, I can promise you nothing. I am glad you told me about the Dark King, and the demon," he assured her quietly. "Will you tell us anything else—about Murat's intentions, for example?"

"His intention was to leave Tasavalta quietly, before you began to attack us."

"To leave, taking you with him."

"Of course."

"To Culm?"

"That I will not tell you."

Mark turned away and started to leave the tent.

Then he halted as Kristin spoke again.

"I say again, to you my uncle and you my former husband, that I wish neither of you ill. But it is not for your sake that I warn you about the demon—and about the other, the man who sees with demon's eyes, and who is worse than any demon. What I tell you is for my lord's sake."

"We understand that," Karel murmured.

"If I do not hate you, who are his enemies," she said, "it is only because *he* does not. I tell you that my Lord Murat wishes no one any harm—not even you, who are now bent on killing him."

Mark stared at her. Before he could answer, a guard put

his head into the tent to whisper that young Stephen had wakened, learned his rescued mother was now in camp, and was demanding to see her.

"Let him come in," sighed Mark. Earlier he had spoken to his son about the possibility of frightening changes.

When the boy entered, a few moments later, Kristin stared at her son, then held out her arms to embrace him.

Leaving mother and son alone for the time being, Mark and Karel walked out of the tent. When they had gone a few paces, and were out of earshot of the sentries, they began conversing in low tones.

Mark asked, "How long will it be, magician, before she's my own wife again?"

"That I cannot say, Prince," Karel answered heavily. "We may hope for some favorable change in a few days."

Before Mark could speak again, Stephen, on the verge of weeping, came bursting out of the tent. The boy walked quickly away, avoiding his father when Mark would have spoken with him.

Mark let him go. After a final word with Karel, he retired to his own tent to try to get some sleep, leaving word that he wanted to be called as soon as there was any sign that Murat had awakened.

Sleep came quickly to the exhausted Prince, but his rest was soon troubled by strange dreams. It seemed to Mark that he was wandering, fully armed, but with only ordinary weapons, in a strange countryside. His path led him beside an unknown stream. Eventually it came to him that this must be the Aldan, the small river on whose wooded banks he had grown up. Having made this discovery he tried to walk faster, in hopes of catching sight of the mill operated by his foster-father, Jord, or hearing the familiar groaning of the wheel.

The stream might have been the Aldan, but every detail about its banks remained stubbornly unfamiliar. At last, on rounding a bend, Mark came upon his father the Emperor, leaning against a flowering tree with his arms folded, and regarding Mark as if he had been waiting for him to arrive. The Emperor looked no older than the last time Mark had seen him, and now for the first time it struck Mark that this man, his father, looked somewhat younger than himself.

Standing a little behind the Emperor was Ben. Ben's massive arms were folded like the Emperor's, and he was regarding Mark with a strange solemn silence.

The Prince did not hesitate, but strode toward the Emperor in an angry mood, ready to challenge his assumed authority—as indeed he tended to do in waking life, on those rare occasions when he actually saw the man.

Mark halted two paces away from the waiting, imperturbable figure dressed in gray.

"You are my father," Mark said. The words came out like an accusation.

"Yes."

"Very well, then, I need your help."

The middle-sized man in gray looked sympathetic. "What kind of help?"

Mark had not realized until this moment what kind of assistance he meant to ask for. But now he did not hesitate. "I want you to lend me Soulcutter. I know you have it."

The father who appeared to be no older than his son now seemed to be regarding the younger man with disappointment if not distaste. "How do you know that?"

"Because that Sword was in your possession when it was last seen, years ago. You picked it up on a battlefield and carried it away. Who else should have it now if you do not? Did someone take it from you, or have you given it away?"

"The answer is no."

"No?"

"No. I did not remove the Sword of Despair from that field only to give it back again. Besides, that weapon does not belong to me. But even if it were in my possession, I would categorically refuse to loan it to anyone, especially my son."

"Why?"

"I need give you no explanations, Mark, but I will. The best way to put it is that you don't know what you're asking for."

Ben, looking gloomy, having nothing to say, remained standing in the background. Mark understood that this dispute was to be only between father and son.

The Prince moved a step closer, looming over the smaller man in gray. "Will you for once give me a straight, complete answer when I ask you a question? Will you for once admit that I might be right?"

The Emperor smiled faintly at him, and said nothing.

Groaning, muttering in exasperation, Mark moved to seize the Emperor by his garments and shake him. But somehow it was hard to obtain a solid hold.

"You are a bothersome son, sometimes," his father said. And Mark himself, to his surprise, was grabbed in a grip of incredible strength, and jerked about until his teeth rattled.

At that point he came struggling out of the dream to reenter the real world, to find that someone was really shaking him, albeit much more gently than the Emperor had done.

The eastern wall of his campaign tent was glowing in the rays of the newly risen sun. An officer had come in with an urgent report: Ben of Purkinje was unaccountably missing from the camp. Missing with Ben were two riding-beasts, an undetermined amount of supplies, and the Sword Sightblinder.

SIXTEEN

SOMETHING—he had an impression of distant shouts or screams—awakened the Crown Prince well before dawn, and he could see by moonlight that the door of Kristin's bedroom was standing ajar. Only a quick look at the empty bed inside was needed to confirm that she was gone. Had intruders, treading in supernal silence, stepped over him as he slept? There were no signs of struggle in Kristin's room. And it ought to be impossible for anyone, here in the central glare of the Sword's full power, to intrigue against Murat, to kidnap his beloved. But still the bedroom window was wide open. . . .

Trying to think clearly, but still fighting a hideous drowsy lethargy, Murat struggled to his feet, stepped over the still-inert form of Vilkata farther down the hall, and began to stumble downstairs, leaning on the farmhouse wall to keep his balance. In the process of making his way down the narrow stair, the Crown Prince shifted the Sword very carefully from one hand to the other, being very careful lest it fall from his cramped fingers. With the transfer he felt only the slightest alteration in the effortless flow of magic. But not for an instant did Murat cease to hold Skulltwister. There was no moment in which even the swiftest enemy might have been able to penetrate his defensive field and strike.

Except, of course, by some other magic, operating from a distance. Now he understood that the slumber from which he struggled to extricate himself was certainly unnatural.

Having reached the dark hall at the foot of the stairs, Murat turned toward the kitchen, passed through it and went out into the night. But when he found himself outdoors he was unable for the first few minutes to do much more than stagger about the farmyard like a sleepwalker. Groggily the Crown Prince strove to free himself fully from the toils of Karel's slumber-inducing enchantments.

And it was in the farmyard, before he was fully awake, that he heard for the first time eyewitness testimony of Kristin's departure. One of the sentries, seemingly the only man in camp who had not been entirely overcome by sleep, swore that he had watched her go, alone.

Swiftly mounting anger helped Murat break free of the clinging tendrils of soporific magic. And as soon as he felt confident of being able to think coherently, he strode back into the farmhouse, climbed to the upper hall, and in a cold fury started trying to rouse his supposed magician.

He went at the job with ruthless energy, but still it took him a few minutes to get Vilkata fully awake. When the Crown Prince was satisfied that the man could hear him, he informed his vanquished wizard that the Princess was gone.

"One of the sentries," Murat grated, "reports that she walked out of the camp alone, apparently of her own free will. Up the path toward two mounted men who appeared on that hill."

The wretch who had once been the Dark King, now sitting on the floor in a moonlit corner of the little upstairs hall, pressed his pale albino's hands, incongruously backed with dark hair, over the bandage that crossed the upper portion of his face.

His voice sounded muffled. "You say the man reports her leaving, my lord? Why didn't he stop her?"

Murat could answer that, having already briefly interrogated the sentry who had witnessed Kristin's departure. The soldier swore that he had been in a helpless state that kept him from doing anything about Kristin's departure—or would have prevented his interference, had he considered it his duty to interfere. Actually, as the shaken trooper had pointed out, the sentries had been given no orders to keep the Princess in the camp. Rather, everyone had been commanded to grant her every wish. Murat, raging in the farmyard, had been forced to realize that in justice there should be no punishment for the sentry.

Indoors he continued his dialogue with Vilkata, but, as it seemed, to little purpose. When presently the two men descended into the farmyard again, Murat vented his anger on other people. He beat one man with the flat of his Sword when the fellow could not be awakened by less violent means.

And he continued to be angry at his magician for allowing Karel to prevail and put them all to sleep.

"Scoundrel, charlatan! Where is your demon? I suppose the vile beast is sleeping too?"

"I do not think so, Great Lord." Vilkata's tones were full of misery. "But where he is at the moment I do not know."

"Then summon him, and let us see!"

With this end in mind, Vilkata and Murat went alone behind some outbuildings, so that the simple soldiers should not be unduly terrified, and there the Dark King went through the brief necessary ritual.

Akbar when summoned appeared promptly, a blurred and shifting figure in the center of a muffled glow that soon outshone the moonlight and then quickly died away. An almost-convincing human shape was left: the simple maiden's form which Murat had seen during the previous manifestation.

On being informed of Kristin's departure, the demon professed surprise, and started trying to console Murat for her loss.

"Ugly monster!" the Crown Prince roared back hoarsely. "I do not want your sympathy! What I want is to know where you were at the crucial time!"

Akbar, cringing again, replied in a small maiden's voice, explaining his absence by saying that he had wanted to keep out of the way of Mark, whose approach to the encampment he had detected, and who was known to have a knack for dealing ruthlessly with demons.

"I thought this was in accordance with your orders, sir."

"Could you not at least have warned us that we were all being put to sleep?"

The demon cursed and groaned, hoarse tones and coarse words dimming the illusion of maidenhood, admitting that Karel must have been too subtle for it.

"I failed to understand what was happening, sir. I thought the two men were only scouting."

Soon Murat ordered Vilkata to dismiss the useless creature. There was no sleep for anyone in camp during the remainder of the night. By dawn Murat's rage at his enemies, his sleeping sentries, his incompetent wizard and cowardly demon, and at Fate, for failing to prevent Kristin's departure, was threatening to become irrationally, murderously violent.

At last the sight of his son, who was watching him with frightened eyes, sobered the Crown Prince somewhat. Carlo was the only one in his company at whom he had not grown angry.

The royal anger persisted, though over the next few hours it tried to fix itself upon serious targets and grew more calculating. The Crown Prince was now in the process of consciously deciding that whoever was not firmly with him was most definitely against him. By degrees he was coming around to the conviction that whoever did not support him without reservation really did not deserve to live.

He told a small worried gathering of confidants, including his son Carlo and Captain Marsaci, that almost anything bad that happened to such people could be regarded as a just punishment for their wrong attitudes and willfully bad behavior.

Again and again during the course of the morning, while Marsaci, Vilkata, and others waited for meaningful orders, the Crown Prince called the unfortunate guard, now completely wide awake, back into his presence and demanded to be told all the details of Kristin's departure.

The formerly somnolent sentry, his nerves dissolving under the barrage of repeated questions, informed his master over and over that he had been unable to see any details of what had happened up on the hill. But he had heard several screams from up that way, a few minutes after the Princess had walked out. Yes sir, those yells could have been made by the Princess; it had sounded like a woman's voice.

By now it was thoroughly confirmed that all of the other sentries—indeed everyone else in camp—had been sound asleep at the time. Murat suspected that some of them might have been inclined to deny it, except that any who admitted to being awake when the Princess was spirited away feared being held culpable for having failed to prevent such a calamity.

Around noon Vilkata, on being asked by the Crown Prince for his advice, urged strict enforcement of the military code concerning simple soldiers who slept on sentry duty.

"It will be easy for my lord to replenish his ranks, should they be depleted in the course of justice."

Murat, looking at the other sourly, declined to follow his

advice. "Perhaps recruiting more soldiers, even if that were my object, would not be that easy. Think about it. The enemy, fearing to come near my Sword, will certainly retreat in haste from any offensive move we make. They'll run away swiftly, and leave me to waste my energy and scatter my forces into uselessness if I am so inclined. No. No, thank you. When I order a march at last, I'll move to better purpose than that."

Adding to Murat's difficulties of the day was the fact that now his pair of flying scouts, who were too unintelligent for the Mindsword to have any effect on them, had somehow been lost. It was not surprising, when he thought about it, that the beasts should have been lured away or killed by other flyers, or by Tasavaltan handlers, beastmasters more skilled than the lone expert in the small force of his defectors.

But the loss of the beasts was a substantial blow. Murat saw that without good scouts he should have no chance of catching up with Kristin, or Mark, or any other well-informed and well-mounted individual. He hesitated to send out any more human scouts; it would be a waste of time, now that his camp must be surrounded—at a prudent distance—by numerically overwhelming Tasavaltan forces.

Shortly after midday, Vilkata timidly informed his master that he suspected Karel had found some way to make visible the field of influence of the drawn Mindsword, at least to some of the enemy, including of course Mark himself.

The Crown Prince cursed fluently. It was truly maddening to have the power of the Mindsword in hand, and be unable to strike with it effectively. But the most tormenting aspect of the situation was Kristin's behavior. In truth, he had been hesitating in camp for more than half a day because he was endeavoring to make up his mind about Kristin.

Try as Murat might to disregard it, an unquenchable suspicion had begun to gnaw at him. His doubts had begun the moment he heard that she was gone, that she had evidently walked up the hill to meet her abductor willingly.

Her chief abductor, of course, must have been her former husband. The Prince of Tasavalta, armed with Sightblinder, had dared to approach the camp of the Crown Prince closely. Perhaps the Sword of Stealth had shown him to the Princess in the guise of Murat, presenting an image that she might not have been able to distinguish from Murat himself . . . that was a comfort to the Crown Prince, to think that his beloved had remained loyal, but had been treacherously deceived.

Carlo, when consulted, argued in favor of this interpretation. But as much as the Crown Prince wanted to believe it, he suffered persistent doubts.

Vilkata, in his sincere desire to serve his master, was permanently suspicious of all other servants and advisers, including Carlo. Perhaps these others meant well, but what did this youth and these ignorant soldiers know about intrigue, what understanding did they have of the great game played with Swords? Only he, Vilkata, the wizard and former king, had the experience and foresight to offer proper guidance.

Therefore, the Dark King, in a mode of thought as natural to him as breathing, mentally prepared ways in which he might discredit other advisers. In his heart he was firmly convinced that the dear and glorious master really would be better off if he came to rely on the Dark King above all others. . . .

And Murat, as the hours of the afternoon dragged on with no orders given, no decisions made, could not get the suspicion out of his mind. Could she, could she, after all, have been lying to him all along? Only faking her conversion by the Sword?

Kristin's uncle, after all, was a mighty wizard; those versed in such matters counted Karel one of the world's best, though he did not seek fame and seemed to care little for his reputation. Might Karel have been able to provide his Princess with some special help, some protection that would grant her immunity even to the Mindsword's powers?

But no, no such magic existed anywhere. The Crown Prince was ready to stake his life on that.

Except, of course, in the Sword Shieldbreaker.

Kristin, while she was with him, had not been carrying any Sword. But for all he, Murat, knew, Mark or Karel might possess the Sword of Force. And if they could somehow have transferred the power of that mighty weapon to her—

No. Kristin would have told him if Shieldbreaker was somewhere in Tasavaltan possession. No, Murat would not, never could, never would, believe that his beloved had been lying to him about her love.

Vilkata, when Murat again questioned him closely, assured his beloved master that yes, years ago, Prince Mark had seemingly defied the Mindsword's power for a time. Oh, for a matter of minutes only, an hour at the most. Vilkata's only explanation was that, somehow, on that distant day, Sightblinder's power of allowing its holder to see things and people as they really were had worked as an effective antidote to the force of Skulltwister.

Murat growled. "And what the Sword of Stealth has accomplished before, it might be able to do again."

"No one can deny it absolutely, my lord. But I think it could not have enabled Mark to enter your camp last night, and go away again."

Murat thought the situation over, and suffered helplessly, and thought some more. His men continued waiting anxiously for orders, but in his uncertainty he let them wait. His intellect assured him that Kristin's conversion to loving him must have been genuine—hope whispered to him that such a transformation might have, must have, would have taken place, even without the Mindsword's power to assist.

But he found his intellect essentially helpless against the seed of doubt, once planted.

A cunning and evil turn of his imagination showed him the Princess and her husband, even now, embracing each other, slyly laughing at him together.

After a few moments of that tormenting vision, Murat took himself firmly in hand, telling himself that there was no reason to suspect, let alone believe, anything of the kind. For a time he managed to put his doubts aside.

But whenever the Crown Prince tried to bring back in memory those predawn screams, supposedly Kristin's, heard by himself as well as by the sentry, they persisted in turning into shrieks of joyous, spiteful laughter.

Calling the abused former sentinel yet once more before him, Murat questioned him for what seemed the hundredth time.

"You say she went out from my camp willingly?"

And for the hundredth time the frightened soldier gave essentially the same answer.

"Yes, my gracious lord, willingly as far as I could tell. But then when she had joined the two men up on the hill—"

"Never mind. It is enough. She went out willingly."

SEVENTEEN

As the hours of the afternoon passed and still no marching orders were given by the great Lord Murat, no definite decision of any kind announced, Carlo grew increasingly worried about his father. And the Princeling became to some extent concerned about his own safety as well. He considered his own safety vitally important, and not for purely selfish reasons. The truth was that none of the others in camp knew Carlo's father as he did. And, Sword-magic or not, none of them could be expected to serve the Crown Prince as well as he, who understood his father's every mood and whim, who knew when the Crown Prince really meant an order and when he spoke only out of anger and might soon regret his words.

Certainly no evil magician, and no demon, could be entrusted with the responsibilities of acting as second in command. Carlo meant to do everything he could to minimize the influence upon the great Lord of such unworthy ones.

Vilkata spent most of the afternoon alone in an upper room of the farmhouse, engaged in deep thought. Though he realized intellectually that his bondage of helpless service to the Crown Prince had its roots in magic, still he was conscious of no slightest wish to escape that bondage.

Now established in a more or less honorable and trusted position, he was dutifully doing his utmost as a schemer and intriguer to make plans in Murat's favor, to ensure that no one else did anything to harm the lord. And one person in particular soon claimed the burden of his thought.

Before the Dark King had been many hours a faithful servant of Murat, it had crossed his mind that Kristin's eventual removal from the scene might be required. When, before dawn this morning, he had discovered her flight, his first thought was that the departure of the Princess was likely to prove a blessing in disguise. Might Kristin, as Murat's consort, have been ultimately a harmful influence upon the lord, bad for his career?

The Dark King pondered long upon this question, but the more he pondered the less certain he felt of the answer. Many rulers benefited from the presence of a faithful, loving consort.

Perhaps things would have been different in his, Vilkata's life, his own period of real kingship much prolonged, if he had possessed such a dependable helpmate in the days of his own glory. . . .

. . . but all that was ancient history now. Shaking his head, he who had been the Dark King brought his thoughts eagerly back to the present. His present career, in the service of the One True Lord, Murat, was far more glorious and important than anything he might have achieved in promoting any other cause, including his own.

If Princess Kristin was, or would have been, of doubtful value to the Lord Murat, then what of his son?

Carlo, now . . . the presence of a grown and potentially rebellious son . . . it was hard to discover any positive value at all in that. Of course Carlo, while gripped in the Sword's power, would find it impossible to be openly rebellious against his father. But in the future, someday when the Sword had been sheathed again, or the son had been allowed to travel for some time outside its influence . . .

The Dark King's head ached when he thought of the possible risks to Murat's power in such a situation. Coldly he pondered. Sooner or later, he decided, Carlo would probably have to go.

Meanwhile, Murat was nursing some new suspicions of his own. He wondered whether Vilkata had been able to resist Karel's sleep-making magic, but had for some reason pretended otherwise. And had the cunning Eyeless One somehow induced Akbar to go along with that pretense? The possibilities for intrigue seemed endless.

The Crown Prince tried his best to put these new worries out of his mind, telling himself firmly that they were nonsensical for any holder of the Mindsword. But despite his best efforts he could not entirely disregard them.

While Murat and Vilkata brooded separately, one of the converted troopers was asking Carlo, in genuine puzzlement, why his royal father had not taken the woman to his bed when he'd had the chance. Why should any woman believe that a man really wanted her when he'd refused to do that?

Carlo could find no good answer.

Indeed, Murat himself had now begun to think along the same lines. What a chivalrous fool he'd been! But never mind, he'd get Kristin back. And if—*if*—her loyalty had been fraudulent the first time round, well, it wouldn't be on the second.

He'd find a way of making sure.

There was no reason why the holder of the Mindsword should be forced to endure treachery.

Vilkata, still closeted in the small bedroom he had been granted as his own, weighing as best he could the benefits and problems attendant upon each possible course of action, was coming around to the conclusion that Kristin would be, at least for the time being, a desirable mate and ally for his lord. Every great lord should have a queen, or empress, and no one more fitting than the Princess of Tasavalta was likely to become available to Murat in the immediate future.

The next problem, of course, would be to get her back. The Perfect Lord would no doubt soon declare that as his objective, and Vilkata began racking his brain to find the best way to accomplish the goal.

Later on, of course, Princess Kristin could be replaced if, for reasons of state, a different consort should become more desirable.

Vilkata did not mention this last consideration when, late in the afternoon, he was again called to consult with his lord.

But the former Dark King, speaking from experience, did repeatedly urge deviousness and caution in moving against Mark and the other resistant Tasavaltans, even though it was also necessary to avoid prolonged delay.

"As I see the situation, sir, it will be best if we can somehow lull the enemy into thinking that we are ready to talk peace. Then, advance upon them quickly, strike like lightning with the Mindsword!"

Murat shook his head gloomily. "Mark will not be lulled so easily. Nor will his chief advisers."

"True." Vilkata thought a moment longer. "An alternate plan would be to occupy the enemy capital, then negotiate. If we move quickly enough into a heavily populated region, particularly Sarykam, all of the local people will not be able to avoid your Sword. You will acquire a great number of hostages."

Murat rubbed at his once-neat beard, now grown untended. There were specks and small streaks of gray among the black.

"When I entered the capital a few days ago, it appeared to be completely deserted."

"Indeed, sire. But Your Highness did not use the Sword when you were there." The wizard's tone was gently chiding.

"True, I didn't want to use . . . yes, true. There might have been people, many people, hiding within its range. At that time I didn't want . . ."

Murat's words trailed off, as if he had now forgotten what he had then been trying to avoid.

"But this time you will enter with Sword drawn, as swiftly as you can ride."

The Crown Prince sighed heavily. He squinted in the direction of the other man, as if at something difficult to see. "It might work, but—hostages?"

"Hostage-taking can be a very effective measure, when properly carried out. I myself have on a number of occasions—"

Murat blinked. He appeared to rouse himself from a dream. In a changed voice he demanded, once more: "Hostages?"

Vilkata blinked also. Sensing unwillingness in his master —worse than unwillingness, a rapidly growing anger—he tried to change his approach.

"They are forcing you to such measures, Master," the Dark King murmured defensively. "What the enemy forces you to do is not your fault."

Murat, grieving for his lost Princess, suddenly found himself plunged into horror at the very sight of this man whom she had so violently hated and feared. This man who *had once even tortured her.* Who—

The Crown Prince had a sudden thought: Perhaps it was the very presence of Vilkata and his demon that had forced Kristin to desert his camp.

He roared at the wretched demon-handler: "I will answer for my own faults! I find your advice distasteful. More, I find the sight of you disgusting!"

"Sire, I only—"

Lunging forward impulsively, striking hard with the black hilt, Murat knocked down the object of his wrath. Then the Crown Prince stood over Vilkata, shouting at him, while the fallen magician, his forehead bleeding, struggled to regain his senses.

"In fact, foul man, I find you and your schemes inhumanly repulsive, and I wish to see you no more. Out of my sight!"

Vilkata crawled, then stumbled to his feet. More shocking than the blow itself was the realization that he had so angered his beloved lord. In the face of such wrath the Dark King did not dare to argue, or to delay his departure; he simply ran, as fast as aging legs could carry him, while turncoat troopers and former bandits stared. Vilkata's first thought in this emergency, reeling and weeping at rejection as he was, was that he must not allow the master to kill him—because if that should happen, how could he serve his faultless master anymore?

Reeling past the barn and the adjacent corral, with blood from a forehead wound still trickling into his empty sockets, the Dark King made no effort to claim a mount, but stumbled out on foot into the lately unworked fields surrounding the farm buildings.

Even now, from the very beginning of this unhappy exile, even before he began to consider where he himself would find his food and shelter, Vilkata was planning ceaselessly for some way to continue to help Murat—and of course to win himself back into Murat's favor, so that he could serve to much greater effect.

About a kilometer from the farm, in the steep side of a

narrow creek's tall earthen bank, the wizard found a kind of cave, recently abandoned by some small animal, and in imminent danger of complete collapse. Here was immediate shelter. Here, he thought, his arts and a minimum of practical craft should enable him to keep himself alive and free for the time being. Soon, in no great number of days and hours, his master was going to have grave need of him again. All the strength that the Dark King could muster was going to be needed, he was sure.

Forcing his body back into the tiny cave as far as possible, Vilkata muttered spells meant to conceal himself from discovery, and to strengthen the crumbling earthen roof through which the pale roots of wild grass depended. That he might have warning of any approaching danger— or opportunity—the Dark King spent his next half hour in the summoning and deployment of a score or so of minor powers, half-real and insubstantial beings that were at the command of any practicing magician.

In Vilkata's endless concern to be of service to his incomparable lord, it had not yet crossed his mind that in a few days, now that he had left the Mindsword's field of influence, he would begin to recover from its effects.

That point had already occurred to Murat, and within an hour after the departure of the Eyeless One; but such was the ruler's contempt and hatred for the magician that when the realization came, he did not consider trying to get the foul one back.

Another and more sobering realization, coming to the Crown Prince only after Vilkata had departed, was that he, Murat, did not possess anything like the magical knowledge he assumed would be necessary to summon his demon of supposedly constrained loyalty.

At that point Murat did briefly consider trying to get his magician back. Probably, he thought, the man would show up in a few hours on the perimeter of camp, begging to be reinstated. Should he be allowed to return?

After a little thought the Crown Prince shuddered, and permanently rejected the idea.

Shortly after sunset, the Crown Prince went strolling a little apart from his men, outside the boundaries of the farmyard, his Sword in hand as usual. He had not gone far before, to his considerable surprise, he beheld the demon quietly, almost unobtrusively manifesting itself in front of him.

Murat halted in his tracks, warily twirling Skulltwister. Addressing the slight image of the maiden who now stood before him, he said softly: "I had thought that I would have to summon you."

"It is my experience, Great Lord," the image replied modestly in its young girl's voice, "that anyone who really wants to meet a demon on friendly terms is likely to get his wish. Or hers. In one way or another. Whether magic is employed or not."

The maiden did subtle things with her eyelids and lashes, and briefly showed her pearly teeth. Her dress this evening was somewhat disarranged, even slightly torn, so that it threatened to fall away completely from one fair, rounded shoulder.

The Crown Prince, gazing at Akbar in this guise of a simple young girl, knowing well what it was that he really gazed upon, still found himself, to his own disgust, being aroused by the sight.

With an inward shudder, and a violent effort, Murat put such thoughts and feelings from him.

He said: "Wretched One, I have dismissed your partner, Vilkata. What have you to say to that?"

The girl made a point of rearranging the dress that still kept slipping—oh, quite unconsciously—from one shoulder. She murmured: "Only that I am not surprised, Great

Lord. In my own humble view, that man was far from being satisfactory in his capacity as your adviser. Certainly he was not worthy of preferment by a ruler as glorious as yourself."

"Why do you say that? What did you see wrong with him?"

The maiden's eyes twinkled. "I express my opinion, Lord, only because I have been invited to do so. As to the Dark King's deficiencies, evidently you have discovered them for yourself—as I was confident you would, in your great wisdom."

"Then I take it you are not of the opinion that I should try to get him to return?"

"Your Lordship will be the best judge of that. I await your commands." And the demon-image curtsied deeply.

"You know where the Eyeless One is now?"

"I believe, Great Lord, that he has concealed himself. And he is a magician of some accomplishment. Still it is possible that I might find him if I searched."

"Does he still enjoy the vision that you provided for him?"

"He does, and will, until I seek him out and darken it again. Shall that be my task?"

Murat found himself heartily tired of the subject of Vilkata. He hesitated, and sighed.

"What that man does now, or what he sees, is not a matter of the greatest importance. But should you, while carrying out your other duties, happen to discover his whereabouts—let me know."

The maiden waited, poised, hands gracefully clasped in front of her. "It shall be as you say, Master."

Silently Murat took note of the fact that Akbar was now beginning to assume a rather different personality than the one he had presented in Vilkata's presence—calmer and less terrified. Less—*pressured*, perhaps.

That wasn't all. It seemed to the Crown Prince that there

was now something vaguely—*larger*—about the demon.
Not an increase in physical size, no, the image of the
maiden looked much the same, slender and delicate.
But . . .

Murat found it almost impossible to define the difference, even to himself. But it was there.

"May I inquire, Master, what strategy you now intend to
adopt?"

"I have not yet decided. Before the vile Vilkata left, he
suggested a lightning attack, directed at the city. . . ."
Murat, with an ambiguous gesture, let his words trail off.
Despite his own reaction to the idea of taking hostages,
when the Dark King had suggested it, he now found
himself admitting inwardly that there was some merit in
the plan. Either Kristin had left him willingly, or the
Tasavaltans had kidnapped her. In either case, someone in
this land deserved to be punished.

Akbar persisted gently. "I take it the plan is not merely
for a lightning attack with thirty cavalry, against the city
walls?"

"Of course not. An attack with the Sword, in my own
hand."

"Despite its source, Your Majesty, the suggestion may
have some merit." The demon seemed to be echoing the
man's thoughts. "May I ask how such an assault is to be
accomplished, according to that lately banished one?"

"I hadn't really thought about it. I suppose, by riding
swiftly. . . ." Then Murat, noting the amused expression
on the demon's girlish face, allowed his words to die again.
After a pause he asked: "You have in mind some means
better than an advance by riding-beast? I suppose Vilkata
must have meant something other than that."

The demonic maiden moved a step closer to the man,
spreading her open hands in a kind of invitation. Her dress
had slipped again, her shoulder was bare, her full bosom
rather more than suggested.

The girl said: "I myself will be honored to carry you, Master, you and your Sword together, swiftly as the wind. No one in the city will have a chance to flee your righteous wrath before we are upon them."

"Swiftly as the wind, you say?"

"I understate my capabilities, Master. We might travel more swiftly than that, by far."

Murat, despite his innate dislike of this creature, found himself tempted by its suggestions. "And what of Mark's power to banish you, that you feared so greatly?"

"I can smell that one at a good distance, and I'll stay safely away from him. While at the same time I'll drop you and your Sword close enough to bother him a great deal—till the Prince of Tasavalta becomes your worshipful servant. Trust me, Master!"

Carlo, looking for his father, caught up with him shortly after the demon had been dismissed.

"Father, who—what was that, that fled just now when I came up?" The youth sounded horrified.

Murat was annoyed at his son's reaction. "One with whom I had business."

"Father—"

"You will tell me not to deal with demons. I tell you that they are no worse than people."

Carlo had nothing to say to that.

Slowly making his way with Carlo back to the farmyard, the Crown Prince also came back to his bleak thoughts of Kristin. Tenderness had been replaced by wounded anger. He'd have this enigmatic Tasavaltan woman yet, whether or not she was really laughing at him now!

In his heart Murat knew that the most decent and trustworthy adviser remaining to him was his son—but he had to admit that Carlo was perhaps not the most competent.

When the two men were back in the farmhouse again,

and the demon, as far as they could tell, was well out of sight and hearing, Carlo engaged his father in an urgent discussion.

"I am worried that you dismissed the Eyeless One."

"Really? I thought you had no liking for him."

"I hadn't. But at least he stood between you and—that other."

To himself, Murat thought that his son really had no idea what the Dark King had been, or what he very well could be capable of being once again.

The Crown Prince said: "You need not worry about that man. We shall manage quite well without him."

"What I worry about is you, Father."

"The Sword keeps me safe."

Carlo did not seem reassured, and Murat was irritated. But the Crown Prince, still full of tender feelings for his son, considered sending Carlo home to safety before launching his swift attack on Sarykam.

He made a tentative suggestion along this line, but it was swiftly rejected.

"No, Father, my place is here with you."

Murat rejoiced inwardly to hear those words, and immediately decided to entrust his son with some key role in the coming attack. On making this decision the Crown Prince realized that he had now already, perhaps unconsciously, decided to follow the plan of attack suggested first by Vilkata and then by the demon.

Murat in starting to elaborate these plans at first considered marching his men away from the farmhouse, to get a little closer to the city before he struck at it like lightning. But before long he came around to the view that it might be wiser to stay encamped as long as possible where he was, amid plentiful supplies and with good shelter for people and animals.

Ominously, he had received no communication yet from the Prince of Tasavalta.

It would seem that Mark had no intention of arranging a parley, or Murat would have heard from him long before now; but perhaps it would be wise to take the initiative in that regard himself? He could send Carlo to talk to the Tasavaltans under a flag of truce. He'd not go himself to any meeting without the Mindsword, and as long as he had that the other side would not care to come close enough to talk.

That night Murat got but little sleep. At first light, having made up his mind to his proper course of action, he ordered his men, just for practice, to break camp at once.

In the midst of the flurry of activity produced by this command, the Crown Prince, Sword still in his hand, stalked about among his troops, looking around him sharply, wondering if any of his men were laughing at him when he wasn't looking. They could very well be laughing at the way he'd been cheated out of his woman. To his face the men all seemed overtly sympathetic, but—

A new suspicion had been born. Murat couldn't help but wonder.

. . . and then, after he'd had her, enjoyed her fully, or perhaps even before he'd done that, would come the punishment of Mark. That punishment would consist of, or reach its climax with, the obliteration, or at least the removal from the Great Game, of the stubbornly undeposable Prince of Tasavalta.

Having countermanded his order to break camp, Murat looked once more with affection upon Carlo.

"You, my son, are the only person with whom I really enjoy talking anymore."

"I wish I could be of more service to you, Father." It seemed a heartfelt hope.

"You are. And you will be." Serenely, and without transition, the Crown Prince went on to ask: "Tell me, am I the one who is destined by the gods to gather all of the Blades of Power into my hands?" The question seemed to have come into his mind from nowhere.

"The gods are dead," his son commented, after a pause, in worried puzzlement.

EIGHTEEN

VILKATA, dozing uneasily in his cramped earth, was awakened by a little occult thing, a messenger invisible to ordinary eyes, come gibbering in terror to whisper an urgent report into the magician's ear. This creature was one of the tiny powers he had set to guard him as he slept, and the burden of its whispered, fearful message now was that a strange and utterly monstrous demon, far more terrible than Akbar, was lurking near the wizard's hideaway.

Whatever personal anxiety the Dark King might have experienced on receiving this intelligence was swallowed up in an awful concern for the dear Lord Carlo. Immediately Vilkata, his body stiff and bent, muscles aching from yesterday's unwonted exercise, came creeping out of his small mud-walled cave to investigate. The bruised scrape on his forehead still throbbed faintly. He emerged into a dull sunless morning of thick mist and beaded moisture everywhere.

Hastily applying several tests, the wizard, somewhat to his surprise, could detect no traces of a demonic presence in the immediate vicinity. He considered calling his other sentinel powers to him for interrogation, but soon discovered they all had fled beyond his reach—in itself an ominous sign, to say the least.

Climbing the creek bank with some difficulty, then walking warily in the direction indicated by his small frightened sentinel, Vilkata had not far to go before his demonic vision showed him a rider in the mist. The man was moving slowly, wrapped in a dark cloak to suit the weather, and leading a spare mount equipped with its own saddle.

"A demon? Hardly that!" Vilkata breathed, studying the rider's figure from the rear with a demonic intensity of perception. In another moment he had let out a little cry, surprisingly childish, and was hurrying forward to overtake the mounted man.

Actually running again despite his aching limbs, the wizard as he approached the other called softly: "My lord! My lord, am I forgiven? Do you come seeking me?"

The rider halted his mount and swung round in his saddle, presenting to the approaching magician's keen demonic vision the noble, thoughtful visage of Murat. But for a moment the Crown Prince did not reply to his banished servant.

"My Lord Murat! Forgive my offenses, and allow me to be of service to you!" Then Vilkata paused, staring in belated realization. "You have sheathed the Mindsword again!"

There was the black hilt at Murat's side, the bright steel muffled in dark leather.

"I considered that I did not need such protection at every moment," the Crown Prince responded at last, allowing his right hand to rest briefly on that hilt.

The Dark King had now caught up, and stood gasping after his brief run.

"I trust Your Majesty will not have cause to regret the decision. I fear that you have many enemies. Only a moment ago I had warning of a tremendous demon in the vicinity."

"Indeed?" But for some reason Murat did not appear to

be impressed. In a moment he had dismissed worrisome demons with a careless toss of his head.

"As for your desire to be of service, magician, why, I accept it gladly. I suppose our falling out was not entirely your fault."

Vilkata, his heart pounding with joy to hear these words, bowed deeply. "I rejoice to hear you say it, sire, but I must insist that all the blame was mine."

The wizard was now standing close enough to his master's mount for him to be able to cling to the other's stirrup, and he longed to do so. But at the same time he feared another rebuke. Instead of clinging, he clenched his hands together.

"Master, what plan have you decided on? Have you marched your handful of men forth from the farm yet?"

"Not yet."

The Eyeless One breathed a sigh of relief. "Then what of the plan that I suggested?"

The Crown Prince, looking thoughtful, once more shifted his position in his saddle. He said: "Explain to me once more the advantages of your suggestion."

Rapidly Vilkata rehearsed the advantages of surprise, of striking rapidly with the Mindsword at the enemy heart.

"Yes, of course. But how did you intend that I should transport myself and my Sword to Sarykam?"

"Riding on the demon, Majesty!" the Dark King explained triumphantly. "Naturally I will accompany you to make sure that nothing goes wrong. Together we can reach the enemy capital from here in only minutes, instead of days or hours!"

"That mode of transportation would never have occurred to me." Murat's expression was solemnly guarded.

Terrified lest he might have offended again, Vilkata hastened to offer reassurance.

"Of course it will be necessary to control Akbar sufficiently to make our passage absolutely safe—I can see to that—and with your Sword it should present absolutely no problem anyway. . . . Has Your Highness seen anything of the demon since I—since I left camp?"

"No. No demons at all."

"That's good, sire, very good. As I mentioned a moment ago, very recently I have received a warning—one cannot be too careful with demons. I should be present at your next meeting with Akbar—shall I return with you now to camp?"

Murat evidently found that this question required some thought, reinforcing Vilkata's growing impression that the master today was in a strange, new, preoccupied mode.

"No," the Crown Prince said at last. "I can manage whatever demons may appear for myself, with the Sword. But managing the creatures is one thing, and . . . and the truth is that I have a special mission for you elsewhere."

"Sire, with all due respect, and having your own safety always foremost in mind, I must protest. The management of demons is—"

The Crown Prince, looking haughty, cut him short. "Do you wish to continue in my service or not?"

"Of course, Lord, of course I do! Tell me of my special mission. Where am I to go? I'll go anywhere! And to do what? Anything my lord commands!"

"Calm yourself. The task I require of you is a simple one, though I suppose it will not be easy. I want you, somehow, by your art, to destroy the demon Akbar."

"Ah!"

"You seem surprised. You should not be. When you ruled as the Dark King, you were a powerful magician. Are you still great enough to find this horrible creature's life and snuff it out?"

"To find—" Vilkata goggled.

"To find its life. And put an end to it. Any idea how to go about that job?"

"But—but—in your Sword, Great Lord!"

"My Sword? What do you mean?"

"Is not the foul beast's life still there, where Akbar himself confessed that it was hidden?"

Murat, face turning blank again, cast a long look down at the black hilt by his side.

Then he turned an unreadable gaze back at Vilkata. "I suspect," the great lord said at last, "that the beast has relocated its life elsewhere since it made that confession."

"Ah—or that the demon—lied to us about it?" Silently Vilkata cursed his own gullibility. Even a man could lie, under the Mindsword's power—provided the motivation were to help his lord. And if a man, certainly a demon. Or might there be some other possibility . . .?

"All I know," said the Crown Prince, "is, somewhere, somehow, there has been deception." He paused as if considering weighty matters. "Can you still see well enough? I mean—despite Akbar's absence, you are still managing to function without eyes? You found me, and recognized me, without much trouble."

Vilkata raised a hand to his face-bandage. His fingers felt that the cloth was in place, but it was not apparent to his own sight. "Yes, Master. Once granted me, the demonic vision is quite independent of Akbar's presence."

"Then take this mount," ordered Murat decisively, shaking the reins of the spare that he was leading. "There are food and other necessities in the saddlebags. Also an edged weapon or two attached—though one of your talents will probably prosper better by not relying on such crude implements. Go where you want, do what you will, take as much time as necessary. Only locate the demon's life and slay him."

Almost unconsciously Vilkata accepted the offered reins. "Perhaps I will be able to find where his miserable life is hidden now. Perhaps I know a way. . . ."

"You will find it!"

"Yes, Lord!" Under the piercing gaze of his Master, the Dark King straightened up. "As you command. And when I have slain Akbar, Lord? What then?"

"That's better. That's what I like to hear, confidence." Murat smiled and nodded. "Accomplishing such a task should keep you busy for a while. When the demon's dead, and not before, come look for me again."

"Let it be as you command, Master."

Under that commanding gaze Vilkata mounted quickly, and rode off in the general direction of Sarykam; before the mists swallowed him, he turned for one more brief look at his beloved Lord Murat. Then he was gone.

Waiting quietly in his saddle until the other was out of sight, Ben of Purkinje released a long breath, and slowly sheathed the great Sword Sightblinder.

Around midday, Crown Prince Murat, who had not left his camp for a moment during the misty morning hours, was again closeted in consultation with the demon Akbar. For this purpose Akbar had been allowed inside one of the upper rooms of the farmhouse. So far the demon's indoor manifestations had been restrained, though not entirely without effect upon the people in the other rooms. Once the sounds of distant retching carried into the conference chamber.

Today's discussion between slave and master had not made very much progress before Akbar respectfully inquired of the Crown Prince whether the great lord had had any contact with the villainous Vilkata since dismissing him.

Murat was only slightly interested. "No, I still consider myself well rid of that scoundrel. By the way, does he still enjoy the eyesight that you provided?"

The demon's imaged maiden had seated herself on the

edge of a narrow bed. Her peasant skirt was creeping up toward her knees, and today her form was a little fuller and more provocative than yesterday. The changes had been subtle, but Murat had noticed them, though he had not yet decided whether to remark on them or not.

In answer to the question about the banished magician's eyesight, Akbar temporized. It was, he claimed, not easy to reclaim such a gift.

"Unless the miscreant himself should fall into my power, and if that happens I will do with him whatever Your Majesty might like me to do."

Murat frowned. The whole subject was still distasteful. "Never mind him for the moment."

The discussion moved on to other matters. Murat, before finally committing himself to the plan suggested by Vilkata and now enthusiastically seconded by Akbar, was trying to anticipate any problems likely to arise in its execution.

One thing in particular bothered him.

"But when it comes down to you, or any other demon, actually carrying me, and perhaps my son—"

"I pray you, Master, do not consider any other member of my race for the job."

"—what I want to know is, are you going to assume some solid form, capable of flight? Take the shape of a great bird, I suppose? Or what?"

"A bird, yes, if that should be the master's preference." The maiden paused, smiling. "Would you like to see?"

"No, never mind." The Crown Prince brooded for a few moments. "The important thing is, you are certain of being able to transport me—or us—in safety?"

"Absolutely certain! If you do not like the idea of riding on a bird, you—we—could be invisible in flight. I can carry several people, or a number of objects, about with me at any time, in secrecy. Trust me, Lord!"

"I think we understand each other on the matter of trust—exactly where is Princess Kristin now?"

"I cannot be entirely sure, Master, but Prince Mark has—I think almost certainly—taken her back to the palace in Sarykam."

Murat took thought for a while, shifting his Sword from one hand to the other as he did so. By now this action had become habitual, automatic, almost unconscious.

"And," he asked at last, "if I decide to bring Prince Carlo with me to Sarykam?"

"I can carry several persons, Great Lord. As I have said. In perfect safety."

"I know that human wizards, even those powerful enough to control demons, are not wont to ride upon demons. Griffins are the magic steeds of choice, for those who can obtain and master them."

"I believe the reason griffins are preferred is, as Your Majesty so wisely points out, that great wizards are inclined to be distrustful of my kind. Because, my lord, those inferior people lack the means that you possess, of enforcing trustworthiness."

The Crown Prince nodded; that sounded only reasonable to him. He muttered, so quietly that even Akbar had to attend carefully to hear him: "I trust no human being any longer, even if their intentions are good toward me."

"I am overwhelmingly honored, Master, to think that *I* am now the one to be so honored, so—"

"Cease your babbling! If I trust you at all, fiend, it's only because you're much simpler than any human being. Pure malignance—but channeled by the Sword now, so all the ill intentions must flow away from me. What do I trust? This Sword, as long as I can hold it in my own hand. And that's about all."

The maiden bowed silently, even while remaining seated on the bed, making her figure an archetype of humility.

Murat told the pretty image: "I have decided that I will

probably bring my son with me when I attack. And I will certainly go with the Sword sheathed, when the time comes, because otherwise Karel will be able to track me by the radiant magic of this Sword, and will know at once where I am going, and when, and probably by what means of transportation. Do you concur with my decisions?"

"Regrettably, Master, as regards the need to muffle the power of your Sword, I fear I must."

"But then, when I sheathe the Sword, Karel may very likely know that too."

"It does not seem possible to conceal very much from that one, sire, when his full attention is upon us, as it is now, and we are the focus of all his skills."

Murat considered whether to try to make the sudden quenching of the Mindsword's magic, from the view of watching Tasavaltan wizards, less suspicious by deploying his handful of cavalry in a deceptive sortie at the same time. Give the enemy something else to watch and wonder about.

He wondered whether the best deployment, in such a scheme, would be in a number of small groups, sallying out quickly in several directions from a center.

"The enemy," Murat explained to his son and Captain Marsaci an hour later, when starting to reveal the plan of his attack to them, "will think I am still with you, marching with my Sword sheathed, hoping to keep the identity of my particular group a secret."

"And where will you really be, sire?" asked the captain.

"I'll explain about that a little later. At the last minute."

"It's true," agreed Marsaci, "that if our little band is split up into small groups, the enemy can be expected to waste time trying to avoid the Sword. They won't know which groups are safe to attack. They may well retreat in all directions."

"What would your orders be, Captain, were you commanding the other side?"

"Against the tactic we just discussed, sir?" It seemed that the captain had already given the problem some consideration. "I'd most likely retreat from all these small forces, and let them do what ravaging of the countryside they might. I'd have massed archers and slingers ready, at a distance. That's what I'd say ought to worry us, sir. Bows and slings don't need accuracy as individuals if they come in thousands. I imagine General Rostov must have some such plan in place."

"Very likely, Captain, you are right."

Murat waited until he was alone with his son, before he confirmed his decision about the attack.

"You are actually planning to ride the demon, Father?" Carlo had trouble believing it.

"I see no reason why I shouldn't. The Sword will keep the foul one loyal to me. Only, when I am in Sarykam, surrounded by enemies, I'll need one person with me whom I can trust, even without the Sword. Now there is only you."

Carlo was stunned, and turned pale at the mere thought of being carried on Akbar's back, but he could not refuse. Only for his worshiped father would he agree to be transported by a demon. Despite his loyalty, he feared that the experience when it actually came might be too much for him.

Murat and the demon had agreed between them that Kristin's exact location should be easier to establish than Mark's. She had left several tokens of herself, including a hunting knife and even strands of hair, in the farmhouse. With such aids to magic Akbar felt confident of being able to locate her quite handily.

At the end of his conference with Akbar, Murat dispatched the demon on a reconnaissance mission to make the attempt, if it should be possible without alarming the people in the city.

The demon, in the course of carrying out this mission, happened to observe Vilkata, riding well mounted and equipped, and by now halfway to the city.

His interest awakened, Akbar drifted closer, curious as to how his former partner had managed to outfit himself so quickly and so well, and what his current goal might be. Obviously banishment by the master had not brought about collapse.

The demon thoughtfully observed the wizard's steady progress. At first he was content to watch the man from afar, but soon decided to draw nearer, feeling almost careless as to whether his presence should be detected or not.

On the first part of his journey toward the capital, Vilkata had been busy formulating new plans to help Murat. But gradually those efforts had ceased. A day had now passed since he had been dispatched on his secret mission by Murat, and two days since he had last been exposed to the power of the Mindsword. For the past several hours the old wizard had been experiencing strange and frightening moments, mental flashes and foretastes of thinly disguised malignant hatred and contempt for his great lord.

These fits, moments when the Dark King hovered on the brink of forbidden guilty anger, so far had departed as quickly as they came, leaving him feeling shaken, trembling in horror. Each time he forced the incident out of his mind, until the next occasion came. So wrapped up in his calculations was the Dark King that the true explanation of these terrifying episodes had not yet dawned on him.

But whatever his feelings now toward Murat, Vilkata's

suppressed hatred of the demon Akbar was coming to the fore. All of the magician's art and all his instincts insisted that his best chance of finding this hated demon's life lay in proceeding to Sarykam. Sooner or later, whether the foul creature still labored faithfully in Murat's service, or now sought to disrupt his plans, it was sure to leave its traces there.

Frequently during the past few hours the Dark King's concentration had wandered from his assigned mission. The Dark King became aware of Akbar's surveillance almost as soon as it began, though at first he pretended to have noticed nothing. He was not particularly surprised by Akbar's interest; no doubt the demon, whether faithful or treacherous toward their common master, was as suspicious of him, Vilkata, as he was of it. Nor did he allow himself any false hopes that this encounter might provide a chance for him to destroy it; the thing's life still might be hidden almost anywhere.

At last Akbar, giving free rein to his curiosity, and believing that by this time he had probably been observed anyway, openly approached his former partner.

Vilkata raised his eyes, and reined in his mount, as if only at this moment had he become aware of the other's presence.

"Well met, partner," he said at last.

"Well met, as you say." The demon paused. "It seems, great magician, that you are prospering in exile."

"Fate has not been unkind, so far."

"So I see. . . . Tell me, former partner, has our glorious master's glory begun to dim for you as yet? You have now been for some days out of the reach of his Sword."

Vilkata pretended more shock than he felt. "For me the glory of the great Lord Murat will never dim. Is it not the same with you?" And even as he spoke Vilkata felt one of the twinges, a moment of rebellion, coming on. Whatever he felt, he was going to conceal it from this beast that faced him now.

"Of course. Great is our lord." To the magician the words sounded rather perfunctory. And the demon hovered, in the form of a small black cloud, as if it were uncertain of what action to take next.

"Yes, great. I . . ."

Vilkata suddenly fell silent. He stretched up in the saddle, pale hands raised to cover the eyes that he had not possessed for many years. His mount, sensing an abrupt change in its rider, came to an uncertain halt.

"Is something wrong?" Akbar's voice was innocence itself.

"The Mindsword . . . " whispered the man. His tone, and attitude, suggested terrible pain.

This time the demon answered nothing, but only waited silently.

When at last the man brought his hands down from his face, he seemed to have weathered a crisis. His next words were spoken almost calmly.

"You are with me now, Akbar, because I summoned you."

"Indeed?"

"Indeed. It was a subtle summoning, and I am not surprised that you may think you sought me out of your own volition. But here you are, in nice accordance with my latest plan."

At some point since its arrival the black cloud had settled to the earth, where it now assumed the form of an inoffensive dwarf. As the dwarf seemed to bow, something of the old fawning attitude came back into Akbar's manner.

"What, mighty Dark King, does that plan involve?"

"You told us once, the master and I, that your life is hidden in the Mindsword."

"Indeed."

"Well, I am absolutely certain that it is there no longer."

There was a silence. The dwarf was staring, with penetrating, very human-looking eyes, up at the mounted man.

"If it ever was there," continued the Dark King. In a moment he added: "Are we going to reform our partnership?"

At last the demon answered. "Are you on your way to Sarykam?"

"Perhaps."

"The glorious master will soon be there."

Moments after delivering that somewhat enigmatic statement, the demon had departed. And Vilkata, the last shreds of his loyalty to Murat gone, a slowly building rage giving him new strength and new confidence in his reborn abilities, took the first steps toward summoning some other demons.

He was the Dark King, and enslaved no longer. And now he meant to sate himself with power and revenge.

NINETEEN

ON the morning after recapturing Kristin, the Prince of Tasavalta had withdrawn temporarily to the capital, bringing with him, under heavy escort, his estranged, mesmerized, and captive wife. The Princess, making the journey in a covered wagon, was kept under observation day and night by teams of magicians, nurses, and armed defenders. Mark established this strict guard not only to forestall any further attempt by Murat to communicate with the Princess, but because he feared what she herself might do under the lingering pressure of the Sword of Glory.

The day-to-day management of military affairs had been left in General Rostov's hands. Mark's concern continued to be more for Kristin than for the country whose rule he shared with her, though he well understood how inseparable the two were. He wanted to keep his wife with him, and at the same time was eager to remove her to a place where she could get better care, remote from the dangers of the battlefield. Violent conflict now seemed unavoidable.

Also, as Mark confided to his friends and aides, the farther Kris was kept from Murat, the more she would be spared continual reminders of her lover's presence nearby. And the less likely that—Ardneh forbid—she would ever be exposed to the Mindsword again.

Another need, in itself enough almost to compel Mark's return to the capital, was his postponed meeting with the governing Council. He had to admit the Council was right in demanding to see him soon.

The royal couple and their party traveled swiftly, but by the time they came in sight of the capital, it seemed to him that Kristin's affliction had already lasted an eternity. The Prince found it necessary to keep reminding himself, as the wagon bore his wife in through the great city gates of Sarykam and toward their familiar quarters in the palace, that three full days had not yet passed since Kristin had walked away from her lover, taking herself out of the range of influence of the Sword of Glory.

Only when at least that length of time had elapsed, so Karel had repeatedly warned Mark, would he have any right to hope that his wife would begin to show some basic change in her attitude of utter devotion to Murat.

Another major concern for Mark was Ben. Nothing had been heard from the huge man, or of him, since his disappearance from Rostov's headquarters encampment, at the same time that Sightblinder vanished. He would have had unchallenged access to the tent where the Sword was kept. The only reasonable assumption that could be made was that Ben had stolen Sightblinder and carried it away.

Almost no one who was even slightly acquainted with Ben would have questioned his loyalty in ordinary circumstances, and Mark had often enough trusted him with his life. The inescapable conclusion was that Ben, in the course of the skirmish fought during his last patrol, must have fallen foul of the Mindsword.

"Therefore," said Mark to Karel, as they were entering the city of Sarykam, "the report he gave us on his return from the patrol must have been all lies."

The old wizard shook his head. "Perhaps not entirely lies."

"Meaning?"

"Well, for example, it might very well have been Carlo and not Murat who was really leading the enemy squad—just as Ben reported. Information from the other survivors of the patrol confirms that."

"Then Ben would have become enslaved to Carlo—but do you think Murat would have entrusted his son with the Sword?"

"It's possible. And consider, Prince—if it were Murat to whom our comrade became bound by the Sword's magic, then Ben's first act on returning to our camp would most likely have been to attempt your murder."

Mark, considering, had to admit that that seemed probable.

"But in fact," Karel continued, "Ben attempted nothing of the kind. Which would seem to mean that he does not consider you his master's most important enemy."

"Then what *is* he doing, to serve Carlo?"

"I have been pondering that. Were I fanatically devoted to that young Culmian's welfare, I think I should consider either Vilkata or the demon his worst enemy—with his own father perhaps not far behind."

"Ah. Yes." And Mark rode for a little time in silence. Then he said: "At least Ben's three days should be up—very soon, if not already."

"My Prince, there is no magical significance to that precise period of time. Recovery from the Sword's power may come more quickly for some people. Or it may not come at all. But at least after about three days we may begin to hope."

Once it became apparent that Ben must have fallen victim to the Mindsword, Karel had hastened to make sure that none of the other loyal Tasavaltans in Ben's patrol had been similarly affected. The wizard had tested these men carefully for indications of Skulltwister's influence, with negative results. Those surviving troopers had been questioned closely before the royal couple and their escort started for the capital, but they were able to add nothing substantial to the information they had already provided.

Ominously, all the men involved agreed that Ben had been separated from them for a considerable period during the skirmishing. For all they knew, their leader during that time might very well have encountered someone armed with the Mindsword. What little information they could offer about the commanding officer of the enemy patrol indicated he might very well have been Carlo and not Murat.

Karel and Mark speculated on the possibility of taking advantage of divided loyalties among the foe, if Carlo as well as Murat was making personal recruits with the Sword. But so far no way of exploiting the division had suggested itself.

Ben of Purkinje, his mind in turmoil, was riding methodically toward home.

He had accomplished something, with Sightblinder, setting a powerful and dangerous wizard the task of killing a—possibly—even nastier demon. One of those enemies would surely destroy the other, and whichever perished, the blessed Lord Carlo would be more secure.

Beyond that, Ben wasn't sure that he had achieved anything at all for his great lord.

There had been moments during the past day—moments coming more and more frequently—with the grip of the Sword of Glory beginning to loosen from his mind, when he was not quite sure, not only of his loyalty to Carlo, but of who he was himself. Such uncertainty of his identity was no great novelty for Ben, who'd been a foundling. Even the last part of his name didn't really belong to him; the "Purkinje" had somehow become attached when, as a youth, he began to rise out of the obscure poverty of his beginnings; no one of any importance could be called simply "Ben." The extra name had stuck, and after years of desultory efforts to disown it, he'd given up.

Today, brooding Ben was riding almost careless of any danger he might encounter on the road. His way was guarded by Sightblinder, his huge right hand resting on the hilt of that sheathed weapon. Steadily toward Sarykam he guided his mount, through farmland and over pastures, threading narrow strips of forest. Mentally he was free to concentrate upon his problems.

Today there were stretches, some of them hours in duration, when the obligation of devotion to Carlo still held sway. Magnificent Carlo, the Princeling of Culm, that young lord unequaled in his glory, who'd drawn the Mindsword only when Ben, encountering him alone in the field, had tried—crime unthinkable—to kill him or compel his surrender.

Then magnanimous Carlo, with the mandate of the gods flashing in his hand, had spared Ben's life, and ordered him to serve the great Crown Prince Murat. Ben had tried at first to persuade the Princeling to pursue his own advantage. But very soon it had become obvious that Master Carlo was under some kind of an odious enchantment, which compelled him to serve his unworthy father.

And today there were other stretches of time, each so far no more than a few minutes in duration, when he was assailed by doubts as to whether he should be serving Carlo at all. Terrible, grave doubts . . .

With an inward shudder he put such frightening uncertainties aside. How, Ben had wondered, was he truly to serve a master so afflicted by bad magic as Carlo was? Certainly not by simply following orders. No, in a case like this, one nodded and smiled when the master gave orders, assenting to all that was commanded—and then one went and did what was obviously best for the glorious lord, who in his present state could not be trusted to know that for himself.

It seemed to Ben that the most immediate threat to his glorious master Carlo was neither Mark nor the master's overbearing father, but the demon Akbar. That creature now, according to Karel's best intelligence, seemed to be gaining some kind of ascendancy in Murat's camp.

Once that demon had been eliminated, Ben decided, Carlo would also be well served by the death of both Murat and Mark—Carlo's father now presented, in Ben's judgment, at least as great a threat to Carlo's success as did the Prince of Tasavalta.

Besides . . . Ben's ugly, deceptively stupid-looking face grew sad at the mere thought of having to eliminate Mark. He could see, though, that such an act might well become necessary at some point, since Carlo's welfare was at stake. Ben had known Mark and counseled him and fought beside him for many years, since they were both boys, long before either had seemed likely to amount to anything in the world's affairs, and therefore Ben was sad about the situation. Not, of course, that such considerations would keep Ben from killing the Prince, if glorious Carlo might benefit from such an act. Naturally, no personal attachments could be allowed to count for anything against the master's welfare or the advancement of his marvelous career.

Naturally . . . though once more doubts arose. . . .

The idea of eliminating the demon, of course, engendered no sadness in Ben. Nor would he be sorrowful to see Murat depart. Once the Crown Prince could be put out of the way, Carlo would not only be freed of his ridiculous enslavement to his father, but ought to inherit his father's claim to the Culmian throne—and if either Sightblinder or the Mindsword, or preferably both, could then be put into Carlo's hands, he should be able to make that claim good.

But any Sword given to Carlo under present circumstances, as Ben realized perfectly well, would be quickly
passed on to his megalomaniac father. Therefore, Ben had
made no effort to enter the enemy camp and place
Sightblinder in his glorious master's hands.

Besides . . . he was beginning to have doubts.

Murat, keyed up by gradually heightening excitement as
the hour of his planned attack drew near, was keeping
firmly in mind the necessity, at all costs, of maintaining his
control over Akbar. From the moment he, the Crown
Prince, sheathed the Mindsword, that control would inexorably weaken. For the rest of Murat's life, or until he could
find some way to destroy the beast, he would have to draw
that Blade again at least every couple of days, or risk having
Akbar escape from his control.

And in his darkest dreams Murat could hardly imagine
any outcome worse than that.

The Dark King was raging quietly as he rode at a steady
pace, continuing his methodical progress toward Sarykam.
He fingered the sore place on his forehead, still raw and
throbbing despite his magical efforts to heal his own flesh.
He knew how poisonous the Mindsword's blade was said
to be; even the hilt, it seemed, was capable of causing a
particularly nasty wound. An injury that cried out, with
every throb, for special vengeance.

The last vestiges of Vilkata's magical enslavement to
Murat were now dissolved, and he was trying en route to
decide on the best way to strike at his enemies, the Crown
Prince now definitely included among them. But Vilkata's
anger did not cause him to forget his enemies' strength.
Ideally, he would destroy them all by getting them to
eliminate each other. Obviously that was easier said than
done.

Vilkata's most recent encounter with the demon had

.done nothing to help his composure. Whether the renewed contract would facilitate his plans remained to be seen. His difficulties were compounded by the fact that in attempting any intrigue against Akbar he risked the loss of his demonic vision. For this reason, the wizard had already summoned other demons to his aid; but how many of their number were going to arrive, and how much help they would be when they did, was, to say the least, still problematical.

Murat felt confident that he and his son, riding aboard the demon, would have an excellent chance of taking the defenses of the Tasavaltan capital completely by surprise. Of course, the Crown Prince reminded himself, Karel's cunning should never be underestimated.

Having been a guest in the Tasavaltan royal palace a year ago, Murat had the general layout of that edifice clearly in mind. Originally he had hoped to have Akbar carry himself and Carlo to some point actually inside the palace, but the palace was not huge, as such constructions went. Logic and memory combined to assure the Crown Prince that no point within the building could be more than a hundred meters from Kristin's bedchamber.

Murat had therefore considered several alternate landing places, but none of these would offer sufficiently quick access to the Princess—not even if he were to use his Sword at once on landing, establishing for himself a zone of dominance inside the very heart of the enemy headquarters. Still, physical obstacles in the form of walls and locked doors would intervene between him and his goal.

No, he must command the demon to bring him very close to Kristin. But he was determined not to draw his Sword, this time, until he had an opportunity to speak to her. And Kristin had a chance, a final chance, to answer him freely. . . . Of course, it was possible that circumstances should once again compel him to draw his Sword at once when he arrived.

Murat stared bleakly into the distance for a moment. Then his thoughts moved on.

As soon as Akbar had delivered his two passengers, he was to hasten away to a safe distance from Mark, who would very likely be somewhere nearby, and stand by for another summons.

As for Murat himself, once he had spoken to Kristin, she would grant him—he devoutly hoped—her free devotion.

Only after she had done that, and with her blessing, would he once more draw his Sword.

On the other hand—

There was still the possibility—

If she *should* refuse him—not likely, granted, but just suppose—if this time the Princess refused him, thereby confirming his worst suspicions about her treachery . . . but no, she was not going to refuse him.

No, she would not.

Murat smiled to himself. It seemed that one way or another, under conditions of acceptance or denial, he would be drawing the Mindsword again shortly after his arrival in the palace. With that act he would inevitably assert his power over a large number of people, including a good fighting force of soldiers—just as in his dream.

Some of that herd of new supporters, the Crown Prince thought, with stone walls between themselves and him, wouldn't even realize at first that he, their new, glorious leader, was nearby. But he had no doubt that their conversions would be just as thorough.

Not only would his new followers be eager to fight for him from that moment forward, but perhaps many of them would prove very useful as hostages. Willing hostages, people who would never try to escape . . . yes, there were many favorable possibilities.

Presently Murat's thoughts turned to his son. Exactly what task he would assign to Carlo when they had landed was, Murat now decided, impossible to determine until the time arrived. Suppose they should encounter a sentry in a corridor, or some servant or official, on the way to Kristin's chamber; why, two men armed with ordinary weapons— Murat meant to bring along his battle-ax as well as his Sword—had a much better chance than one of removing the difficulty silently and with dispatch.

And what if on the way they should encounter Mark? Or if Mark should be in Kristin's chamber when they arrived?

Murat looked forward to that meeting.

Alone in the farmhouse bedroom that had briefly been Kristin's, the Crown Prince, alternately sitting, lying down, and pacing, dreamed and planned through the slow early hours of the night. As the time approached for launching his attack, Murat over and over again imagined himself entering Kristin's room in her Tasavaltan palace. Most particularly he imagined her reaction—delighted, perhaps just a little frightened—at the moment when she saw him come in.

Immediately he would assure her that she had no cause to be frightened. Not if she were loyal.

Sometimes, in Murat's imagination, the Princess was alone and asleep when he entered, and he had to touch her bare shoulder to awaken her.

Again, Kristin would be wide awake despite the lateness of the hour, sitting with her candle at a writing table, and her eyes when she raised them to behold her lover's entrance were filled with the most exquisite joy. . . .

There was another version of this scene that Murat did not welcome to his imagination, but which still would not be denied: one in which Kristin was in bed, but not alone. . . .

Several violent conclusions to that version ran through the mind of the Crown Prince, but for the time being he refused to allow himself to dwell on any of them.

He had thrown himself on the bed, and his waking dreams soon faded insensibly into those of slumber. Troubled sleep brought the Crown Prince visions quite different from the scenarios constructed by his anxious waking mind. Here were experiences of orgasmic glory, in which millions of people gathered to worship him. Yes, millions, hordes beyond counting, joined by other beings who were more than human—joined perhaps by the gods themselves, returning to earth. They had all assembled to give worship to Murat, as it was said that once even the gods had come to give adoration to the Dark King.

The Crown Prince groaned in his sleep. He had never known the Dark King in his days of glory. Vilkata, that filthy beggar? That debased and terrified old man? If the gods themselves could be made to worship *that*—

Then Murat's dreams turned more closely to his own situation. He'd completed his demon-flight to the palace in Sarykam successfully, and a sizable, no, a huge military force in the palace and the surrounding portion of the capital had been caught and converted. His only problem now was that these most recently converted troops could not be made aware that their master was actually present, within the very walls they guarded. Murat shouted and beat with his fists on the stone walls of the palace, to no avail.

Of course, once his new worshipers knew how close to them their glorious new master really was, they would defend him to the death. More than that, they'd fan out eagerly beyond the hundred-meter limit to conquer a whole kingdom for him. And in the future, when the Crown Prince had sheathed the Sword again, the great bulk of these converts would of course remain his loyal subjects. And most of the Tasavaltan leadership—all those who survived—would do the same.

Meanwhile there was a new threat, the stone walls of the palace seemed to be closing in—

In the deepest hour of the night Murat was awakened, just as his dreams were starting to go bad, by the demon, returning from a final reconnaissance flight. To deliver his report Akbar had assumed the by-now familiar form of a young maiden, who sat provocatively, wearing tighter and scantier clothing than ever before, on the edge of Murat's simple borrowed bed.

Akbar in his report now confirmed that Prince Stephen, as well as Mark and Kristin, was among the members of the royal family on the scene in the palace in the Tasavaltan capital.

The Princess herself had been located with quite satisfactory accuracy—she seemed to be spending most of her time in the bedchamber which she shared, in more ordinary times, with the Prince. This chamber was located high in the palace on the eastern side, overlooking the city and the harbor.

Murat was impatient. "I know where her rooms are. And are they sharing one bed now?"

Akbar considered the question carefully. Slyly he seemed to take his time. "That I could not determine, Master, being mindful of your warning to avoid discovery."

Mark, having seen Kristin settled as comfortably as possible into their old quarters, was sleeplessly working alone in a room just down the corridor. In more peaceful times he used this chamber for a study; just now it was something like a command post.

The Prince was standing at a map table, poring over some documents by lamplight, when there was a knock at the door.

When he barked an acknowledgment, a sentry, his face wearing an odd expression, put in his head. "Someone to see you, sir."

"Someone? Who? What do you mean—"

Then Mark fell silent, staring with wide eyes. The door was pushed in farther. Just behind the sentry stood the Emperor, smiling at his son.

Slowly Mark turned to face his visitor.

"Leave us," he told the sentry in a low voice.

"Sir—"

"Leave us, I say."

The soldier backed out. The Emperor came in, and closed the door. He stood with hands clasped behind him, and his gray eyes moved past Mark to the table.

"Is that an accurate map?" he inquired.

Whatever opening statement Mark might have expected from his father, it wasn't that. He could only gape for a moment in astonishment. "The map? I suppose so."

Turning back to the map, gazing helplessly at the documents spread out on it, the Prince was astonished when in the next moment a sheathed Sword appeared, flying through the air almost over his shoulder, to crash down in the middle of the map.

The Prince spun around—to behold not the Emperor but Ben, Swordless and grinning at him heartily, his huge hands spread in greeting.

At that same hour Kristin, sitting in her chamber alone save for an ever-watchful nurse, was greeting a less surprising visitor.

It was Stephen, come visiting in his nightshirt, hopefully, wistfully, to see if his mother was getting better.

"How are you, Mother?"

She held the boy and stroked the rough texture of his hair. "I'm quite all right. I'm going to be quite all right."

"Are you—are you and father still—?" Stephen couldn't quite manage to get the terrific question out in any form.

"I'm here now," Kristin answered at last, softly. She held her son and rocked him, back and forth. "And your father's here too. No one can promise you anything about tomorrow."

"Mother—"

"No one ever can do that."

The boy seemed about to speak again, when a muffled commotion erupted somewhere out in the corridor. There were distant cries, and running feet. Kristin sighed, and kept to her rocking chair. Stephen hurried out to investigate, to return in a few minutes with the good news that Ben was back, and unharmed, and that he had brought Sightblinder.

"Isn't it good news, Mother? Isn't it?"

The Princess was standing now.

"Yes," she said. "Of course. It's good news, Stephen."

In another moment Karel, accompanied by a physician, was coming in to see her.

"Gentlemen, you still hope by your arts to keep me pleasantly controlled?"

Her uncle bowed sadly. "Madam, we want nothing but your own best good."

Kristin was weeping.

An hour later, and once more after that, Mark too looked in on his wife. The first time he found her sleeping, and he retreated patiently, eager as he was to speak with her joyfully of Ben's return.

At the time of her husband's second visit Kristin was awake, and as they conversed she held Mark's hand and gazed at him ambiguously, as if she were trying to communicate something beyond the limited power of words.

Once or twice she also snarled at him in anger.

TWENTY

A T the hour when Murat was receiving from the demon his last scouting report before the flying attack was launched, Ben, sitting in a high room in the palace in Sarykam, was describing to the Tasavaltan leaders his encounter in the field, several days ago, with Carlo, and his more recent meeting with Vilkata.

Vilkata, when Ben had seen him last, had been mounted on a riding-beast, headed in the direction of Sarykam.

Given this information, Karel decided to establish a watch for this evil wizard at the city gates. So far the gates were still being kept open on a normal schedule, despite the general state of readiness imposed on the capital. But the watch at each entrance would be doubled.

Mark, before leaving for an extensive tour of the gates himself, commented: "The Sword's effects on our friend Vilkata will be wearing off, as they did on Ben. We can't be sure he'll still be trying to serve Murat."

"We can be sure," said Karel, "that he means us no good."

As for Murat and Carlo, Ben could tell his comrades no more about their plans than could anyone else in Sarykam. He could only suppose that the Crown Prince intended some bold stroke, and that the Princeling, under continuous pressure from the Sword of Glory, would still be slavishly following his father.

Murat, immediately after receiving his last briefing from Akbar in his lonely farmhouse bedroom, began his final personal preparations for the attack. The Crown Prince armed himself with a knife, in addition to his Sword, and stowed in pockets and pouches a very minimum of other equipment. He thought not much was necessary. He meant to conquer the palace and all the supplies it contained, or else die quickly in the attempt.

Putting on garments and taking them off without for a moment ceasing to hold the Sword was something of an accomplishment, but by now the Crown Prince had had several days in which to practice. For him the necessary maneuvers had already become something like second nature.

Only when Murat was fully dressed and ready did it occur to him that the time had come, according to his own plan, for him to sheathe his Sword. After a momentary pause he did so. Though there was no one in the little room to see him, he performed the act with a ceremonious gesture.

Then the Crown Prince at once left his room. After a perfunctory tap on the door of the adjoining chamber, he entered quickly. Inside he found a sleepless Carlo already up and armed.

The lad looked tired and pale, but bravely he announced his readiness to go.

In the upstairs hallway, father and son encountered Captain Marsaci, who had come for them, bearing a torch, promptly at the appointed time. With the captain lighting the way, all three men proceeded downstairs.

Some hours before Murat had decided that to launch their flight from inside the farmhouse would be impractical. He had chosen the hayloft, in the barn, as offering the best security from observation.

The demonic maiden, who had disappeared from Murat's room a few minutes earlier, sat waiting upon a bale of straw for the three men as they climbed a wooden ladder. Behind her the big doors through which hay was normally loaded were standing open to the night.

Marsaci sneezed, on entering the dim, dusty space. Then the captain started to sneeze again, but the spasm was aborted when he belatedly caught sight of the demon waiting for them. Despite the demure appearance of the image, Marsaci did not for a moment mistake it for a real girl.

"Are you ready, my lord?" the maiden asked, addressing Murat as she got to her feet.

"Ready."

In an instant her form had swollen to several times the maiden's size, and changed into the shape of a giant, winged reptile, crouched on two hind legs that looked too heavy for anything that could fly. A wicked head, armed with long yellow fangs, turned on a long neck to grin at the waiting men. The torch shook in Marsaci's hands, and he mumbled something.

Blaspheming various gods, Murat clapped his hand on his Sword-hilt and snarled an order.

"A bird! Let us have a bird, vile creature!"

"As you say, Master." And in a twinkling rough scales were replaced by sable feathers. A giant black bird, with yellow eyes and curved raptorial beak, crouched ready to be mounted. No saddle or bridle were in evidence; perhaps that meant none would be needed.

Boldly Murat stepped forward, and without hesitation straddled the creature's back. He turned his head to stare at his son.

Reluctantly Carlo clambered aboard behind his father, clutching the older man around the waist with both arms.

There was no delay. The Crown Prince barely had time for a last word to Marsaci before father and son were swiftly carried into the air.

Carlo groaned and gasped.

Murat gasped too, a sound of triumph rather than of fear. Then he let out a loud yell of exultation. They were being borne upward at breathtaking speed, into an aerial realm of clouds, sluiced with cool mist and shot with intermittent moonlight.

The night air howled past the travelers at a terrific velocity, but the Crown Prince soon discovered that his journey was not, after all, going to be swifter than the wind. Carlo behind him was suffering a fit of terror, and came near plunging to his death and dragging his father with him.

His father, getting little or no help from Akbar, was forced to struggle awkwardly to hold his son on the bird's back.

Shouting at Carlo did no good, and Murat directed his yells at the demon. "Stop! Return to the earth! Land, I command you!"

At last, in response to bellowed orders from the Crown Prince, the rush of air diminished. The dark earth rose to meet them, and a landing was effected in some farmer's field.

Disembarking from his black, feathered mount, Murat dragged Carlo whimpering and almost sobbing aside, the pair of them trampling waist-high corn. In the distance, toward the city, thunder grumbled and rain was threatening.

The Crown Prince shook his son, and cursed him.

"What are you afraid of? Not heights, don't tell me that. I have seen you stand on a clifftop without whimpering, and climb a castle wall where there were no stairs."

"It is the demon—the demon, Father—the touch of it is horrible—"

"Nonsense. The touch of defeat, of failure, is the only real horror. Pull yourself together, be a man!"

Carlo managed to establish some measure of self-control. "I can only try, Father."

"You can do more than that. You can succeed!"

They were on their way back to where they had left Akbar, when Carlo suddenly put a hand on Murat's arm.

"Father, I have a confession to make. Something you must know, in case I die before I have another chance to tell you."

Murat stopped in his tracks. "What is it?"

"Once, on patrol—the time we fought the skirmish—I once used the Mindsword."

Stopping in his tracks, the Crown Prince stood for a moment as if paralyzed. Then he screamed: "How could you lie to me? How many converts did you make? Where are they now?"

"Only one—only one, Father. The man they call Ben of Purkinje. I do not know where he is now."

Murat started to choke out more abuse, then paused. "There is no time now to settle this. How could you betray me in such a way?"

"No, Father! There was no betrayal! I swear it! I ordered him to help you."

"To help me? How?"

But his son did not answer. The Crown Prince could see Akbar, at a little distance, still in bird-form, crouched and undoubtedly listening.

"Later we will settle this," Murat grated at his son. "Mount! We are going on."

Carlo, almost fainting, once more climbed aboard the silent demon. In moments they were airborne again. This time the Princeling did not struggle in the air, or show any signs of terror. Rather he rode as an inert weight, as if he were already dead.

The rushing flight continued, in darkness and near-silence. Presently Akbar turned back his bird's head to announce that they had almost reached their destination. Neither of the human passengers was quite able to believe this. But before either of them really thought it possible, the city appeared.

"Sarykam," the demon informed them, its voice a guttural grinding through the rush of air.

Indeed, there lay ahead, still far below the sable masses of those mighty wings, a vast sprawling darkness beneath the clouds, a region vaguely distinguishable from the ocean to the east, and from the fields and farms and orchards to west and north and south, picked out by specks of random firelight.

The distance to the capital was diminishing at a speed that seemed incredible to Murat. Already individual structures could be distinguished. Lower and even more swiftly flew the demon. The walls of the city took shape out of the darkness and rushed beneath the demon's wings. And now more stone walls, even higher barriers, loomed just ahead.

These, unmistakably, formed the south flank of the palace.

Both passengers flinched involuntarily as the massive construction hurtled closer. The ramparts were marked with a few high narrow windows that looked too small to admit their flying bodies. One moment a violent crash seemed unavoidable. In the next—Carlo closed his eyes and did not see how the trick was done—the outer wall and its open windows were behind them, and he and his father were enclosed within a high and otherwise deserted corridor. Already they were on their feet, staggering to establish their balance upon a solid floor as the great black shape of their carrier dissolved to nothingness beneath them.

Murat barely had time to deliver a last command, in a fierce whisper, before the demon vanished utterly.

The two Culmians were alone in a long hallway of wood and stone, lighted at intervals by high lamps. The palace was quiet around them, and it seemed that their arrival must not have been observed.

Murat, hand on Sword-hilt, needed only a moment in which to get his bearings. "This way!" he muttered, and directed Carlo with a nod.

But the Crown Prince and his son had taken only a few steps in the indicated direction before a door opened ahead of them, and they stood face to face with a maidservant, her arms piled high with linen. Her eyes opened wide, enormously, and her mouth worked as if she might be about to scream.

Murat backed up a step, ready to draw his Sword at once. "If you are holding the Sword of Stealth," he growled at the maid, "drop it at once, or—"

Before Murat could finish speaking, Carlo reacted more practically, stepping forward and striking the woman down with the butt of his own sword.

The two men stared at the maid, who now lay dead, or unconscious, on the floor.

Then Murat pulled his suspicious gaze away from her. "Come!"

Father and son moved on toward Kristin's quarters. Then, peering warily round a corner, Murat discovered guards posted in a place that would make a final approach through the corridor impossible.

When he relayed this information to his son, Carlo whispered: "Father, now is the time for you to draw—"

"Quiet. This way."

Murat pulled his son down another angle of hallway, then through a door, into a room which proved dark and untenanted. In another moment they were leaving this room again, through a window opening to a balcony.

From this balcony others to right and left on the same

high level were visible, and accessible, if one was not discouraged by the need to cross sections of sloping, slate-tiled roof.

"The Princess's suite connects to at least one of those balconies," Murat whispered. "Follow me."

The passage across the slippery roof had to be carefully negotiated, but it was quick. Then Murat and Carlo were on another balcony, then boldly entering what the Crown Prince proclaimed to be the Princess's room.

It was a large, well-furnished bedroom, simply decorated, well lit by several candles. The bed was empty, though covers had been turned back, and Kristin was not to be seen. A middle-aged woman dropped her knitting and rose from a rocking chair to stare at the intruders.

She had time to utter only a slight preliminary noise before Carlo was beside her, holding his knife to her throat.

The Crown Prince, hand on Sword-hilt, stood frozen, gaze focused in the distance, obviously listening for something with a full intensity of concentration.

Carlo heard a small noise, as of a hastily closed door, from one of the connecting rooms.

"Kristin?" Murat, calling the name softly, lunged through a curtained doorway toward the sound.

Carlo suddenly found himself holding the body of an unconscious woman; the attendant had fainted. He lowered her body to the floor, and leaped to bar the door that he assumed led from this bedroom out to the corridor. A moment later he had followed his father into the next room. This was another bedroom of some kind, too dark for him to be able to make out much of its contents. Here a door stood partially open to another balcony, and to the summer night.

The young man hastened to bar the hall door of this room too; almost immediately afterward the handle was tried from the outside, and immediately after that someone out there began a heavy pounding on the door. Now the alarm was being raised in earnest.

Murat was looking warily out onto the balcony of the darkened bedroom. Now he stepped out onto it.

"My love," his son heard him breathe.

In the next moment the Crown Prince began to draw his Sword. Carlo, approaching his father from behind, saw with astonishment a half-grown boy, wearing only a long nightshirt, step from behind some draperies beside the doorway and hurl his body on Murat's right arm.

The Crown Prince was taken by surprise, and the Sword of Glory, glittering faintly in the light of candles in the room, escaped from his grip.

Immediately magic informed the air. The voices of a multitude, inspired and invisible, sounded in the mind of every human near. Murat could only watch as the naked Mindsword described a smooth arc, clattered briefly on the dark slates of the nearby roof, and then went sliding swiftly down out of sight.

Before the Sword had struck the roof, Murat went lunging after it. The unreal voices, chanting glory, mocked him. His convulsive effort to catch or retrieve Skulltwister knocked the night-shirted child aside into a corner.

The Princess Kristin, dressed in a delicate robe, stepped into Carlo's field of vision, clutching at the arm of the Crown Prince. But Murat, groaning and muttering, thrust her roughly aside too, and in the next moment had vaulted lithely over the balustrade. There he crouched, in an exposed position on the roof's edge, staring intently down into the near-darkness of a courtyard, trying to see where his Sword had fallen.

The Princess, murmuring and crying, would have climbed after him, but Carlo stepped forward to hold her back. Then for a moment neither of them was able to act effectively. Both were stricken, stunned, half-entranced by the wordless, soundless flow of the freed Sword's magic.

Others, all around them, were affected too. And the mundane silence of the night had been irretrievably shattered. Whether from one source or several, the alarm against intruders was spreading.

Carlo, holding the Princess with one arm, looked around and drew his own sword, momentarily expecting a rush of guards from somewhere. But as yet nothing of the kind materialized.

In the next instant Kristin, with a surprisingly strong effort, had broken free from Carlo's grasp and was bending over her son. The bare-legged boy in the nightshirt lay moaning, half-stunned, his upper body leaning against the wall in a corner of the balcony.

Murat, maintaining his precarious position a few meters away, at the very edge of a section of roof, had just turned his head to call to his own son, when a crackling noise and a brief glare of light roiled the air eight or ten meters above their heads.

Carlo looked up to see an image of the wizard Vilkata, borne in midair amid a small swarm of half-visible demonic shapes. These descended with their burden, as the Princeling watched, to deposit the Dark King upon an angle of roof. The Eyeless One's landing place was one level down from where Carlo and his father were watching, that much closer to where the fallen Sword had lodged.

Having conveyed their wizard-master to the place of his choosing, the demonic forms melted away into the damp air.

Vilkata—there was no doubting the solidity of his body now—straightened up, his fists on his hips in a royal pose. He called out mockingly to Murat: "Have you lost something, Great Master?"

There was no answer.

A moment later the eyeless man went on: "My ethereal servants, who dwell in air and darkness, inform me that within the last minute a certain treasure has ceased to belong to you, Crown Prince." The magician laughed, and made a pretense of peering around him. "Where can it have gone, I wonder?"

Before Vilkata had finished speaking, the rain that had been threatening broke from low-flying clouds, a steady downpour certain to make the footing on slate tiles even worse.

"Don't fall, Murat! Careful, glorious Master! Ha ha!"

Murat, hanging awkwardly at the brink of the perilously steep and slippery roof, finally answered his quondam magician—with a curse.

Then, for the moment ignoring the wizard's threatening presence as if Vilkata did not exist, he turned back to his son. In an almost conversational voice he said: "I can see the Sword, Carlo! It's only a little way down. Guard me while I climb down and claim it."

"Father, don't—"

"I can reach it, and I will. None of these swine can keep me from it."

But Vilkata, starting from his lower level, was already moving toward the prize, and was plainly in position to reach it first. The man descended carefully, with a certain unnatural slowness in his downward movements, as if he had provided himself with magical protection against a fall.

The Crown Prince looked up at his son again, in desperation. "Carlo, your sword! Throw it! Stop him, kill him!"

Abandoning the Princess, whose attention was still focused on her son, Carlo obediently climbed over the balustrade. He had no particular fear of heights.

"Stop him!" It was a scream of agony.

Carlo, only having got down a meter or two, stopped where he was, clinging by one hand to a drainpipe, his feet braced precariously on small stone knobs he could not really see. With his free hand he drew his sword, and hurled the weapon at the Dark King five or six meters distant; a drawn blade was one of the strongest moves any nonmagician could make against any magical operation in progress. But either Vilkata's magical protection was equal to the challenge, or else the missile simply missed him. In any event it fell harmlessly. And for a long time. They all heard it strike, at last, on pavement far below.

Vilkata was within two meters of being able to grasp the Sword of Glory when the demon Akbar appeared, standing on another balcony, on the far side of the fallen Sword from the magician, but as close to it as he was.

Murat, slowest of the three active contenders, remained hopelessly distant from his prize. Now the Crown Prince paused in his slow progress, just as he was about to lower himself from a roof drain, to see the outcome of this new confrontation. In a moment Murat had hurled his own knife in the direction of the wizard, with no effect. His shouted orders to the demon were ignored.

Now Murat, gesturing fiercely, shrieked again for his son to go and seize the Sword, to sheathe it and bring it back to him, to fight the demon, to do something.

Carlo smiled vaguely, nodded his perfect obedience to his father, and moved as quickly as he could toward the Sword. He could see Skulltwister, caught from its fall by a small projecting cornice, leaning hilt uppermost against a wall in a precarious position.

In the next instant his feet slipped from an impossible foothold, and then his grasping fingers slid from the edge of the slick roof.

Falling, he had several seconds in which to think, to fully realize his failure.

Murat, as if he were not yet aware that his son had plunged to the ground, still barked orders at Akbar, commanding him to put the sheath back on the Sword. "Then bring it to me, to me, your master!"

Akbar, posing on the balcony in the form of a maiden, sent an amused glance toward Murat.

"I have decided," said the maiden, "that someone besides you, my Lord Murat, should bear the Mindsword from now on. I'll carry it myself, for the time being, though I don't look forward to all the attention it will bring me."

The Crown Prince, unbelieving, made a strange sound in his throat.

Akbar continued: "Because you—you, my gr-r-reat Master!—live increasingly in a world of your own megalomaniac fantasies. Therefore, in my judgment, you are becoming undependable."

"You are to serve me! I command you—I charge you—"

"Yes, yes. I know you are convinced you are my master. Most humans who deal with me willingly are under some such illusion. But very few indeed can keep the relationship in those terms. Very few. And you are not one of them."

"—by the Sword's power, I command—"

"Fool. What are mere Swords to me?"

Mark, who had been in a distant part of the city when he was alerted to what was happening in the palace, was hurrying desperately in that direction now. As he passed, he could see swarms of troops and magical assistants gathering, torchlit ranks forming, at somewhat more than a hundred meters from his invaded quarters. These defenders, under good discipline, were deploying somewhat outside the range of the Mindsword's effective action.

At least no one who now held the Mindsword within the palace would find there an army ready-made to fight for him.

"Such delusions are very common when one of my kind—forms a relationship—with one of yours," said

Akbar—the maiden was sitting now on the balustrade, modestly swinging her shapely legs.

The demon was obviously toying with his enemies before he reached out to pick up Skulltwister.

Meanwhile Vilkata, only five or six meters from the demon, was almost gibbering at it, plainly trying one spell after another. Plainly none of them were working.

Akbar went on, speaking in leisurely tones: "*After* I pick up this weapon—*after* that, I say—you will, each and all of you, be delighted to serve me, for the rest of your miserable lives. And I intend to see to it that—at least in your case, great wizard, and your case, glorious Master—those lives are very long. But, sadly, it is only now, beforehand, that I can enjoy your anticipation of that prospect."

Fuming and raging, now standing recklessly on a minute ledge in a position where moments ago he had been clinging with both hands, the Crown Prince would not listen, would not understand.

Angrily, with demented determination, he once more ordered the demon to crush Vilkata, and to properly sheathe and deliver the Sword of Glory.

"I think not, Master—but no, it no longer amuses me to call you by that title. I am wearying of this game. 'Fool' is a much better name for you, I think. I am not, and never was, compelled to take your orders. What is the power of a mere Sword, to *me*?"

Murat's speech was becoming unintelligible.

Akbar went on: "The fact is, I do not want to crush the man you call Vilkata just yet. I may well find some better use for him." And the maiden cast a speculative look in the Dark King's direction.

Vilkata was about to say something, but before he could speak the maiden's slender hand gestured in his direction.

"There. I withdraw my gift of vision. You, my dear

Vilkata, shall be blind—for the time being at least. You must be made to understand what the true nature of our partnership is to be."

The Eyeless One clapped hands to his face. Now truly blind, he groped and whimpered helplessly on his slippery roof.

"Be of good cheer. If you were to grovel properly in supplication, I might be willing to shorten your period of darkness."

But instead of groveling, Vilkata ceased to whimper. Drawing himself up, he regained and maintained some dignity in the face of this threat.

He muttered a few words in a low voice.

"Calling for help, great wizard? Feel free to do so. I can repel your—" Akbar's voice broke off.

The Dark King had risked all, diving bodily forward, over empty space, in a blind lunge aimed at the Sword he could no longer see; his right hand and arm, groping, grasping for treasure or for a life-saving grip, made violent contact with the razor-keeness of the Blade. The impact gashed Vilkata, and knocked Skulltwister from its perch.

The Sword fell again, once more passing out of everyone's immediate reach.

Vilkata, his gamble lost, clung blindly to the cornice for an instant, with his uninjured hand. Then he fell—but not to his doom. The shape of his newly summoned demon blurred through the air, catching him in mid-tumble.

The maidenly human shape of Akbar was leaning over the balustrade, watching the Sword fall, when a bulky man burst into view behind it on the balcony and grappled the demon from behind.

Murat, still single-mindedly intent, resumed his infinitely determined, crawling descent. He could still see Skulltwister, which this time had come to rest point uppermost, hilt and pommel stuck down into a drain on a roof's corner. Again his Sword had not fallen far, and he thought he could quickly get within reach.

In the instant of being seized by human arms, Akbar the demon let out a little sound of genuine fear. The maiden's shape vanished in an eyeblink, to be replaced by the semblance of a great ape. A violent struggle began.

Murat, his immediate enemies vanished or distracted, had needed only the space of a few breaths to get within reach—or almost—of the Sword. From the wall to which he clung, the man, stretching his right arm out to the uttermost, might have barely touched Skulltwister's point. It was impossible to clamber any closer, without going an impossibly long way around.

Drawing in his body, pressing himself against his own wall once again, the Crown Prince took a moment's rest. If only Carlo could help. But Carlo . . .

Concentrating totally on his goal, working as swiftly as he could, Murat unhooked the long empty sheath from his belt. As when he had once before picked up and claimed the naked Sword, he would now have to work the sheath onto the Blade before he dared try to seize the god-forged thing, whose unstemmed tide of magic now bathed him at close quarters.

Sheath in hand, Murat stretched out again. One last effort brought leather sliding over steel. But in making that effort he had reached too far, and felt his supporting fingers slip.

He fell. No intervening cornice here.

The last clear thought of his life was that the sheathed Sword was tumbling after him, and that he might still have a chance to catch it in midair.

Kristin screamed. She had been out on the roof, trying to make her way closer to the scene of action, and at the same time trying to compel her son to stay back on the balcony, to save himself.

Karel had at last appeared inside the royal quarters, and then upon the balcony; the old man was in time to keep Stephen from rushing out onto the roof after his mother, but not in time to hold the Princess back.

Madly scrambling over the wet tiles toward the place from which Murat had fallen, she did not stop at the roof's edge, but plunged down after him.

TWENTY-ONE

DESPITE warnings to depart, given by Karel and others, a few servants and a handful of soldiers had gathered and were still gathering on nearby balconies and in windows, to watch the struggle for the Sword of Glory.

Stephen and Karel watched from their balcony, the old man's powerful grip restraining the boy from rushing out on the roof after his mother.

Upon a balcony in the next wing of the palace, the dark and apelike shape of the demon Akbar struggled desperately, but to little avail, as if the strong man who had seized it were really more powerful than any mere human could possibly be. The combatants swayed back and forth.

Karel had no trouble recognizing Ben, who was not only maintaining the solid hold he had obtained at the start, but was gradually improving his advantage.

It was not long until Karel, at least, understood what must be happening.

"Shieldbreaker!" he muttered to Stephen, who still struggled in his grip. "The demon must have it!"

The moon emerged briefly from behind rain clouds, and swiftly retired again. For long moments the struggled was conducted in darkness and near-silence. A faint glow of light, from distant windows and courtyards, still made shapes and movements dimly visible. The hideous demon thrashed about and made noises as if it were trying to scream. But the human limbs that held it were tightening inexorably.

Now those who watched could see that something was wrong with Akbar's right hand, or with the image of a right hand that the demon flailed ineffectually at his opponent.

Moment by moment the image of that bestial hand and arm became a little clearer. There was a solid object at its end.

Presently it could be seen that Akbar was gripping a bright-bladed, dark-hilted Sword. With this weapon he attempted to punish and to slay the one who wrestled with him, but the slashes and thrusts directed at an unarmed foe accomplished nothing.

Again and again that shimmering blade and point penetrated the clothing and the flesh of the man who wrestled with the demon. But no blood was drawn, and the wrestler remained uninjured.

Karel muttered again: "The beast indeed has Shieldbreaker! But it must rid itself of that Sword, or lose this fight."

Ben had come to the same conclusion earlier, on seeing and hearing how the demon defied the Mindsword and Vilkata's spells. Now the huge man steadily increased his advantage—as he had expected. He knew the demon would lose this match against even the weakest barehanded human opponent—unless Akbar could manage to rid himself of the pernicious Sword of Force before it was too late.

Once he, Ben, had outwrestled a god under similar circumstances; no mere demon, handicapped by Shieldbreaker, was going to defeat him.

The demon gurgled, a hellish sound, as if the foul thing were being forced to try to breathe. And waved its right arm frantically—no longer slashing and thrusting. Now it was as if the demon strove to free its hand from the bite of a clinging serpent.

And at last—to Ben's horror and surprise, well after he had thought the feat impossible for Akbar to achieve—the Sword of Force flew free.

Vilkata, bleeding and weakened by the gash inflicted by Skulltwister, had been forced to withdraw temporarily from combat. Now, somewhat recovered, his vision restored by a new demonic partner, he came rushing back, borne through the air again by captive powers.

The sheathed Sword of Glory in its last plunge had fallen all the way to the ground, landing not far from the inert bodies of Murat and Princess Kristin.

A few people, emerging from doors at that level of the palace, had just started out into the paved area, heading toward the bodies and the Sword. But the sight of Vilkata and his onrushing escort drove them back inside in panic.

The demon Akbar, in the next moment after ridding himself of Shieldbreaker, had regained strength enough to hurl Ben aside.

Then Akbar gathered his energies for an effort to beat Vilkata to the Sword of Glory. But he saw that he was going to be too late.

Karel was and had been doing his best to repel all demons, but edged weapons had been drawn, and at the moment the old wizard's best was not going to be adequate. Vilkata, stooping from the back of his demonic mount, had just scooped up the Sword of Glory in his uninjured hand—

At that moment Mark, gasping for breath, came running out onto the balcony where his son and Karel stood.

"In the Emperor's name!" the Prince of Tasavalta bellowed hoarsely at his foes—and had to pause to gasp again.

In fact no more words were needed. A swirling blast, as of a hurricane, erupted out of the steady rain and darkness. In a moment the storm had gathered around all the demons, Vilkata caught up in their midst. Nor was Akbar spared. In the matter of a few heartbeats the whole roaring, twisting mass of air and cloud, now shot through with lightning, had mounted high above the palace, then whirled away. Before Karel could draw a deep breath, it was gone, vanishing at last far out to sea.

Silence fell on Sarykam, broken only by a distant rumble of thunder. Then another roll more distant yet, and beneath those sounds the steady plash and drip of rain.

The invasion had been repelled. The demons, including Akbar, were all gone. So was Vilkata. And so was the sheathed Sword of Glory, which the Dark King had just picked up.

Karel feared that, sooner or later, in one pair of hands or another, Skullwarper would be back again to plague humanity.

Right now the wizard, at the moment feeling very old indeed, was confronted by more immediate problems.

Prince Mark, leaning on the balustrade, slowly regaining his breath, was looking around for Kristin.

Tentatively he called her name.

Stephen was already gone into the building, running for the stair that would take him down to where his mother had fallen.

Karel could see (though not with his aging human eyes) how her body now lay there, twisted, resting partly on stone and partly on softer matter. On another body, whose heart no longer beat.

The right hand of the Princess moved, as if it sought to grasp something. Then it was still again. Of the three who had fallen, she alone still breathed.

"Prince," the magician said softly, "she fell from the roof. She is still alive, and she may live. But—there are terrible injuries."

Before Karel had added those last words, Mark was already gone, racing after his son.

Left alone, the old man was in no hurry to run anywhere. Ignoring the rain, he let his body sag on the stone railing. His eyes were closed, but lids could not shut out the visions of his magic.